FOLLOW THE SUN

FOLLOW THE SUN

R. Gordon Gastil and Janet Gastil

Sunbelt Publications
San Diego, California

Follow the Sun

Sunbelt Publications, Inc.
 First edition 2006

Edited by Jennifer Redmond
Book design by Thompson Type
Cover design by Bonomi Design Graphics
Cover photo by John Gastil
Project management Jennifer Redmond
Printed in the United States of America

Please direct comments and inquiries to:

Sunbelt Publications, Inc.
P.O. Box 191126
San Diego, CA 92159-1126
(619) 258-4911, fax: (619) 258-4916
www.sunbeltbooks.com

09 08 07 06 05   5 4 3 2 1

LIBRARY OF CONGRESS CATALOGING-IN-PUBLICATION DATA

Gastil, R. Gordon.
  Follow the sun / by Gordon and Janet Gastil.-- 1st ed.
      p. cm.
  Includes bibliographical references.
  ISBN-13: 978-0-916251-74-1
  ISBN-10: 0-916251-74-8
  1. Voyages around the world--Fiction. 2. Travel, Ancient--Fiction. 3. Explorers--Fiction. 4. Travelers--Fiction. I. Gastil, Janet. II. Title.

PS3607.A7875F65 2005
813'.6--dc22
                          2005019471

DEDICATION

This book is dedicated to the memory of Thor Heyerdahl.

His life work was an inspiration to us. When he received us at his secluded home in Guimar, Tenerife, Canary Islands, February 2001, he expressed his belief that the journey of Follow the Sun, 3,200 years ago, was not only possible, but likely.

TABLE OF CONTENTS

POEMS

FIGURES

Preface

EACH YEAR, AFTER THE SUMMER field season ends and before fall classes begin, our friends gather at an ancient stone lodge deep in the woods of New England, to renew our acquaintance and exchange ideas. I am an academic geologist by trade, but an archaeologist by inclination. Our group includes Henry and his wife Hilda, archaeologists; Bruce, a geographer; Sarah, an engineer; my wife Janet, and Sylvester, a graduate student emeritus. Henry and Hilda have organized important digs on three continents and are widely recognized for their knowledge of bronze age civilizations. Sarah has made a career of stone engravings and quarrying, the ancient technology of cutting and carving huge blocks of rock. Bruce, a paleo-ecologist, studies the migration of flora and fauna. Sylvester is enamored with words and computers, and—to make sure you understand—he can speak Mandarin Chinese backwards. We call him "the mad linguist" because he sees everything as a language and he believes that with a computer he can understand all patterns of language, art, music, mathematics, and life.

UNRECORDED ANCIENT TRAVEL

I promised Hilda that tonight we would take up the topic of ancient travel. "Go ahead, Hilda, it's all yours."

"I've been wondering for years," began Hilda, "why the colonization of the New World took so long to happen."

Our group chewed on this question for a while. Is it something human, to possess sufficient curiosity for travel into the unknown? Have men not explored the Amazon basin, darkest Africa, and the frigid poles, long before helicopters and GPS? Must we accept that, given several millennia to try, no one made it across the Atlantic Ocean in its less inclement middle latitudes?

Bruce expressed his opinion: "We have no idea where men traveled in ancient times, because few records have survived. We don't know when people first reached the New World. There was no news service. Many a voyage went unrecorded. Many a sea captain could write his name, but not write well enough to keep a journal. The first voyagers to cross the Atlantic could have been pirates."

Watching the fire dancing in our fireplace at the old lodge, we continued our discussion about remarkable trips that might have succeeded, given the technology of their times, but the records of which have been lost. Many may have crossed an ocean, but never returned.

In 1804 through 1806, Lewis and Clarke trekked across the North American continent from St. Louis to the mouth of the Columbia River, and back. One vivid impression of their account is the almost daily "escape" from the perils of charging bison, dangerous bears, unfriendly native people, and undiagnosed, untreated infirmities. One slip, and one of the party would not have survived. But they all did survive, except for one, Sergeant Floyd, who succumbed to "biliose" illness (Ambrose, 1996). But Lewis and Clarke were not the first. In 1793, Sir Alexander McKenzie traveled from Montreal to the Pacific Coast, and back (Gough, 1997).

Was this a unique and marvelous expedition, or was this one of many journeys: the others unrecorded, unsung, and undocumented? How many trappers had followed down the rivers to the Pacific, using their woodsman craft rather than a military detachment and instruments for navigation, oft-times living with the native people for much of a lifetime? Is the spread–diffusion, if you like–of culture, language, and technology a result not so much of conquest or education but of lonely trappers marrying local women? How many had attempted ambitious, lengthy expeditions? How many realized that they had accomplished anything particularly remarkable? How many had succeeded, and how many had failed?

When Cortez and his crew landed at Veracruz, they found local people who could help them communicate with Montezuma. When the pilgrims landed at Plymouth Rock, there were several native Americans living there who could translate for them. One of them, Squanto, had been taken to Spain and could speak three languages. These examples imply earlier, uncelebrated travel.

How long ago would a voyage across the central Atlantic Ocean have been possible?

Henry raised a more difficult question: "How long ago could a traveler have made it around the earth in one lifetime?" We tossed this question about. After much discussion, we agreed that the biggest obstacle was not inadequate technology, but the false concept that we live on a flat earth.

Could such a voyage have succeeded in the classic period of 500–300 BCE, when the warships of Greece, Egypt, and Crete were at their peak? Or even earlier, in the late bronze age, the thirteenth century BCE? More than three thousand years ago, the eastern Mediterranean people were building stout ships and had knowledgeable navigators, capable of carrying them around the Mediterranean, perhaps around Africa, to western Europe and the British Isles (Rabbi Zvi Ilani and others, undated). These were the seafaring days of Ulysses, the well documented civilization of Egypt, and the short but important reign of the Hittites in Anatolia. This age also saw the domestication of horses and the first use of iron (Macqueen, 1986).

Could one have crossed the sea in a ship like the ones made over 3,000 years ago? We believe that the answer is yes. We discussed Thor Heyerdahl's Ra expeditions: Heyerdahl and his crew built replicas of ancient reed boats and successfully completed an Atlantic Ocean crossing on them, using only ancient technology (Heyerdahl, 1971).

Sarah, the civil engineer in our group, told us she had read that in 1997, 24 teams of rowers raced across the Atlantic from Tenerife, one of the Canary Islands, to Barbados, in 41 to 100 days. All arrived safely (Regatta, 1997). Sarah also told us about Victoria Murden, the first woman on record to row solo across the Atlantic Ocean, from Tenerife to the Caribbean island of Guadeloupe (Adept, 2004). Sarah told us that the crossing is now an annual event.

We had already learned that the silk road, the route used for ancient trading of silk and other goods across central Asia, was begun much earlier than previous historians had believed. The discovery of Chinese silk in Egypt, used in the 16th century BCE, suggests the very early existence of the silk road (Lubec and others, 1993). This long distance trade should have provided recognition of the immense size of the earth.

Hilda said, "Looking back at Olmec civilization in Mexico, we know that by 1450 BCE, there was obsidian trade between Cuba and Yucatan. Trade with Cuba means that they could navigate ships across the Caribbean, a dangerous place to paddle. The Olmec civilization was the earliest so far recorded in the New World, and I consider it in some ways more advanced than the civilizations of the Mayans and others that followed. Some of the ages revealed by carbon dating show us that civilizations in greater Mesoamerica developed several hundred years earlier than is commonly supposed. For example, the phonetic alphabet used by the Mayans was derived from a proto-Mayan (Olmec) language of which we have little record (Breiner and Coe, 1972).

"Travel in ancient times from Mesoamerica north to the Colorado delta country would be unknown to us, were it not for the discovery of ancient trade goods, including advanced strains of maize" (Cordell, 1984).

My wife, Janet, and I had recently visited the Pacific northwest, and I reminded my friends that few places in the world of the thirteenth century BCE had better craftsmen, artists, and fishermen than those of our Pacific northwest. On the Makah Reservation of northwest Washington we had recently asked a Makah widow, 98 years of age, if the many languages spoken by the northwest Indian peoples didn't make communication difficult. Her Canadian husband was a native of northern Vancouver Island. "We had no trouble understanding each other in our native Indian languages," she told us.

We went on discussing ancient peoples, until well into the night. Henry took delight in instructing us about the ancient world. We were all eager to participate in the discussion, and we remember much of what was said.

In the year 1279 BCE, most of the habitable earth was occupied by humans, millions of them, speaking a variety of languages, with sophisticated writing systems in use in several isolated regions. The level of learning, technology, and accumulated knowledge varied widely. People in parts of every populated continent were engaged in agriculture, many groups employed beasts of burden, and of those who lived near water, many were excellent boatmen.

In those areas where food was plentiful and society was organized, a small portion of the population was free to indulge their curiosity and wonder about the world they lived in. They recalled the history of their people, speculated on cosmology, and listened attentively to those who had traveled great distances.

As in every age there were a few so bright that they quickly learned many of the languages they encountered, and traveled widely to learn of the world around them. The peoples in the lands adjacent to the great inland sea (the Mediterranean) made boats propelled by both sail and oar. These ancient travelers had sailed north to the British Isles, east to India, and where else we cannot be sure. Their log books are lost—or were never kept. The people of this age were better at leading camels and steering ships than at writing in books.

I proposed to my friends that a young man, particularly talented in language and diplomacy, could have traveled around the earth as early as the thirteenth century BCE. All of us were intrigued by this radical idea, so much so that Janet and I proposed to replicate the journey, and our fireside friends challenged us to go.

About then Hilda remembered that she had some months ago received a few ancient tiles from a colleague working on an archaeological investigation in Morocco. She recalled, "Some farmers in a small village near the Atlantic coast were building a new irrigation system, and they stumbled across an ancient vault containing thousands of clay tiles. Local scholars did not recognize the language, recorded with symbols pressed into the clay. The archaeologist who sent me the sample tiles is an old fellow, not well known in academic circles, and therefore not immediately followed up."

Hilda kept talking, "I know that box of old tiles is somewhere around my office. The writing is pretty well preserved all right, but what language were they writing? It is not in any standard cuneiform script. There were also a few drawings to illustrate the text. The old archaeologist who sent the samples has proposed that these tiles are a tale of travel. Now I remember, maybe I put a few of those tiles in my car, to show a friend."

Sylvester, proud of his recently acquired cyber skills, boasted, "Just find me that box of tiles. With our newest computer programs, I'm sure we can decipher any ancient language. I'll have it figured out in no time."

Our excitement was mounting. Bruce, our paleo-ecologist, suggested, "Maybe someone really did travel around the world in ancient times. Chances are, their record was hidden or lost, so their endeavor was forgotten." Suddenly we were hoping that perhaps at last such a record had been rediscovered.

In a few minutes Hilda returned from searching her car, with three tiles in hand. When Sylvester looked at the tiles, he exclaimed: "Look at this! Do any of you recognize the dots and bars? These are proto-Mayan numbers. We have early Mayan numbers in a Moroccan vault. We could have a record of the first traveler around the world, right here, on these tiles!"

Hilda looked again at the tiles, a little chagrined. "Yes," she said, "You are right. I should have recognized those symbols myself."

As the only geologist present, I took this opportunity to fill my friends in on current dating methods. I asked them, "Have you been reading where we are in millennial scale calendars? We can now use isotopes of uranium, thorium, rubidium, neodymium, beryllium, and potassium (U, Th, Rb, Nd, Be, and K), in addition to carbon (C). Carbon dates are being calibrated by comparing them with lake varves, dendrochronology, and rock dehydration. Carbon can be used for dating materials and events up to 50,000 years old. Potassium can be used to date older objects and events. Events between 50,000 and 100,000 years ago cannot be accurately dated with today's technology. Within decades, we will have a calendar that goes back 80,000 years with an uncertainty of perhaps 40 to 50 years."

As our fire died down to a few red coals, we retired for the night, each of us expressing enthusiasm for learning more about ancient travel.

≋

One month later, the box of tiles had been found, in spite of the fact that finding any missing object in Hilda's office at the university almost required a major dig. Not only had she found the box, but after an exhaustive search she had found the address of her colleague in Morocco and had arranged to visit the site where most of the tiles remained, waiting to be uncovered.

After her trip to Morocco, Hilda sent samples from the weathered timbers protecting the tiles to State University for carbon dating, and the preliminary analyses indicated dates between 3,300 and 3,200 years before the present.

Reading the tiles was difficult, but the early Mayan numbers helped to put the tiles in sequence. Sylvester was not able to read the tiles "in no time," but ten months later he excitedly reported to us that these tiles did indeed contain records of travel to distant lands: travel with horses, camels, on foot, and by canoe. Sylvester combined old and new technology, when he used his digital camera to photograph the writing on the tiles from several directions, making it easier to read the ancient inscriptions. Here were clay tiles, over 3,200 years old, now viewable on an enhanced computer screen! The ancient writer had braved many dangers, learned many languages, and made remarkable scientific observations. We had discovered the world's first geologist and natural scientist!

≋

Janet and I took up the challenge of following the routes described on the tiles, and we began our preparations. Not having a full lifetime ahead of us, we agreed to make the journey using modern transportation, seeking knowledge of both ancient and modern times. During the following two years, we visited the New World from Cuba to Mexico to Alaska, and the Old World from China and Uzbekistan, to Anatolia, Egypt, Morocco, and the Canary Islands. We rode in airplanes and buses rather than on camels or primitive ships. All the while we tried to view our journey as it would have appeared to the ancient traveler.

Figure 1. Ancient Berber Script

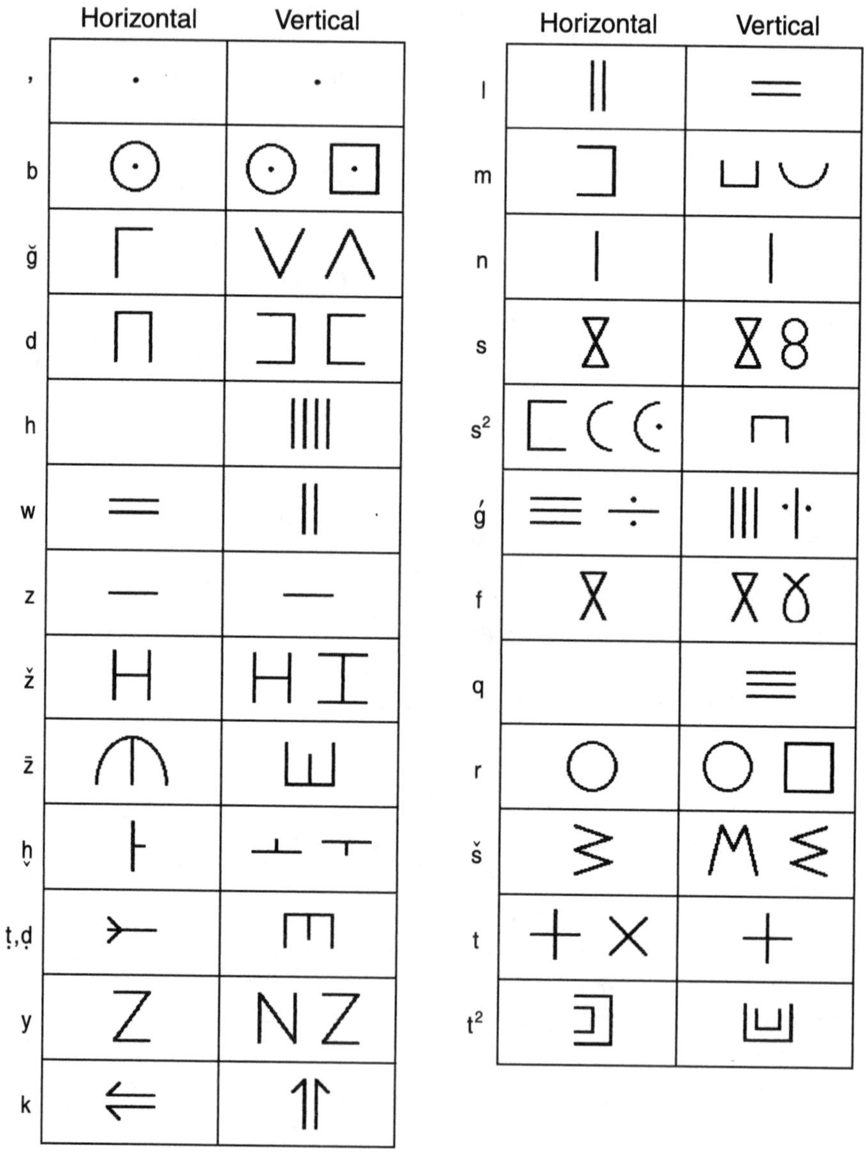

	Horizontal	Vertical		Horizontal	Vertical
'			l		
b			m		
ğ			n		
d			s		
h			s²		
w			ǵ		
z			f		
ž			q		
z̄			r		
ḥ			š		
ṭ,ḍ			t		
y			t²		
k					

xxii

Frequently along the way we asked local scholars, "What would this land have been like three millennia ago?" Surprising to us, we were often told, "Not really a whole lot different." Yes, in many places the older folks are still spinning yarn and weaving rugs.

THE TEXT AND ITS TRANSLATION

The task of translating the tiles was multi-layered. We had to identify both the language and the system used to write it. Our traveler could have expressed himself in Greek, Egyptian, Chinese, Berber, or any one of several languages he learned in the New World. He could have used the cuneiform writing system, ancient Egyptian, ancient Berber, or Chinese.

Until recently, linguists knew little about ancient Berber, and they believed it was unwritten. However, modern scholarship shows that it was written. (The chief curator of the Royal Museum of Morocco, in Rabat, Morocco, showed us examples when we visited there in the year 2000.)

Although the ancient traveler and writer was competent in many languages, he believed that ancient Berber was the best of languages, and he wrote most of the tiles in the ancient Berber script. Little did he imagine that his favorite language, ancient Berber, would be limited in subsequent millennia, and the ancient Berber script would almost completely disappear. The ancient Berber script does exist to this day in remote communities of northwest Africa, where it is used primarily for writing romantic letters and poetry.

Figure 1 shows examples of the ancient Berber script (Lo, 2003).

These symbols may be written in a horizontal line from right to left, or vertically, from bottom to top, sometimes with consonants only. Variations in the writing system were almost as common as the number of scholars who wrote it.

The traveler had also mastered cuneiform writing, a widely used ancient system in which the scribe used a stylus to imprint a variety of wedges and dots on clay. The writing on some of the ancient ceramic tiles was in a cuneiform system. Writers of many languages in the 13th century BCE wrote with cuneiform characters.

To make his account more scholarly, the ancient traveler included a few hieroglyphs, mostly for place names from Greek, Chinese, and Egyptian. On a few tiles, he chose to use Greek or Egyptian script.

When he did this, we don't think he was trying to hide his meaning, but rather to be more precise. A few tiles repeat in ancient Berber phrases that were in common usage in Egyptian or Greek, thus helping us to decipher both the writing system and the meaning.

The following chapters are the text of the tiles that have been excavated and translated. The account written here is in the words of the translator—that is, the team of translators. Considering the uncertainties of translation, our text is very liberal, written in the parlance of contemporary America. Place names are nearly all modernized, to facilitate understanding by today's reader. The translator has adopted a metric system of weights and distance, albeit with some uncertainty concerning comparable values. The translator's commentary, written with knowledge not available to the original traveler, is in brackets [. . .]. Longer commentaries are placed in a box.

To aid the reader we have in many cases added dates, in the calendar system which is in common use in the western world today. That is, a number followed by the letters " BCE" means the number of years before the common era. For example, "1000 BCE" means 3,000 years ago. The letters "CE" following a date mean "common era;" these dates are the same as a year number followed by "AD."

The Ancient Traveler

We have learned little about our traveler prior to his epic journey. We do not know his name before he became known as Follow the Sun. At birth he was given an obscure name in ancient Berber, that means something like "unstoppable"—but that could be just another good story. For signing documents, he used a device of his own creation. As for his appearance, there are no drawings extant. We know that his dark hair was shoulder length. He was tall, slender, and athletic, and he had an insatiable thirst for scholarship. He left us no record of how he dressed, except his reference to accepting a gift of clothing suitable for his Alaskan travels. From that we infer that he wore the garb most suitable to the climate where he was trekking, and as close as possible to that of his contemporaries around the world.

THE MODERN JOURNEY

As Janet and I have followed the path of the ancient traveler, we have added our own observations on life as it is today in the places our ancient traveler visited. These observations are placed in boxes at the end of a chapter, with titles, such as "Egypt today."

We have also added commentary on parts of the ancient journey. Our additions to the ancient text are, like the commentary of the translator, placed in boxes or in brackets [...], to avoid confusion with the text found on the ancient tiles.

REFERENCES

As we have been studying the ancient text, we have also tried to learn from other sources about the ancient world and about modern life in the places visited by our ancient traveler. Where the work of modern scholars has confirmed or added to our ancient traveler's observations, we have noted the author's name, and the date of publication, in parentheses. The complete references are cited at the end of the book, grouped by subject.

WE NOW BEGIN,
IN THE WORDS OF OUR ANCIENT TRAVELER,
AS TRANSLATED FOR US.

≋

CHAPTER ONE

NORTHWEST AFRICA

1278 BCE

THE PEOPLE OF northwest Africa [Morocco] and the islands to the west [the Canary Islands] lead a simple life. Those on the islands live primarily in volcanic caves. The islanders' contact with the rest of the world is limited to a few rare trade boats from the Mediterranean. The Moroccans' contacts are primarily caravans bringing gold and other trade goods from the Kingdom of Mali, far to the southeast.

In our part of Morocco, people live in small mud brick houses, speak a local dialect of Berber, till the soil, and herd animals. Only the king, his family, and a few important individuals can understand written language. Among those few, more important than a general, was a mysterious old miner, perhaps age 50, who walked with a cane and who could tell you about the rocks that hold up the mountains, the rivers that wash them down, and the origin of metals and precious stones.

This old miner, with his long gray beard and a bald spot on the top of his head, was my father. As a teenager, I had accompanied him to the Kingdom of Mali, where we studied the occurrence of gold placers and developed methods for determining where gold occurs and how to find it.

I was born in Morocco. My mother died while I was very young, so her older sister took care of me. My aunt was married to a member of the royal family, so we had access to the royal library, the best collection of literature west of Egypt. She and I studied there every day. In the library I learned Egyptian and Greek. I spent most of the daylight hours with my aunt, jotting down notes with my quill pen and translating the manuscripts into Berber. Often in the cool of the early morning I went out running with my friends, but as the sun grew stronger, I inevitably headed for the library and my scrolls of papyrus.

Our king often needed money to pay his soldiers, to provide dowries for his daughters, and to display his wealth to neighboring potentates. At such times he would call the mysterious old miner who walked with a cane and practiced such earth study methods as "following a contact," finding a lode offset by a "fault," and "panning up-stream." As his son, I worked as his principal assistant and soon became an avid student of the earth. I was interested in every line of knowledge, and I was greatly pleased to exchange ideas with scholars who visited from great distances. Nothing pleased me more than learning new truths about the world of which I was a part.

In the year 1279 BCE a young man, only partly of royal blood, became Pharaoh of Egypt and took the name Ramesses II. In the first few years of his reign he was confronted with repeated invasions of "Sea People" who came from the west of Egypt. The Egyptians ultimately prevailed, but the young monarch, allied with the Minoan civilization on the island of Crete, vowed to build the world's most seaworthy ships, learn about the people and lands to the west of Egypt, and gain control of them, or at least accommodation.

In this vein Ramesses II outfitted a capable vessel and sent a group of scientists to survey the lands west of Egypt. Their ship passed through the strait between the great limestone sea towers [Strait of Gibraltar] and they viewed the northwestern extent of Morocco, where I met them. They knew little of my native language, Berber, but from my studies I could converse in Egyptian or Greek. I introduced these visitors to our king, and the Egyptian scholars carved out for us a document of mutual friendship and peace.

Word of my father, the mysterious miner, and word of my great eagerness to learn, had reached all the way to Egypt, and the pharaoh had instructed the delegation of scientists to study with us. One day they were explaining to me how they could be sure that the earth, the sun, and the moon were spherical bodies. They explained how tall ships and steep hills along the shore disappeared from view, first in their lower part, and then the upper part as well, as the distance separating them from the viewer increased. They told me that gifted astronomers in Egypt had calculated the circumference of our earth to be about 40,000 kilometers.

That night, after hearing all this talk, I slept very little. The following morning I told our guests, "I am ready to travel. If the earth is a sphere of 40,000 kilometers around, and I can walk or paddle 40 kilometers a day, I will return in a little more than 1,000 days."

The wise men laughed. "No one," they said, "has gone around the earth, because there are great oceans with monstrous sea storms that can destroy the ablest ship, and sea dragons that can tear a ship in two and devour the crew. There are high plateaus with fields of ice and snow all year long, and hot, steamy jungles where it rains almost every day. Not to mention the lions and tigers and beasts you have never seen, and barbarous people who will run you down and gnaw your bones."

Day after day I persisted with my proposal, and gradually I convinced the visiting scientists that this was a worthy effort. Had not the great Pharaoh sent them to find the western edge of the earth?

They taught me everything they could think of that I would need to know: how to navigate by the stars and planets, how to read the weather, how to strike a fire, how to make shoes, why to boil water before drinking it. Ultimately the eastern scientists agreed to take me, with several companions, back to Egypt to obtain the blessings and support of the Pharaoh, and to learn about seaworthy ship construction and the existing knowledge of geography.

Before leaving for Egypt, we talked to seamen who knew about the Canary Islands and the westerly currents that had taken many a voyager to "the edge of the earth." But alas, these African seamen did not wish to travel west to oblivion and refused to be part of our proposed expedition.

Then came a stroke of good fortune: one seaman told us that on one of the Canary Islands [Isla Gomera] was a group of shipwrecked fishermen whose home was apparently to the west of the great western ocean [the Atlantic Ocean]. These shipwrecked people had neither the resources nor the ability to construct a ship for a return voyage across the ocean. To them, our proposed voyage would be their only hope to travel home. To me, it would be an opportunity to see the islands west of Africa, learn a language totally different from those in my known world, and take an important step on my journey around the earth.

The scientists from the eastern Mediterranean had heard about fiery volcanoes at "the edge of the earth," on the same islands as the shipwrecked fishermen. Their Egyptian boat having withstood the storms of the Mediterranean, they decided we could sail it to the most active volcanic island of the Canaries [Isla Tenerife] to see the erupting volcano for ourselves.

≋

CHAPTER TWO

THE ADVENTURERS

1277 BCE

A GAIN, AGAIN, AND AGAIN, geysering fountains of molten stone. They burst out of the vent and hurtle hundreds of meters into the sky. On their way up the stones are red. Then they fall back to earth, turning black as they fall, and they accumulate on the walls of the vent. The sound of eruptions is deafening, and occasional large bursts light up the whole volcano.

We sit in the protective shadow of a giant block of stone, which only a week ago was not here. This is the highest peak on these islands. Periodically the escaping gases ignite, producing a shower of ash and bombs, filling the sky. For a moment there is comparative quiet, and we can see the viscous lava erupting from near the top of the cone, running down the steep slopes, red liquid beneath, and a breccia of angular black blocks riding above.

If we look carefully we can see that the ropy-textured rock on which we rest has the same structure as that which is pouring forth to build the cone. For days, weeks, months, the eruption continues, building the island. A small vent near us conveniently heats our tea water.

We are visiting Tenerife, one of seven volcanic islands that have built up, eruption after eruption, from the floor of the Atlantic Ocean.

[Translator's note: The ancient traveler often wrote of past events as if they were taking place in the present. He did this whenever the events were especially exciting or important to him.]

5

Our party of young adventurers consisted of three groups. My group included inhabitants of these islands and the adjacent coast of Morocco. We were native speakers of the [ancient] Berber language, and we understood the hieroglyphics etched long ago on the rocks of the Canary Islands, and the mountains of northwestern Africa.

The second group included the scientists from the eastern Mediterranean. These visiting scientists came to Morocco and to these islands in a large ship marvelously constructed of fitted cedar planks, so that they flex with the force of the waves, and rarely leak. Unlike the native Berber dugouts, this Egyptian boat was propelled by both sails and oars. The scientists were eager to view the volcanic eruptions, which had been described by others as the end of the earth.

The third group spoke a language far different from anything spoken by either the local inhabitants or the scientists from the eastern Mediterranean. These young men had been washed up on the shores of Isla Gomera about ten years ago. They still dreamed of returning to their families, who they told us live on large islands far to the west. Since coming here, they had learned the Berber dialect of the Canaries, with difficulty. They were fishermen, while the Berbers were hunters and herdsmen, and locally farmers. Thus, their occupations were complementary, and they got along well.

The red/black volcanic fragments began to fall closer. It was time we moved to greater safety. The native Canary Islanders and some of the Moroccans had visited active volcanism before. But the shipwrecked fishermen and the eastern Mediterranean scientists have only heard of such activity, never viewing it first hand. Sometimes the ground shakes with fury.

These are wonderful islands. Fruit, berries, dates, and a variety of vegetables—for example, giant asparagus—are ample for all who come to gather them. There are numerous goats, rabbits, large birds, sea mammals, and an abundance of fish. Cloud banks on the northern shores of the islands provide a warm, moist climate for tropical plants. Forests of long-needled pine cover the intermediate elevations. Semi-arid flora cover a large part of the islands. In spring the islands are decked in wildflowers (Bramwell, 1997).

The population on the islands is sparse, and generally friendly. Occasionally traders row or sail the 100 kilometers from the closest island to the coast of Morocco. From the islands they trade sea mammal pelts, stone and ceramic cookware, and salt. From the Moroccan coast the traders bring objects of copper, brass and woven cloth.

≋

A year had passed, and I had learned many things from the Mediterranean scholars: astronomy, geography, and mathematics. Like those scientists, I was convinced that the earth is a sphere.

I decided that we should demonstrate the shape and size of the earth, for our ship's crew. One of the Canary Islands is steep sided and about two kilometers in elevation. We sailed the scientists' ship to the south side of this island and steered directly out to sea, carefully measuring the distance traveled, using a float and a sand clock. As we left the beach we could clearly see the entire island. But as we moved away we lost sight of the shoreline. Then we lost sight of the lower, arid portion of the island, then the higher, pine-covered portion of the island, and finally we could see only the small snow-tipped summit. When we saw the last of the island, we were about 160 kilometers out to sea. I tried to explain to the crew that we were losing sight of the island because the curvature of the earth produced a barrier to our view of the lower portions.

Back on shore I drew a picture [Figure 2] showing the island, our ship 160 kilometers out to sea, and the surface of the water. I pointed out that if the ocean were flat we could look from the ship to the island, and see the entire island. The curvature of the surface of the earth amounts to approximately two kilometers of height in 160 kilometers of distance on the surface. And this would be true if we had sailed north from the island, or west from the island, or in the Mediterranean, or on the Nile, or anywhere. [These scientists were unaware of the refraction of light around the curvature of the earth.]

The visiting scientists told of similar measurements obtained from approaching the cliffs that rise on both sides of the strait separating the Mediterranean Sea from the Atlantic Ocean [the cliffs later known as the Pillars of Hercules, on both sides of the Strait of Gibraltar].

Back on the island beach, the Egyptian mathematician showed us how to calculate the distance to the center of the earth. Drawing in the damp sand, he said, "You have measured the height of the mountain as two kilometers. Let's call that height h. And you have measured the approximate distance out to sea, where the snow-capped tip of the mountain disappeared, as 160 kilometers. Let's call that distance d.

7

Now think of a giant triangle. One side is the distance we just called *d*. The second side is the distance from our ship on the water, down to the center of the earth. Let's call that side *a*. The third side of the triangle is the height of the mountain, *h*, plus the distance from the beach down to the center of the earth, *a*."

FIGURE 2. MEASURING THE CIRCUMFERENCE OF THE EARTH

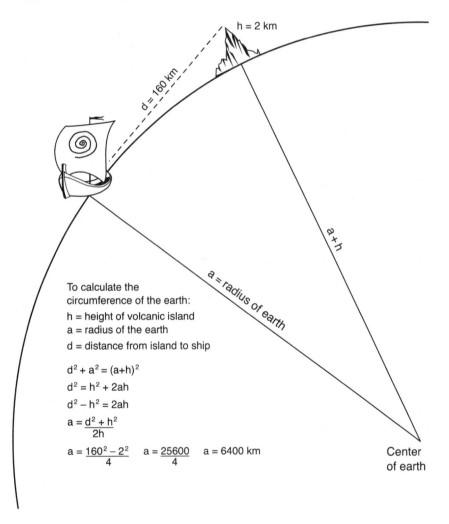

h = 2 km

d = 160 km

a + h

a = radius of earth

To calculate the circumference of the earth:

h = height of volcanic island
a = radius of the earth
d = distance from island to ship

$d^2 + a^2 = (a+h)^2$

$d^2 = h^2 + 2ah$

$d^2 - h^2 = 2ah$

$a = \dfrac{d^2 + h^2}{2h}$

$a = \dfrac{160^2 - 2^2}{4}$ $a = \dfrac{25600}{4}$ a = 6400 km

Center of earth

He finished drawing the big triangle for us, in the sand [Figure 2]. He puzzled over the diagram for a moment, lost in thought, and then informed us, "There is a constant mathematical relationship between the length of the sides of a right triangle. When we know the length of two sides, we can calculate the length of the third side. One side of our triangle is *a*. One side is *d*. And the longest side is *a-plus-h* . In my studies at home, I figured out a secret formula, so I know that *d* squared plus *a* squared equals *a-plus-h* squared."

He drew his special formula in the sand. He rearranged the figures several times, taking care to separate out *a* from the other symbols. Then he substituted the numbers for the symbols *d* and *h*, which we already knew, and he was able to calculate the value of *a* for us. That's how we learned that it is about 6,400 kilometers to the center of the earth [Figure 2].

A crewman said, "But we still don't know the circumference of the earth [at this latitude]."

"Now that is comparatively simple," answered the mathematician. "You will find that it takes 6.3 radius lengths to complete the circle. This is true of any circle, including the earth."

This made sense to me. The others practiced measuring circles in the sand, and sure enough, every circle had the same relationship between the distance around it, and a line drawn from its outside to its center.

I stayed out on the beach a long time, reviewing all this, until I was satisfied that the mathematician's special formula really worked, every time.

CHAPTER THREE

PREPARING FOR THE GRAND VOYAGE
1276 BCE

S EVERAL OF US, including three of the stranded fishermen, accompanied the eastern Mediterranean geographers on their return trip to Egypt. The voyage from Morocco to Egypt took 35 days.

Soon after we arrived in Egypt, we presented a proposal to Ramesses II, for a voyage west from the Canary Islands to the western shore of the Atlantic Ocean.

Not only did the pharaoh feel very positive toward the proposed trans-Atlantic voyage, but he gave it high priority and personally participated in the planning. He would commission a state-of-the-art, ocean-going ship, and would employ the best, most knowledgeable navigator. To the pharaoh, discovery meant conquest—and conquest was his life.

After questioning the shipwrecked fishermen, our navigator explained what had probably happened to them, and how we would steer safely across the Atlantic Ocean and back. From his travels, and those of others, he believed there was a strong westerly current that traveled from the Canary Islands west across the Atlantic Ocean. On the western edge of the Atlantic—and our stranded fishermen were evidence that a western shore exists—there is a current traveling northeast. This current travels across the Atlantic until it reaches the shore of western Europe. The current then turns southeast, past the Strait of Gibraltar, down the coast of Morocco, and on to the Canary Islands. Thus it travels a circular path, the way the stars appear to rotate around the polar star [clockwise]. Our navigator said we could return the fishermen to

11

their homes, deliver me to the shores west of the Atlantic, and return the rest of the crew to Morocco and the Mediterranean.

Our stranded fishermen, according to their account, came from one of several great islands, which they say form the western edge of the Atlantic Ocean. So what could we do if we reached these islands, and could not communicate with anyone, or perhaps met people unfriendly to our fishermen? Neither I nor any of the scholars from the eastern Mediterranean had ever encountered a language that had no relation to any other known language. To address this problem I learned the native tongue of the fishermen, in hope that their language was one of a family of languages that we might encounter west of the Atlantic—and indeed, it was.

EASTERN MEDITERRANEAN DEEP WATER SHIPS

The shipwrights and shipyards of Egypt have had thousands of years of experience, both in the construction of reed boats, and of cedar plank boats. The earlier Egyptian ships were primarily shallow draft boats for travel on the Nile. The first ships (3000 BCE) sent across deep water to Syria were adaptations of the large river boats (Jones, 1995, and Casson, 1995).

Queen Hatshepsut (1500 BCE) sent ships to the land of Punt, to trade for myrrh, ivory, ebony, monkeys, greyhounds, and slaves. (Some believe that the land of Punt was what we call Somalia today.) These ships had a keel but no ribs. The mast was erected mid-ship. The ship was 25 to 30 meters long, and driven by 30 oarsmen. It could be sailed in half wind.

The queen's barge for transporting huge granite obelisks measured at least 63 meters long and 25 meters wide. The sails could be raised, and the mast could be lowered while traveling. The barge carried the obelisks from the granite quarries at Aswan to lower Luxor. The obelisks at the Karnak temple stand almost 35 meters high and weigh 350 tons each.

Deep water commerce was so important that ships sailing the Red Sea were dismantled and carried overland from the Nile. But this transport was so arduous that the Egyptians dug a canal in the Wadie

Hamamat from the Nile to the Red Sea. Seafaring was so important to Egypt that one account tells of sending 40 ships to a port in Syria. Documents from Babylonia tell of canals linking all the major cities and transporting grain, oil, fruit, vegetables, cattle, fish, milk, wool, stone, bricks, and shoe leather, as well as passengers. An illustration of the period shows bearers unloading a ship of its precious load of ivory, gold, myrrh trees, and greyhounds (Jones, 1995, and Casson, 1995).

The principal timber used in these boats was cedar from Lebanon, where trees grew as tall as 66 meters. A sharp adze was used to cut the logs into planks, which were attached edge to edge with wedges and dovetails. Shorter boards were cut from native acacia and sycamore. Oil was applied to make the boards flexible and asphalt was used to waterproof the boats. The asphalt was brought from Mesopotamia.

By the reign of Ramesses III, the Egyptians had borrowed the ship-building technology of the northeastern Mediterranean (similar to the technology used by the "sea people"), and with these ships, about 1190 BCE, Egypt succeeded in decisively defeating the invaders, in one of the greatest sea battles of all time.

We took an active part in the fabrication of a deep sea ship designed especially for our trip. The ship built for us to cross the Atlantic was designed to make optimum use of the sea and wind currents, depending on oars only as need be to stay abreast of the currents. Two smaller sails were stowed in case the principal sail were destroyed.

Our ship as designed for the Atlantic crossing was 22 meters long, 4 meters wide, and boasted a giant cedar keel 20 meters in length. The large cedar timbers were shaped by careful adzing, then split by wooden pegs and joined by wet wedges and splices. The craft was designed primarily for sail drive, but was outfitted for six oarsmen on each side and two men operating the till.

We packed dried food—sausage, jerky, hardtack, dried fruits and vegetables—to avoid the necessity of hauling fuel for cooking. Fresh water would be a limiting factor. When filled, the water containers made of animal bladders would be sealed and attached to our ship below the water line, thus adding to the buoyancy of the craft. Our ship underwent rigorous test runs from Morocco to the Canary Islands.

In the next year [1274 BCE], the vessel and crew were ready, complete with a document from the pharaoh in four languages: Egyptian, Phoenician, Greek, and Berber. This was addressed to all the rulers of foreign lands, whoever they might be, promising peace and friendship, from the earth's mightiest sovereign: Ramesses II.

From Egypt back to Morocco

After returning to Morocco, we made several trips around and southwest from the Canary Islands to familiarize ourselves with the somewhat predictable habits of the sea. We covered our ship with two layers of animal skins, for waterproofing. For a month we lived on dried food and sea life that our fishermen could catch in deep water, so that we could become accustomed to the fare that we would be enjoying during our voyage. For drinking water we were doubly careful. We took only water from the famous springs on the Island of Gomera. Then we boiled it before packing it in sealed bladders, roped together and partially filled with air so that they could not sink.

As an extra precaution, we deliberately capsized our boat and provisions in the choppy sea. Every hand sprung to action as we had planned and practiced, and our boat was soon righted, without loss of crew or supplies.

The weather was perfect. We planned to dry our fresh fish, as it was caught. We carried a tallow lantern in case we should encounter others on the sea at night.

The sail on our boat was a very sturdy sheet of Egyptian linen canvas, reinforced with stout cord. It was four meters high and five meters wide. We agreed that it should be decorated, perhaps with a glyph of ancient Berber. Our crew chose a spiral, a symbol common

Figure 3. The Right Spiral

to many cultures. While the spiral has been used in many ways, with many communicative intentions, it is generally a sign denoting growth, the recognition that very small beginnings can evolve into great plants, creatures, storms, volcanic eruptions, ideas, and nations [Figure 3]. In our sail, we hoped that an idea would grow into an appreciation of the universe, a combination of thoughts and objectives that would ultimately bring the peoples of many lands together.

A MODERN VIEW OF THE CANARY ISLANDS

The Canaries are idyllic volcanic islands (Araña and Carracedo, 1978). The Spanish built cities there beginning in the 1600s, white-washed and red-tiled like those of Spain and other Mediterranean coasts, providing retirement homes for people from all over western Europe. It is today a modern country, with a large university, modern freeways, and old streets so narrow that it is necessary to park on the sidewalks. The seven Canary Islands are connected by large modern ferries and frequent air service. Bananas and tomatoes, grown in greenhouses, are the principal crops (Bramwell, 1997, Martín-Rodriguez E., 1998).

The Canary Islands are important to this journey, because historically those intending to cross the Atlantic have departed from here, carrying their water from the Island of Gomera, as Christopher Columbus did in each of his voyages, as described in his journal (Columbus, 1492).

Flowering plants native to the Canary Islands decorate gardens all over the world. Even the weeds are magnificent: we found dandelions four feet tall. A shrub, similar in appearance to the chemise of southern California, grows up to 20 meters tall (Bramwell, 1997).

The stone-faced terraces of the Canaries are impressive. They are almost ubiquitous, in some places on very steep hillsides. Most are long abandoned. On the island of Gomera, these terraces rise steeply from the water's edge, to an elevation of more than a hundred meters.

In the town of Guimar, on the island of Tenerife, there are several "step pyramids," which resemble the step pyramids of ancient Egypt. We do not know with certainty when they were built, or by whom. Thor Heyerdahl and other researchers at the museum built there by FERCO believe that these pyramids are about 3,000 years old (Bethencourt, De Luca, and Perera, 1996). But local archaeologists do not hold this view. (FERCO is the Foundation for Exploration and Research on Cultural Origins, founded by Thor Heyerdahl. The website is www.ferco.org.)

The Canary Islands are a mystery. The rocks of these islands are engraved with hieroglyphics of pre-Spanish (pre-conquest) people, apparently of Berber origin (Navarro-Mederos and del Carmen del Arco Aguilar, 1996). We have no record of who lived there or how they lived in the thirteenth century BCE. The western world first learned about the islands second hand, from the descriptions of Herodotus and Pliny the Elder more than two millennia ago. History is then quiet until the islands were "discovered" by the Portuguese in the 1340s CE. What they found were tribes called the Guanches, reportedly Nordic in appearance but possibly of Berber origin. They had no metal tools or weapons, and no boats. Here were Neolithic people, living on the very doorstep of Europe. Apparently technology advanced rapidly, for in 1492 Columbus steered his flotilla directly to the islands, where he stocked up on fresh water and food, and had one of his ships repaired.

≋

CHAPTER FOUR

ACROSS THE ATLANTIC OCEAN TO CUBA
1273 BCE

S PRING IS THE SEASON with the fewest storms, so in April, from the Island of Gomera, by the light of a full moon, we set sail and waved goodbye to our comrades on shore.

One important question that we had not answered was: How far is it from the Canary Islands to the western edge of the Atlantic? Our astronomer-navigator assured us that at the latitudes of Morocco and Egypt, we were far north of the equator and thus need not travel the entire circumference of the earth. But a more difficult question for me was, how far is it from the western shore of the Atlantic to known places, like Arabia or India? Maybe we have several oceans to cross, maybe with continents in between? I resolved to get answers to these questions, not only for myself but for the benefit of future travelers.

Once out of sight of the Canary Islands we could not be sure where we were. We knew by the position of the sun, the moon, and the stars what direction we were headed, and timing a float tossed on the water gave us a rough idea of how rapidly we were progressing.

To get the maximum shove from the wind and the sea currents we were frequently using our oars to steer back into the breeze and ocean current.

Our cook laced our fare with spices that he had brought along from Egypt, some possibly originating in the far east. Some days we gathered edible seaweed that floated on the ocean, but we had to use fresh water to leach out the salt, and to me it tasted bitter.

One early morning, when all we could see was water, one of the crew asked me, "How do you know which direction to go?"

I answered him, "I follow the sun"—and it stuck: from then on, I was called "Follow the Sun," in a succession of languages.

All seemed to go our way: no storms, no sea monsters, no place to fall of the edge of the world. About eight weeks out we began seeing small uninhabited islands [the Bahamas] which our shipwrecked fishermen recognized. This, they said, meant that we were very close to their homeland. We should soon see a long mountainous island [Cuba]. And we did. Our fishermen could understand the language of the local inhabitants, and they rejoiced to be almost home.

We had crossed the dreaded Atlantic on half of the supplies provided for us. Our navigator now had a solid idea of the distance to return across the Atlantic, and of the supplies required.

Cuba

The big island of Cuba extends from east to west about 1,000 kilometers, and is less than 100 kilometers from north to south, forming a barrier between the Atlantic Ocean and the west Atlantic Ocean [Caribbean Sea]. It is separated from the mainland to the north [Florida] by 100 kilometers of water, and separated from another large island [Haiti] by 50 kilometers. We estimated these distances by the time it took us to travel, and from the reports of the local inhabitants.

Cuba is a land of beauty and contrast, warmed all year by the sun. The beaches on the north central coastline are covered in sparkling sand. Large parts of the interior of the island are covered with long-needled pine trees. But most outstanding among the trees are the royal palms, with huge fronds spreading shade for us. Cuba is underlain by cavernous limestone, with streams of water that appear from and disappear into the rock caves [karst topography]. In shadier places within the jungle vegetation we saw many beautiful flowers, white, pink, and purple, some brightly colored and some in more muted shades, with a very complex structure [orchids]. While we were stopped for rest, admiring the many different kinds of orchids, we saw a long snake emerge from the brown mud, grab a small frog, and start to swallow it. Both the snake and the frog were completely covered in mud, of a uniform greenish brown hue.

To our benefit, we discovered there is lively trade across the straits between Cuba and the mainland to the southwest [Yucatan]: gold from the westernmost part of the big island, gem stones and jaguar pelts on their way to Mesoamerica, and obsidian and serpentine for carving and cutlery, to Cuba. In the interior of this island are hard green and blue stones that are sacred to the peoples of this region.

The balsawood and mahogany dugouts from Cuba were as much as 20 meters in length with a crew of up to twenty men. With these boats they traded among the many islands of the Caribbean Sea. The larger boats are constructed from mahogany and used in longer voyages. The balsawood boats are used for local travel and can easily be carried over land, if necessary.

The sea currents traveled northwest, along the north coast of Cuba, then turned back northeast toward the Atlantic Ocean. The current traveling northwest along the south coast of Cuba turned southwest toward Yucatan. Thus one part of the crew with the boat from Morocco would ride the northeast current homeward, while one young Cuban and I signed on with a 15 meter dugout on its way to Yucatan. No boats dared attempt long journeys during late summer or fall because of the fearsome hurricanes.

The people whom Columbus encountered when he landed on Cuba in 1492 were the Taino, farmers planting manioc, maize, casaba, squash, and beans. The villages were as large as 1,000 people, and they used a very accurate astronomic calendar.

The mild mannered Ciboney (Arawaks) were a gifted people who had migrated north from the Orinoco Valley, Trinidad, and the Antilles. Their art emphasized sculptures of demonic creatures/humans, not Olmec or Mayan, but clearly Taino. The execution of their art was very sophisticated.

We know little about who occupied Cuba and the greater Antilles circa 1273 BCE. But we do know that Cuba has been populated for at least 5,000 years, perhaps 10,000 years (Dacal and Rivero de la Calle, 1997), and that the Olmec culture blossomed in what is now southern Mexico, beginning about 1450 BCE.

The people that our traveler encountered were probably Ciboney (Arawak), who arrived from South America more than 5,000 years BCE, and were primarily hunters, fishermen, and plant gatherers. Their art was very different, and included spherical quartz balls, some as large as soccer balls. Their goods traded to other Caribbean Islands included seashells, turquoise, lapis lazuli, jade, and precious metals (Dacal and Rivero de la Calle, 1997).

As an ironic footnote to history, Christopher Columbus arrived in Cuba in the fall of 1492, accompanied by neither soldiers nor clergy. On Christmas day, 1492, one of his ships ran aground. The Admiral of the grounded ship, on receiving help from the native Cubans, had Columbus write this message to the sovereigns of Spain: "I assure Your Highnesses that I believe that there are no better people in the world, and no better land. They love their neighbours as themselves, and have the softest speech in the world, and are docile and always laughing" (Columbus, 1492, translated by Ife, 1990). The following April, Columbus returned from Spain to the same part of Cuba with 17 ships and 1,200 settlers (all men) and thus began the conquest of the New World.

≋

CHAPTER FIVE

MESOAMERICA

1272 BCE

ONE YEAR AGO MY CREW and I left the eastern shore of the Atlantic. Now [in the year 1272 BCE], I have struck out from Cuba with a group of traders, southwest across the open sea for a land few of my fellow voyagers had ever seen, where the inhabitants spoke a language no one on my side of the great ocean had ever heard. We carried jade and serpentine, colored feathers, even the magnificent pelt of the jaguar. These traders hoped to return with cocoa and chocolate, jewelry of gold and silver, rubber and resin of copal.

There were 16 of us in a mahogany dugout canoe 15 meters long and 2 meters wide. Skins were stretched across the boat to shed waves and rain. The sea current drove us steadily southwest, and two days out we could see the low profile of the Yucatan coastline, to the south.

We had a safe journey, but safety on the Yucatan coast requires more than fair weather. Under cover of night we slipped into a coastal lagoon and hid our dugout boat while we made contact with a group of friendly traders known to two of our party. All this peninsula is under the rule of one of several supreme beings, who are continuously skirmishing, collecting tariff from traders, farmers, and craftsmen, and taking slaves to be sacrificed to the gods.

When we had made the necessary contact we were able to row safely into the trading port of Xochimilitun [near the modern city of Merida]. Goods from Cuba were rare, traders bid for them feverishly, and my companions obtained a choice load for their return to Cuba (Clark, 1994).

I had never seen a city like this. There were long stone wharfs for the boats to tie to, walls and streets, and temples all made of stone, many painted red and other colors. There were workshops in which, using only stone tools, skilled artisans carved statuary showing the likeness of ruler-gods, made elaborate pottery, and wove garments of cotton, hide and brilliant feathers. This was the hub of sea trade from places as far away as Panama, and perhaps further [Venezuela and Peru].

It was the practice of traders to include for the return voyage a couple of native speakers to assist with the next trading voyage.

Sea travel on the Caribbean is dangerous even in the most favorable months, but the rewards are spectacular: merchants are among the most wealthy people in the kingdom, and commonly hold political positions.

All of our crew would return to Cuba except for me and a young man named Dzaltu, who had relatives here in Yucatan, and who looked for adventure.

To reach his brother and family, Dzaltu and I took a small fishing canoe up one of the lazy rivers. Yucatan is a low altitude peninsula composed almost entirely of limestone. The vegetation includes a variety of pink and yellow trees (Dirzo, 1994). Very few areas of this kingdom are good for agriculture, and away from the port cities the population is sparse (Stuart and Stuart, 1993).

On the river, the adults wore nothing above the waist, and the children, nothing at all. To fish they threw out a net, and the fishing was good. From small farms near the river we traded for corn, beans, amaranth, squash, avocados, and edible plants that grow wild. The fish were baked with a variety of delicious herbs—I have never tasted better fish.

I noticed that my new companions were always wary of strangers, and I asked why we needed to be so concerned. They let me know that they and the others with whom we traded fish for corn were what you might call "outlaws." Not that they had committed what I might consider a crime, but in the eyes of the authorities they were uncooperative, and to be uncooperative is a sin against their gods.

This took a lot of explaining by Dzaltu: "Some years ago our grandfather had achieved an elite status. His skull was reshaped in infancy, and as he grew, ornaments pierced his ears, lips, tongue, and other parts of his body. He used an obsidian blade to peel skin from his legs and variously tortured himself. The priests encouraged these acts and the pain drove him crazy. Ultimately he achieved the reward of having his head sawed off and his pumping heart cut out and fed to a hungry jaguar. His self destruction gained for his family a status of nobility. But we did not concur with these beliefs.

"When he was 16 years old my brother was awarded the honor of becoming a soldier. He wore a fantastic headdress, carried a sword and shield, and with the other soldiers waited for the morning planet [Venus] to reach the highest point above the horizon, then went forth to subdue those peoples who did not respect our god-king. Unfortunately he was captured by the opponents and made a slave. When he was 20 years old he was sacrificed to the gods of his captors.

"We live on this river and fish because we have babies and the tariff collectors of the god-king are constantly looking for babies and small children so that the high priests can eat them."

One night a splendid canoe came up the river, carrying magnificently clothed and ornamented soldiers. Sitting at the head of the boat was a splendidly attired nobleman, bearing ornaments of gold and jade: this was the father of my friend. He had come to extol the advantage of sacrificing the children to the god-king. The most difficult part for me to understand: Dzaltu's father genuinely believed that he was offering great honor to the whole family—to the parents, to the children, to the extended family—and that only through this total lack of selfishness were we helping to assure good crops and a better life for all the people.

As Dzaltu's father left empty-handed, Dzaltu and his wife were distraught—not just because of the danger averted, but because they loved and honored their elders, and all the people, and lived with great ambivalence regarding "sacrifice" and the degree to which the god-kings, the priests, and the jaguar-people controlled the universe. No threat of torture—and there was none—would cause them to give up the children, but still they felt guilt for their refusal.

A few days later when the trauma of the parents had subsided I asked if all the people of this area were thus terrified by their religion and its representatives. "Oh, no," they assured me. "You have only heard the dark side. There are within a few weeks' travel from here hundreds of thousands, perhaps millions of people, and most of them are relatively safe. There are many kingdoms and a number of related languages. The scholars tell us that we were once one people with one language, and one set of gods."

Ironically, I was to learn that most of the leaders (god-kings) are very bright and remarkably well educated. They are architects, engineers, stone masons, artists, musicians, poets, astronomers, mathematicians (Aveni, 1997). Typically they speak several languages, and appear to have a method of placing the spoken language into pictures on stone, wood, and other materials. [The civilization of the Olmec/Mayans goes back at least to 2000 BCE (Leonard, 1967, and Stuart and Stuart, 1993).]

TABASCO, 1270 BCE

My new friends on the river told me that a relative of theirs, a chief engineer for the king, traveled constantly as an emissary between kingdoms. One attribute of the royal hierarchy was their curiosity about the world. My river friends offered to introduce me to their relative, the engineer, and assured me that my head would be as safe as anyone's. So I met Baltuztal and we worked together for many months, in lands that varied from coastal islands and lagoons to steep wooded mountains.

The engineers had plans for hundreds of temples, pyramids, walls, and highways, under construction by thousands of workers, artists and draftsmen, speaking a variety of languages and paying homage to a variety of kings and gods. The elite were proud of their knowledge and were eager to share it with their peers. Baltuztal would sit down with a group of fellow engineers and discuss the techniques of lintel construction, albeit they worked for different kingdoms and were honoring different gods. They had no fear of being sacrificed.

The magnitude of these enterprises was enormous. Quarries were opened for stone of the specific type desired. Individual blocks of stone might weigh 7,500 kilograms, and in some cases they had to be placed on wooden rafts for transport. Scribes and artists worked with stone cutters to fashion a variety of effigies and altars of all sizes. In one area there were dozens of stone heads each about two meters high, apparently commemorating a group of rulers of related but slightly different physiognomy. Apparently the individuals whose likenesses were carved were not totally appreciated: nearly all of the giant heads and associated altars had been deliberately damaged, and some had been tipped over and buried. All had been carved from black basalt, and some had been transported as far as 80 kilometers (Clark, 1994).

The engineers used levels and plumb bobs, measuring tapes, and in some cases a magnetic compass (Carlson, 1975; Urrutia-Fucugauchi, Maupome, and Brosche, 1985).

Let us digress: the local scholars possessed occult knowledge that gave them their prestige. The magnetic property of lodestone was one of their secrets. They knew that a dense black mineral [magnetite] had the peculiar property of attracting other similar rock or mineral [lodestone]. Not only could it attract smaller pieces of magnetite or other "magnetic" material, but if suspended, as on a piece of cork floating on water, it would always point in the same direction, toward the same star [the North Star]. The best navigators knew that this star, low in the northern hemisphere, appears to remain stationary while all the other stars rotate around it (Breiner and Coe, 1972; Carlson, 1975). [Actually the North Star, Polaris, is also moving, and through the centuries the name, the North Star, has been attributed to different stars.]

Knowledge and curiosity were revered. There were organized schools for the sons (and in rare cases the daughters) of the elite. There was an emphasis on scholarly activity (as I have found to be common in my circum-global travel). The elite were very conscious of their civilized status. They understood that civilization flourished where corn grew plentifully.

Nowhere on my travels did I find a more vigorous middle class, made up of traders, artisans, officials, soldiers, scientists, musicians, artists, poets. And the peasants were not forgotten: these people had an organized system by which surplus crops were collected for distribution to people in need.

At several of the centers of Olmec culture the stone figures of the king-gods were held aloft by dwarfs carved in stone. My guide saw some humor in this: "The kings reach for heaven, standing on the shoulders of little people."

I was invited to visit the field of experimental agriculture. Here were many hybrid corn plants. Some had been selected to grow well in an arid or a swampy environment, and some apparently provided higher nourishment as determined by experiments on animals. A number of wild plants were being tested for domestic use. Avocado trees were being variably pruned to augment production. The idea of enhancing usefulness by seed selection and cross pollination was such a simple concept that I was amazed not to have encountered it elsewhere. Further, the chief agronomist was self-taught. Like only a few others, he had earned his elite status. And yes, he was a lecturer at the school for elite youngsters. Needless to say he made a strong case for education.

I spent a few weeks with the agronomist, visiting other gardens, in some cases bringing cuttings and seeds from distant sources. He pointed out to me the genius of nature. He showed me how the coloring of birds and animals was different in different habitats, for protection, and how both plants and animals had diversified, probably by natural selection, to succeed in different climates. He speculated on how this may have brought about diversity in human beings.

I was invited to be a lecturer. I had to apologize for my unpolished vernacular, but these students were already familiar with several of the Mesoamerican languages. I tried to teach them some geography and geology, but we raised more questions than we could answer. With the students, we considered the physiognomy of people we had seen (even among ourselves), and speculated that their ancestors may have developed in varied environments. Perhaps those with abundant body hair had migrated from a cold environment. Perhaps those with narrow eyes had migrated from an arid environment, and had evolved through natural selection.

It was clear to my students that language, more perhaps than any other attribute, distinguishes humans from animals, and each of the students made suggestions concerning the variation in language even over relatively short distances.

The students pointed out that the development and dispersal of languages, particularly of glyphs, was a necessity for the traders. Some said that there were islands of unacculturated people, with little outside contact, who spoke languages understood only by themselves. Others pointed out that language was power and that some groups practiced secret language. In fact in some groups the men spoke one language and the women another.

Writing language was the most fascinating area of study. The idea of expressing ideas on stone, wood, bark or paper-like materials was exciting to the students. The concept of information transmittal through time or geography was not new. Indeed, the elite were in general the patrons of recorded history, calendars, memorials, astronomy, music and literature. Rendering such information in hard stone was a major commitment of resources. Most of the written record was carved on wood or other materials [long since destroyed in a tropical to subtropical climate].

There was no general consensus on the need to have a widely understood written language. To the students, each carving of glyphs was a piece of art in itself, demonstrating the originality or skill of the sculptor or of the person who ordered it created. Each author/artist depicted his own understanding of the subject, hoping that other viewers would understand—or perhaps not. I could see that while enjoying the incentive for written language they were not prepared to forgo originality in favor of uniformity. So true written language for this culture was a few generations in the future.

≋

The strength of the Olmec culture was found in the artisans (Clark, 1994). No other culture lacking bronze or iron metallurgy was able to fashion the tools and weapons found here.

No other culture lacking the potter's wheel was able to fashion the artistic ceramics produced here. No one else in this era had perfected the variety of weaving in varied and mixed fibers, especially cotton and feathers. No other culture fabricated jewelry of shells and precious stones and precious metals with such artistry.

One question I asked was, how much was created for actual use, and how much for possession or decoration? They made effigies of children, carvings of family pets, tiny toy cradles, and even toy animals on wheels.

Their giving away possessions was similar to the "potlatch" that I observed later in the land of the totem, where the apparent objective was to demonstrate one's social and economic status.

As we journeyed northwest the land became drier and the people had constructed irrigation canals to water their crops. There were great mountains, which in winter were capped with snow. This was the first time I had visited a land with permanent snow. The engineers had triangulated the elevation of these mountains and concluded that the summits were more than 3,200 meters above the surrounding areas.

I was fascinated by the astronomy, mathematics, and geography that these elite understood. For example, they knew that there were approximately 365 days in the solar year, and they had accounted for the necessary correction of minutes and seconds in their calendar (Aveni, 1997).

I told them of my travel from the land east of the Atlantic Ocean. But they told me of another ocean, to the west, to me a second ocean—which I must say was a little discouraging. The people seemed to be vaguely aware of the existence of many distant lands and had met people of very different appearance before. But they were totally unfamiliar with men on horseback, elephants, or chariots.

≋

I intentionally avoided educating those I met, on any subject that might challenge beliefs that were sacred to them. But one day when our small group was discussing the earth, a very knowledgeable elder in our group asked me how far I thought it was to the edge of the earth, and I broke my rule. I responded to him by asking if he thought there was an "edge" to the earth. He replied that he supposed the earth was infinite in extent.

"Where then," I asked, "do the sun and the moon go? If the earth is infinite in extent, must not the sun move back underneath the earth so as to be in a position to rise again the next morning?

"Do you think that the earth, however finite or infinite, is flat? Well, I think that the earth is a sphere. I think that if I continue traveling in a westward direction (following the sun) I will eventually come back to the place from which I started."

"That is impossible," he replied. "If you try to walk across the 'underside' of the earth you will fall off!"

I replied, "If you throw a stone in the air it will drop back toward the earth. Why is that?"

"It is because the earth attracts the stone."

"Exactly. The earth attracts the stone. All I am saying is that the earth will attract the stone wherever you may be on the earth. The stone will not fall off of the underside of the earth any more than you will fall off this side of the earth.

"Do you know how to confirm this? If you journey toward a tall mountain—and you have several in this area—you see the tip of the peak lighted first, and then gradually the lower part of the mountain," I drew for him a curved surface and a straight line of sight, showing why the lower part of the mountain is not visible at a distance.

Next, I cleared a long table. I labeled one end of it "west" and the other end "east." I then placed several small objects on the table. I said the easternmost object was Yucatan. Next was the land of the Olmecs, still further west the Valley of Mexico, and finally the west coast [the Pacific]. I darkened the room, took a small candle and placed it just below the "eastern" edge of the table.

I asked, "Can the people in Olmec land see the candle? Can the people in the Valley of Mexico see the candle? Can the people on the western coast see the candle? No, the candle symbolizes the sun, and it has not yet risen."

Then I raised the candle and it was seen all the way across their flat model of the earth.

"Do you believe this is correct? Do you believe that the sun rises at the same time everywhere? Have you never been outdoors when the sun rises, and have you not seen the shadow of night retreating as the boundary between the light and the dark portion of the earth moves west?"

A young woman of about 20 years jumped up excitedly, saying, "Grandfather, the man is right. The sun does not rise at the same time

FIGURE 4. HOW FAST DOES THE SUNRISE TRAVEL?

If it takes the sunrise .58 minutes to travel 16 km and it takes 1,440 minutes for the sun to travel around the earth, what is the length of that travel distance?

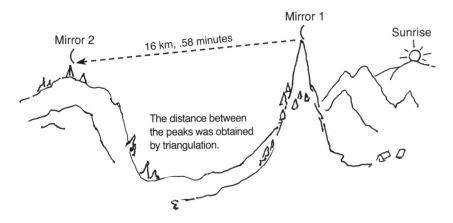

Mirror 1

Mirror 2

Sunrise

16 km, .58 minutes

The distance between the peaks was obtained by triangulation.

everywhere, because the surface of the earth is curved. Get up tomorrow and look at Mount Orizaba. The light of the sun strikes first on the snow-covered tip of the peak, then gradually the light of the rising sun comes further and further down until all of the mountain is illuminated."

Over the next few weeks several of the young people devised an experiment for testing the hypothesis. They established an observation point on a volcanic peak, and put a large hematite mirror there. Then they put a second large hematite mirror on a similar peak, 16 kilometers to the west. One morning before dawn they climbed high on the eastern volcanic peak and waited for the sunlight to strike each of the burnished hematite mirrors. They measured the lapse of time with several devices [clocks], and computed a measurement of time for distance: it took over half a minute for the sun to move across the 16 kilometers.

Knowing the distance between the mirrors, the time it took for the sunrise to travel from the first mirror to the second, and the number of minutes in one day, they tried to calculate how far it would be for the sunrise to go all the way around the world.

The young people thought about this for some days, and talked it over amongst themselves. Then they concluded, "We know that it takes 1,440 minutes for the sun to circle the earth. Our measurement shows that it requires about .58 minute for the sunrise to travel 16 kilometers. So, if the sun goes 16 kilometers in .58 minute, it goes 27.59 kilometers in each minute. Since the sun goes all the way around the earth in one day, which is 1,440 minutes, it must go 39,724 kilometers each day. Therefore the distance around the earth must be about 40,000 kilometers."

I believe the elite of Mesoamerica had come as far as they had, perhaps as advanced in some ways as anywhere in the world, in their day, because they had a critical mass of youthful scientific curiosity and an experimental approach. This would have been impossible had each little kingdom been restricted to communication among its own group of geniuses.

The idea of testing hypotheses had bitten them and they proceeded to measure the distance to the sun and the moon by triangulation. Their answer for the sun was an infinite distance, whereas they could see that the distance to the moon was probably finite. [The difference in apparent velocity between the two bodies may have given pause to some of these youngsters, but we have no record of their subsequent thoughts, and it would be 2,700 years until that problem was solved, on the other side of the Atlantic.]

Olmec astronomers had recorded several eclipses. And the crescent shadow confirmed the hypothesis that the object creating the shadow was either a sphere or a round disc.

The time spent with the Olmecs and their associated peoples raised some other interesting questions. At one of the sites of enormous sculptures [La Venta], the stones used [basalt] were transported over land and sea a distance of about 80 kilometers. Why were these blocks, each weighing 20 to 40 tons, selected for carving? Limestone, far easier to carve, was closer at hand. Could the engineer testing the rock try his lodestone on powder derived from the basalt, and discover that the basalt contained a small but measurable proportion of magnetite, and thus grains of the basalt were attracted by the lodestone, the magic stone that points to the North Star?

MAGNETIC STONES

Many ancient people have cast red specular hematite in graves. Specular hematite is weakly attracted by the lodestone. Is this red mineral, symbolizing the sun and life itself, related to the miraculous ability of the lodestone? Most serpentine also contains a noticeable amount of magnetite. Did Olmecs know this? Is this why it was used extensively?

We tried several interesting experiments with the youngsters and fascinated elders. We sprinkled magnetite powder on a thin sheet of cotton, placed the strongest lodestone we could borrow beneath the cloth, and tapped the cloth gently. Miraculously the grains of magnetite arranged themselves into a pattern. Re-scattered, they rearranged themselves into the same pattern. But if we rotated the lodestone, the pattern also rearranged to conform to the new position of the lodestone.

The elders, some of whom were part of the religious hierarchy, saw in the pattern of grains the face of divinities, and correctly pointed out that this pattern was identical to a glyph which had been given several meanings. Since most of the identified lodestones were in the possession of the religious establishment, it could hardly be contested that the spirit of the universe was in the magnetite and in the glyphs [the recognition of which predated the first known "magnetic" pattern.] To be sure, the scholars and students all subscribed to the miraculous explanation.

It was difficult to depart from this community of scholars, but it was time for me to follow the sun, and I carried messages to the rulers of the furthest outposts of Mesoamerican influence.

To Nyarit and Sinaloa

We followed a west-trending range of volcanic mountains. Some were smoking, but most were tipped with snow. We traveled through forests of oak and pine. The trader trails were well marked and the route was trader friendly. Lodges for food and rest were established at reasonable intervals, and there were posts of soldiers stationed for the protection of trade. The grade of the trail was well engineered, and bridges or hand cables were located at stream crossings.

As we approached the west coast [Nyarit] the vegetation and humidity turned tropical. The largest trees were a species of fig, with buttress-like flairs of roots extending out above the ground, from the base of the trunk. There were orchids and poinsettias, and large colorful birds whose long, brightly colored tail feathers crossed each other [like a pair of scissors].

The edible resources here were fish, shellfish, and an abundance of shrimp. The important items of commerce were ornaments carved from shell, pearls, salt, and cotton. Cotton could be purchased in any condition, from the bolls to fancy woven cloth, including cloth decorated with colorful feathers. In exchange the traders brought ornaments of gold, copper, precious stones, animal pelts, and finely decorated ceramics.

≋

CHAPTER SIX

DELTA PEOPLE

1269 BCE

A T THIS TIME CENTRAL MEXICO, even to parts of the great northern plateau, was under the cultural influence of the Olmec civilization,
with its advanced mathematics, astronomy, and technology. I enjoyed
several years in this country. The area supported a considerable population, employing advanced agriculture and both fresh water and marine fishing.

The Olmec rulers sent me, with an agronomist and a scribe, to
report on the status of occupation in the area of arid land between two
great rivers [the Colorado and Rio Grande Rivers]. We traveled with
three traders, who brought 20 bearers. Bearers are paid according to
the weight they carry. The merchandise being carried north consisted
of an advanced hybrid seed corn, and jewelry crafted of copper, turquoise, and other stones. On their return trip to the south they would
carry uncrafted raw material.

The trails were well worn, and in good spring weather we aver-
aged about 32 kilometers per day. We employed a guide, not to show
the way, but for translation and news concerning the people through
whose range we passed. Most of the people we were meeting spoke
some dialect of Yuman. Some of the languages were more intelligible
to me than others. Our guides were usually known to the indigenous
people—you might call their work "public relations." Every few days
we picked up a new guide, and our current guide headed south, usually with a band of traders. As we traveled northwest, the vegetation
became more desert-like (Fisher, 1992; Dirzo, 1994).

Sonora, 1269 BCE

After several days travel [close to what is now the southern edge of the Mexican state of Sonora], we encountered a group of traders and bearers traveling southward. Their guide told a fearsome account. In the region ahead the people had lost their crops for lack of water and destruction by animals. The famine had produced disease. Most of the people had either died or moved into the mountains to the east. Many were too weak to travel. Trading groups were being ambushed for their food. His group had several skirmishes, lost one man, and had several injured.

This was serious for several reasons. To maximize the weight of merchandise we could transport, we were accustomed to purchasing food along the way. Each traveler carried his basic supply of corn, beans, and spices, which we supplemented with dried fish, shrimp, and sometimes other locally obtained meat or seafood.

Our large shipment of seed corn would be difficult to explain to starving people, yet this superior yield corn was intended to avoid just this kind of famine in the Delta Country to the north. We had resolved to see it delivered.

Our new guide suggested that we travel largely at night, follow some alternate trails, and walk closely spaced.

Soon we were noting how all of the edible wild beans [mesquite beans] and cacti [saguaro fruit and prickly pear] had been stripped. We passed villages that were recently abandoned, and the buzzards circled above.

On the fifth day in this terrible land, we encountered two figures on the trail: a girl of about eleven years and her seven year old brother. As we approached they confronted us on the trail. The girl was carrying a small satchel and a spear. When we came close she spoke in an earnest voice: "I am the granddaughter of the great shaman, and this is my brother." Our guide was able to understand her, and spoke with both of them.

It seems that her grandfather was indeed a powerful shaman revered in all this region, caring for many small villages over a large area. Recently he became too ill to travel eastward into the mountains and he fasted to death. His followers wrapped him in his fabulous hair coat and laid him in his grave. But he had told them to save his wooden tablet, the tablet which contained his great magic, for his heirs. "They placed heavy stones upon his grave." Upon telling this, tears began to trickle down the girl's face. "They placed such heavy stones"—and she looked away, for the granddaughter of the great shaman must shed no tears. Our guide assured her that when the time came her grandfather's spirit would be strong enough to raise the stones. And she looked back at us, hoping so much that it was true.

A couple of days ago she and her brother had fallen asleep, and when they awoke everyone else was gone. For the children they had left a tiny cache of food and a spear. And while she was awakening, holding her brother's hands, the image of her grandfather rose above them. "You are the last," he said. "In your custody now is the magic tablet. Little brother, when you grow up you shall be a great shaman, more so than I. Follow the great trail north—and I shall send someone from the spirit world to look after you both." And reaching into her satchel she produced the magic tablet.

We were perplexed. I knew this meant slowing down the packers, or carrying the children, and sharing our short rations. It meant perhaps that raiders would kill us all. Yet my nature was such that I could not walk past them.

Other members of our party concluded that we were already in grave danger, that we had pledged to deliver our merchandise, and some sentimental action to fulfill a grandfather's magic was irrational. What, they asked, would we do when we encountered two more or ten more, or 100 more? Our guide, however, feared the wrath of the departed shaman. The children were undaunted, and while we deliberated they began walking up the trail. "We have food, we know where there is water, we have light loads—so we can walk. What we ask of you is protection"—and she grasped the spear tightly. "As we walk we are being watched by the great cat, and the buzzards circle low, waiting. And there are people out there crazed with hunger. Let us walk with you."

My companions said that I was the pampered pet of princes and scholars; that I had never faced starvation, and could not make the hard decisions required for survival. The little girl made a brave effort to maintain the pace, and several of us who did not already have enormous loads carried the boy when he could not keep up.

We were hungry and exhausted when we met a group of marine

fishing people. We knew that only thorn forests lay between us and the land of the delta folk, the farmers of the north, also called the basket makers (Cordell, 1984).

Delta People, 1267 BCE

We had mounted a small hill, hoping to see on the north horizon an indication of our destination, when we spied two figures, running! Our guide smiled: "They are Exala and Alexa, identical twin daughters of the greatest shaman of them all." The guide explained to us that when they were born their mother had not enough milk for both of them, and their father, the shaman, using his magic powers found a wet nurse, in thanks for which the girls promised to devote their lives to others. So this group had three shamans, the father and the identical daughters.

Growing up, the girls competed with each other in every activity, especially running. They ran together every day, and no one had ever outraced them.

A few hours later, when it was beginning to cool, Exala grasped my thigh admiringly and exclaimed, "You have strong thighs. You must be a runner." I admitted that I had done some running. "Oh," cried Alexa, "you are pretty good? Maybe you can beat us. Would you like to try? Our village is about an hour's run from here. Let's go." I never had a choice.

They ran along beside me, telling me a great deal about their people and their father. They appeared to be coasting all the way. Finally, when the village was well in sight, one of them said, "Now we shall see!" and they took off like rabbits, racing each other. I came in a ways back, puffing, out of training for this sort of effort. They slapped me on the back and assured me that I had done well. No one beats Alexa and Exala, and they do not mind telling you so.

These people are renowned for their baskets. They made many types of baskets, for different uses. Some were so small you could use them for thimbles; others so large you could hide in them.

The great chief knew who the two children were, and expressed his admiration for their famous grandfather. "You are brave little ones. We pray for the others of your family. The tablet will be very safe here. And when you are grown let us hope that your grandfather's spirit will be renewed, and you shall serve the survivors of your people. I will help you."

36

The following evening there was a great celebration in the grand kiva, a crude-appearing structure of desert willow overtwined with palm fronds and other plants. Hundreds of people came, some from a day's distance: men, women, and children, dressed in their very finest. The great shaman/chief wore a wispy white beard and stood very tall, as he welcomed his distinguished guests. Exala and Alexa stood tall and motionless, on opposite sides of their father, covered from head to toe in furs and feathers and jewelry: not only identical, but in mirror image. Wild flowers had been placed in profusion. There was a feast of wild turkey, fish, and venison, together with a salad of wild bulbs and greens from along the river. With certainty this was ostentation to impress us, as travelers from afar. Gifts of jewelry were bestowed according to social status.

Finally, our agronomist, the wise one from the south, was introduced. He was what we might call an agricultural engineer—a teacher of agronomy who had learned his trade near the Gulf of Tehuantepec, now making his home in the region of farmers, to the north and to the east, where he was not only important, but essential. He explained how the Olmec had selected the finest ears of maize for generation after generation, until they had a corn plant that produced several times the weight of kernels that had been in the original, wild plant. It required no more water, and no more effort, but yielded a great deal more food. He thanked the bearers and traders for undertaking the hazardous journey, and explained how the various elders of the area would achieve a fair distribution of seeds. He promised to personally oversee the planting, protection from animals, and harvest. It was important that these seeds produce new seeds for future fields.

Each morning a group of us went out for a run. The group included the identical twins, several young men from the village, and myself. On these jaunts we got some insider information. The twins considered the first problem of the delta people to be overpopulation. More and more tributaries of the Colorado and Gila Rivers were being diverted, and larger fields were being planted.

Exala explained the problem: "These larger fields gave the elders the feeling that they could increase foodstuffs without limit. A few generations ago much of our food was gathered from wild seeds and roots, deer, rabbits, and fish. Those sources are still available, and still harvested to some extent. But if the maize crops should fail and we were once again dependent on our earlier sources, we would starve, just as the parents of the boy and girl who arrived here with you."

I asked the twins (for you never speak to just one twin) what their daily activities were. Their answer was that their father, although still robust, could not get around to all of the marriages, funerals, puberty ceremonies, and so on, not to mention the political meetings with elders and neighboring chiefs.

"Why," I asked, "does this task fall to you? You have brothers. Why doesn't the task of shaman fall to one of them?"

"A shaman," they answered, "is a very special person, called upon by the spirits to communicate between heaven and earth. We were chosen. We are dedicated, and we do our best."

"Do you have husbands?"

"Oh no, having children is a different responsibility. Our brothers and sisters can handle that. We have enough to do.

"Would you like to follow us around and see what we do? At three sticks [approximately 10:00AM], we meet with a group of expectant mothers, first-time mothers."

"How many?"

"Oh, perhaps ten."

"Really! No wonder you worry about overpopulation."

"Well, between you and us, not all of them are pregnant. Some are wishing they were."

"What do you do for them?"

"We teach them exercise, diet, and we answer their questions. We also talk about what to do after the offspring arrives."

"Then at five sticks [1:00PM] we meet with a group of boys and girls about 11 or 12 years old."

"What do you teach them?"

"Well, we don't pull any punches. You think this is too young? Ha! We tell them that the last thing this pueblo needs is a bunch of babies without parents ready to take care of them.

"We have group meetings for the elderly, the disabled, the mentally disturbed. These people need not be a burden to the group. Many of them have useful hands, and they can contribute. A healthy community is one where all members contribute as they can."

"You mentioned puberty rites. Is that your responsibility too?"

"Well, this is a little complicated. It used to be that boys (and they are quite young emotionally) were given a drink of Jimson weed and they then were expected to have a vision that would show them their life ahead. If they did not get the vision they pretended that they did. We have never drunk Jimson weed as we are female, and this is a male thing."

"But isn't Jimson weed a deadly poison? Don't you actually lose some of the boys?"

"You are absolutely correct, and as shamans administering the potion we are responsible. Don't breathe this, but we make up a potion that looks and smells like Jimson weed, but is harmless. The very act of having drunk something is nearly enough to put them into a trance, but we have learned the art of hypnotism. And we suggest to them what to dream: a brave hunter, a proud father, and so on" (Cordell, 1984).

We have no direct archaeological evidence about who lived around the delta of the Colorado River in 1267 BCE. The people were primarily a hunting and gathering society. It would be over a thousand years before these people started building the rock towers and multistoried dwellings of Arizona and New Mexico, the ruins of which we see today.

However, by using pollen dating and other techniques, we know that maize, beans, and varieties of squash and pumpkins were in the American southwest at least as early as 2000 BCE, and possibly by 3500 BCE. Maize was grown and hybridized in Mesoamerica between 6500 and 4800 BCE, and the varieties planted in the American southwest reflect the progressive plant improvement achieved in Mesoamerica. Maize and a variety of other introduced cultivars gradually became an essential part of the southwestern diet (Cordell, 1984).

Jimson weed (Datura stramonium) still grows wild today in the American southwest.

We conclude that we are visiting the delta just after the transition to irrigated agriculture.

THE TRIP TO THE NORTHEAST

Shortly after our arrival in Delta Land, the shaman and elders determined that it was time for a general gathering of representatives from all the regional groups. For these events all notables were invited: artisans who have made spectacular ceramics, or weaving, or music; athletes: runners, ball court champions; farmers, hunters, and others. This year the conclave was to be held east of the Great Canyon [near what is now the Arizona–New Mexico border]. Prize agricultural products were displayed, and there were workshops or seminars on practical topics: successful medicines, metallurgy, fabrication of stone, bone, and wooden tools.

This was an opportunity for the great shaman to introduce the twins and laud them for their occult powers. It was generally felt that this was a beginning of the relinquishment of his authority in favor of the twins.

We traveled up the Gila River to the high plateau: a land of giant cone-bearing trees, and deep canyons of colored stone.

The twins had to compete in a race. Rumor had it that there was a notable runner from the northeast who many thought could outrun the twins. He had trained at high altitude and the twins lived near sea level. So the twins went north a month early to train for the race.

The day of the race arrived. There were contestants from many areas. The race would be about 5 kilometers out to the turning point, and then the same distance back to the beginning where the audience would be gathered. Initially both twins lay back and the young challenger took the lead. Finally, one of the twins began to pass the field, but the challenger chose not to let her take the lead. She would go faster, so he would go faster. At the turning point the one twin and the challenger were neck and neck, but traveling at an excessive speed. The other runners were grouped some distance back. Finally the second twin broke out of the pack and began to steadily gain on the front runners. Eventually the challenger and the lead twin began to falter, and the second twin won easily.

On the way home the twins conceded that these races were not as easy as they once were. "If our group of villages is to continue winning the distance races, we should teach some of the young people to compete," concluded Alexa.

GREAT CANYON

One morning on the trip back from the race the twins woke us up early: "You have never seen the Great Canyon—you must see it!"

In the past several days I had seen many spectacular cliffs and canyons, and I really didn't think I needed another. But when the twins label something "great," you had better see it. All day we hiked north, from the piñon pine and juniper, to the long needled pine, gradually gaining elevation. The breeze was brisk and small patches of snow persisted in the shadows. In some meadows there were outcrops of white limestone [Kaibab]. Then abruptly the breeze turned warm—and there it was! Did they not call it the Great Canyon?

This is the canyon to dwarf all canyons. Standing near the edge, we could not see the bottom, and the far side was several days' hike away. Within the span of the Great Canyon, whole mountains stood below us. As sunset approached shadows raced from mountain to mountain, from scarlet to yellow to gray.

We climbed down through layer after layer, some sandstone, some shale, mostly red, mostly flat-lying. At the bottom the rocks were tangled and dark colored, cross-cut with veins rich in mica and quartz. Many years later, crossing the mountains of Morocco [the Atlas Mountains] we hiked through a similar sequence, steeply tilted strata, with crystalline rock underneath.

What does it all mean? Anywhere a river cuts deeply into the earth, would crystalline rock be exposed? And what would be found still deeper? The immensity of the canyon dwarfs the most ambitious structures of man. Yet this canyon, impressive as it is, does not compare with the grand features of earth, the oceans and continents. And the whole of our earth does not compare with the lighted stars and galaxies we see in the sky!

Yet the gentle drops of rain wear away these mountains, the rivers carry the sediment to the sea, the stars follow their rigid path, and time passes. As I walked along the path, again southwest, I found it hard to put in perspective the drops of rain, the concept of time, and yes, the limited comprehension of man.

≋

One of the ideas generated among the elders was that foodstuff (corn, beans, wild grains, dried meat) could be destroyed by unusual weather, depredation by wild animals, insects, or disease, but excellent raw material such as paint and precious stones, and craft products such as weaving, sewing, and carving, could be stored for years and exchanged for foodstuff as the need arose, bartered for surpluses generated in other areas.

Thus, some communities with surplus manpower, often people of middle age, could learn trades that provided wealth for the group, whereas other areas with ample and dependable supplies of water and youthful labor could intentionally produce a surplus of foodstuff for trade. I could attest to the viability of this type of economics, since I had experienced it in southern Mexico. But what happens when you have lots of craft work to sell and the agricultural neighbors have little to trade? I could imagine this spawning whole cities of artisans–and ultimately an even worse overpopulation dilemma.

I wrote a report in Olmec hieroglyphics for the scribe to carry back, on his return trip to the south. I described all that I had learned, and he joined a caravan of traders headed south. On the return trip his party was to follow a route far inland from that which we had followed as we came north.

CHAPTER SEVEN

SOUTHERN CALIFORNIA

1265 BCE

To the west lay the delta of the great Colorado River, an area of frightening earthquakes, hot springs, and sometimes geysers. About once every hundred years mud and steam shoot so high in the air that they can be observed from the junction of the Colorado and Gila Rivers [over 300 meters high, according to Strand, 1980]. Beyond the area of geysers are barren white mountains of granite, and at times a great lake [Laguna Salada] with abundant fresh water shrimp, hot water springs, and thousands of palm trees. Few of the delta people have traveled this far, but some of the elders could recall the great hot springs, the cold waterfall, and high on the mountain a fresh water lake. "You follow the river from this lake west to the ocean—where live the giant shellfish with the iridescent shells" [abalone].

The great shaman and his advisors determined that it was time to send a party to the coast of the second great ocean. The expedition would have several bearers, a guide, and would be led by the twins. I joined them, somewhat reluctantly, since my stay with the delta people had been very rewarding. And why? I had spent much time with the shaman's grandchildren, whom we had met on the trail. They had listened so intently, had been so willing to believe, and had asked such remarkably mature questions. I felt as never before that I was tutor to a prince and princess, and that they and all their people might gain from our discussions. I learned that anyone can become a leader, and make a difference, even if they live in a part of the world where people cannot write their names. At this parting the tears were undisguised.

We carried a variety of merchandise, mostly products crafted with skill rather than utilitarian items. We were less heavily burdened because we needed to scale a steep mountain, and our bearers were less experienced. Our first objective was a small black volcano just north of the geysers [Cerro Prieto]. On the west side of the white mountains was a warm spring with small fish, which we caught with a net. Then we crossed a dry salt flat. After several hours on the salt flat, we found a large grove of palms and a shear rock spine that appeared to pierce the horizon.

When we were leaving the delta people, the great shaman had handed me a small package of red paint, saying, "You may find someone out there who needs this."

At the hot springs we were surprised to meet a small group of elderly people. They had come here from many places to enjoy the curative waters. Some wove baskets from palm fronds, some seined the salty lake for fish and shrimp. We had enough food so that we could share and they insisted on giving us some of their weaving. One ancient fellow explained that he had been a shaman, but could not survive without using the magic warm water. He spent his time drawing red and black figures on the white stone [granite], but he had exhausted his red paint. We gave him our paint, and in appreciation he drew a figure for us. It looked like a human, was entirely red on the left side, and entirely black on the right side. We asked him why he had chosen this color configuration, and he became very quiet. He explained that it had been done this way for thousands of years: only the shamans knew why, and it could not be revealed.

Up the palm-lined canyon from the hot springs was a large cold water pool fed by a waterfall. The cold water was most enjoyable to us, even though these palms provided little food. We had been told that a trail leading up the very steep mountain began at the falls, but at first we could not locate it. Finally, one of the very elderly was able to show us the way. It took all day to reach the plateau above.

LAGUNA JUAREZ

Story has it that in times of drought the magic lake of the mountains disappears. But we were fortunate. It was there for us: a gorgeous lake surrounded by white granite and tall cone-bearing trees. There were fish in the lake. A group of people was camped by the lake. They had come from the west coast to gather the nuts of the small pine trees [piñon]. We pulled off our sweaty clothes and dove from the rocks, then stretched ourselves out to dry. How good! That evening the leader of the local band told us the story of how the lake came about, of the magic lake maiden and of the mortal who had wooed her in vain. This is how I recall it.

La Laguna

IN THE FAR LAGUNA VERDE
SHADED BY THE STATELY PINE
IS A WIDE AND QUIET WATER
CAUSED BY SOME UNKNOWN DESIGN.

LEGENDS FROM THE ANCIENT PEOPLE,
LEGENDS FROM THE DAWN OF TIME,
TELL A TALE OF THIS LAGUNA,
TELL A TALE OF THE DIVINE.

VERY, VERY LONG AGO
TWO CHILDREN PLAYED BY THIS LAGOON:
HE WAS THE SON OF MAN AND WOMAN;
SHE, THE DAUGHTER OF THE MOON.

THEY RAN AND SWAM
AND ROLLED THEIR STONY DICE FOR FUN.
AND YET TODAY THEIR TEARS OF LAUGHTER
GLOW AS CRYSTALS IN THE SUN.

THEY LISTENED TO THE WISE COYOTE
TELL THE FUTURE AND THE PAST,
OF THE STARS, AND STORMS, AND CREATURES,
HOW THE MOUNTAIN SHAPES WERE CAST.

AFTER MANY SEASONS LATER
THE CHILD OF MAN RETURNED
AND SEARCHED ACROSS THE WATER
FOR THE MAIDEN OF HIS YOUTH.

SHE AROSE FROM DARK GREEN SHADOWS
AND SAT ON A SUNLIT STONE,
AND SMILED TO SEE THE CHILDHOOD FRIEND
REVISITING HER HOME.

"THE WORLD," HE SAID, "IS CRUEL AND COLD;
THROUGH STRUGGLE ONE SURVIVES;
AND MEN FIGHT WITH ONE ANOTHER
THROUGH EMPTY IGNORANT LIVES.

"I COME TO THIS ROMANTIC PLACE
TO OFFER YOU MY LOVE:
I, WITH THE TOOLS AND SKILLS OF MAN,
YOU WITH THE POWER ABOVE.
"OUR CHILDREN WILL BE LEADERS,
AND TEACH THE WAYS OF PEACE,
OF SHARING AND COMPASSION,
UNTIL GENERATIONS CEASE."

"NO," SHE SAID, "YOU WILL GROW OLD.
IF I SHOULD JOIN WITH YOU
I WOULD BECOME A MORTAL
AND I SHOULD WITHER TOO.

"HERE MY FLESH WILL NEVER WRINKLE.
HERE MY HAIR WILL NEVER GRAY,
EACH SUNRISE IS A MAGIC SPELL—
THE CREATION OF A DAY."

REJECTED, HE CLIMBED THE SPINELIKE HILL
AS HIGH AS HE COULD GO
AND HURLED HIS MORTAL BODY
ON THE GRANITE ROCKS BELOW.

AND FOR A THOUSAND YEARS, AT NIGHT,
THE EERIE COYOTE HOWL
RECALLS TO THE SPIRIT WORLD ABOVE
THE TORMENT OF HIS SOUL.

AND THE GODS SEND CLOUDS OF GRAY
AND LIGHTNING LIGHTS THE SKY,
AND HURLS DOWN ICE UPON THE LAKE
AS IN ANGER THEY REPLY.

THE MAIDEN OF THE MOON'S CONDEMNED
TO SWIM THE LAKE AND WALK THE SHORE:
BEAUTIFUL FOREVER,
BUT VISIBLE NO MORE.

YET SOME HAVE SAID—THAT ON A MOONLIT
 NIGHT
WHEN THE LAKE IS VERY STILL
HER SHADOW CAN BE SEEN,
SILHOUETTE AGAINST THE HILL.

AND THERE ARE ALSO THOSE WHO SAY
THAT ANYONE WHO SWIMS THIS LAKE
IS FREE TO MAKE THE CHOICE:
TO BE BEAUTIFUL FOREVER,
OR TO LOVE—AND TURN TO DUST.

≈

This seemed an enchanted land. Though the inhabitants did not practice agriculture, there were many people and plenty to eat. There were acorns (these had to be leached) and berries of many kinds, bulbs, and greens, and other plants growing in the marshy areas and along the streams (Roberts, 1989). There are deer and bear, and mountain sheep, rabbits and turkeys, possum, coons and beavers. We were impressed by the lack of competition for possession and willingness to share with strangers.

The instructions for reaching the coast were simple: follow the stream from the lake, and along the way, right in the streambed, look for hot springs, most enjoyable. Just downstream from the last hot spring, look for a waterfall from a side stream dropping directly down 12 meters.

Word of our approach was widely heralded. Those possessing a store of abalone shells were glad to see us because abalone shells for trade accumulated much faster than traders arrived to barter for them.

It was a buyer's market. People as far east as the Great Canyon, and perhaps farther, cherished these shells, but few had sent expeditions to trade for them.

As with many groups we visited, the most prized commodity was information. Somewhere within a good day's run they could usually find someone with whom we could talk. While I was being treated in a princely fashion and my cohorts were also being treated well, elders, chiefs, and shamans gathered from far around and outdid one another to gain my attention.

Imagine that you personally have never been more than a few days distant, that you have spoken only to those who have been a few weeks distant, and that while you are convinced that those places are not the end of the earth, you only have the sketchiest and conflicting information about anything further away—and here is a fellow who talks of lands that are continents and oceans away.

Sometimes they wanted to tell me of other travelers, of people in boats with a sail who came down the eastern edge of the second ocean, and on a couple of occasions they showed me small artifacts from such contacts. I did not know then, but now I suspect that these were boats from the orient, perhaps Japan. And once again I was impressed with the contrast between my new hosts who were unaware of most of the planet, and yet at this particular time and place their experience involved contacts with lands far to the west [easternmost Asia].

FROM SAN DIEGO TO THE MOUNTAINS, 1264 BCE

We spent several days on the beach, fishing and riding the waves. People had come from several areas including the offshore islands. They had paddled sturdy boats up to about 10 meters in length, constructed of planks and sealed with asphaltum. Some of their villages were several days' paddling to the north, and they were gathering seashells that they used as ornaments and money. Some of them spoke a Yuman language. Alexa and Exala were apparently related to them, and spent several days catching up on news.

It was time for the coastal people to make their annual trek through the mountains gathering acorns, grass seeds, and berries. I became a temporary member of this band.

This was the daily routine: the men and older boys made a reconnaissance trip to the area ahead, reporting on the abundance of

FOLLOW THE SUN

foodstuffs to be gathered, making sure that other groups were not en-
croaching on what was considered theirs. Then they gathered such
game as they came upon, mostly rabbits and squirrels. The women and
older children gathered acorns, roots, and edible flowers. The acorns
were ground in rock mortars with a *mano*. They were too astringent to
eat without leaching (Ocean, 1999).

One morning before the group was underway, one of the middle
aged women took me aside and showed me a sunny slope where grew
a plant I came to know as the brown lily. She said there were many of
these lilies, and their bulbs were very shallow.

"How do you use them?" I asked her.

"Oh, you can eat them raw, but it's better to put them in a stew.
They make everything taste better."

From that day on I kept my eyes open for brown lilies. All of the
peoples along the trail knew of them, and we saw them again and
again—but more of that later (Moerman, 1998).

> The brown bells are probably *Fritillaria biflora*. Edible lilies would
> appear again in many places along the journey. This species is found
> in southern California today. Their common name is Chocolate Lily
> (Moerman, 1998; Pratt and Jefferson-Brown, 1997).

It was the women's task to catch and roast quail. It was not uncom-
mon to see coveys of 20 or 30 quail. The males have a top-knot, a small
fan of short showy feathers at the top of their heads. When they have
enough to eat, all the quail are plump. To catch the quail, the women
and girls spread a net of about five-centimeter mesh, and sprinkle over
it some grain prized by the quail. The short blades of grass hold the net
off the ground and allow the birds to creep under it. When the quail
are under the net they cannot run. The women gather what they can
eat at a sitting, always letting some of the quail go free.

Near the coast the mesas are covered with bushes. Oaks and sycamores grow only along the arroyos. Most of the people in this group
had made this journey several times and knew every creek and outcrop
of stone as old friends. Times had been good for these people and there
were many children of all ages. One mother had two children a little
too young to hike the trail without help. I asked the leader of the group
if it would be proper to volunteer some child transportation—and he
quickly provided me with a backpack for little ones.

49

In early afternoon, when the sun was hottest, the women would gather around grinding holes (*metates*) in the shade of a large oak tree. Each woman had her particular *metate*: the older women were using deeper basins and the teenagers were working on shallow basins. It seems that each year each woman comes back to use the same *metate*, the deeper ones 40 or 50 years in use. A girl grinding for the first time had to begin a new *metate*.

Seeing a girl working on a shallow basin next to an unused, larger one, puzzled me. I asked her whose basin it was, and why she was not using it. Her answer was simple: this was the *metate* of her grandmother, now deceased, and there were basins of other women, some having remained idle for several generations. "Those who have gone still work here, beside us. We do not see their acorns, just as we do not see them. But if we chose to use the *metates* belonging to them—they would have their way of telling us."

The talk turned to the discovery and use of magic *metates*. Some had seen them, some had not. One elderly woman said she knew where one was and offered to lead us. A magic *metate* was about 90 centimeters in circumference and as perfectly round on the outside as on the inside. These were utensils of the spirit world, not to be used by humans except perhaps in secret ritual, such as when a shaman asked for rainfall. [Some of these are now on display at the Barona Indian Reservation in San Diego County (Barona Cultural Center and Museum, 2004)]. Who ground out these enormous and beautiful *metates*? The people: everyone who was of age had a sacred duty to contribute in a small way to the fabrication. In some places there were more than one of these because when the shaman determined that one was finished a new one was fabricated next to the older ones, and it was the aspiration of each generation to please the spirits by making an even more impressive metate.

As the weeks passed we climbed higher in the mountains, gathering pine nuts, a variety of berries, and sometimes honey. Acorn mush covered with honey is the best breakfast anywhere on this earth (Ocean, 1999). Later in the season manzanita berries and elderberries would be ready to gather, and in the winter they would seek out the bright red toyon berries.

In the broad valleys we could see deer grazing. The men have strategies for encircling them and frightening them into snares. Not only are they good eating, but they also provide garments and moccasins. Deer are very important to these people.

THE MEETING PLACE

Several days' travel north along the mountain crest is a broad valley and a clear stream of water. Once a year the people from far around gather to play competitive games, to sing traditional songs and to retell sagas, seek spouses, and trade. There are people of different languages, and usually the meeting is peaceful, but sometimes in the past there have been accusations and duels.

The people with whom I traveled were particularly interested in trading with the desert people for obsidian from near the great inland sea, and hot spices that grow along the great river to the east. In exchange we brought shells (including abalone), boxes made of cedar, and crystals of many colors.

Nah-ta-hadnah, their overall leader, was a giant man, over two meters tall, with considerable hair on his face. For several decades he had been the leader of this group, but age was catching up with him and he had relinquished leadership to his nephew Nah-ta-ha-hadnah who was not as physically strong, but very wise.

As the annual gathering convened the former chief announced that he was dying, and he did not wish to pass on with hate in his heart. It seems that over his decades there had been many skirmishes between neighboring peoples, young men had been killed, and villages had been burned. While he hoped that justice had been served, he feared that many loathed him. Indeed, he still felt animosity toward others. He wished those who hated him and those whom he hated would smoke the pipe with him before he succumbed. And they came, they came from very far away, and chiefs and shamans met in conference and called upon the spirits for guidance.

I was told that this was an unprecedented event. Soon many of the group were confessing their sins and forgiving those against whom grudges had been held. They washed themselves in the sulfurous hot spring, and many were welcomed into manhood and womanhood, and many took spouses. And for widows without spouses the relatives (especially brothers) of the lost spouse offered to take them into the family.

Sagas of past events, happening many generations ago, were sung, and new sagas were created to commemorate this great event.

It perplexed me why these people sharing much of their culture, living in the same environment, depending on each other for trade and genetic diversity, spoke such a variety of languages, some of which are very different. How difficult to barter in two languages! How difficult to marry a husband who does not understand your tongue!

Some of my quandary was explained. For example, many groups such as those gathered above shared a "trading language," a system of words and gestures that were understood by all, especially for the purpose of trade. There were other specialized languages for different games.

Then there were languages largely limited to ritual, and not used in familiar circumstances as in a family gathered about the fire, commonly not understood by children. The adherence to this formal language distinguished the group of speakers as a distinct band, and without it they simply melt into a generalized population. Without it they lose their identity.

One young man told me that his uncle often walked off by himself and spoke to himself for hours in an ancient language of which now he was the only living speaker. And he asked, "Uncle, why do you spend time speaking in a language that no one else understands?"

His uncle answered, "Nephew, when I go to sleep I often dream, and in my dreams all of my ancestors are speaking in this language. When I pass on I expect to be with them, and I want the language I greet them with to be understood, so I must practice it."

Soon it will be chilly again, and the hilltops will be white. So we pull on our buckskin robes and begin the return journey to the coast.

THE UNTROD TRAIL

THERE IS A TRAIL, SO DEFTLY TROD
THAT WE SCARCELY SCAR THE SOD.
HALF A CENTURY YOU AND I
HAVE PASSED THESE STONES
TO REST IN SHADE.
THROUGH THE FOREST, THROUGH THE GLADE,
TO JOURNEY ON, OLD PARTNER,
THIS IS OUR STORY TO BE SUNG.

EVERY GLADE

EVERY GLADE HAS A NAME.
EVERY SPRING HAS A NAME.
EACH LARGE STONE HAS A FACE, WHICH
    CHANGES
AS THE SHADOWS MOVE—
AND WE INTERPRET THE EXPRESSION—
AN ORACLE IN STONE.

ON A SOUTH-FACING SLOPE IS A SPRING THAT
    GURGLES AND BUBBLES
AND ON A WARM DAY IS VERY ENTICING.
THE KIDS JUMPED RIGHT IN AND HAD A GREAT
    TIME.

THIS IS THE PLACE WHERE THE DANCERS COME
    OUT AT SUNDOWN AND TREAD ABOUT.
EACH DANCER HAS A SPECIAL DESIGN OF PAINT,
WHICH THEY APPLY TO THEIR BODIES—
THE POWDERS MIXED IN CUPULES ONLY THREE
    FINGERS WIDE.

FINALLY, THERE WAS A FEAST FOR ALL.
AND GRADUALLY WE FELL ASLEEP,
AND DREAMED AUSPICIOUS DREAMS.

CHAPTER EIGHT

LAND OF THE CHUMASH

1263 BCE

TO THE ISLANDS

TO THE ISLANDS—OUR BARQUE
SHOVES OFF AGAINST THE ROLLING WAVES,
OUR BOW RISES HIGH, AND SLAPS DOWN HARD.
THEN THE LAST TO BOARD
LEAPS ON—AND WE ARE OFF AGAIN,
FOR THE MOUNTAINS IN THE SEA,
FOR A LAND OF VISITORS LONG DEPARTED
IN UNSPOKEN MYSTERY.

THERE ARE LARGE ISLANDS off the shore of southern California, some so far out that it takes several days of paddling to reach them [San Clemente Island and San Nicolas Island]. Sea mammals are plentiful, and large fish are abundant. All the islands are populated, and the people speak languages that are mutually understandable with those on the adjacent California coast.

The boats are magnificent: typically 10 meters in length, they are elegantly crafted from planks so carefully fit together that they are watertight, then further sealed with asphaltum. We met three boats that had come to trade steatite for obsidian and pine nuts.

ON ISLA CATALINA

We camped near a coastal mountain [Palos Verdes], sharing food with a group of fishermen known to our boatmen. The next morning early we paddled directly toward the mountainous island that we could see to the west [Isla Catalina, 37 kilometers from the mainland]. The giant swells rose so high that in the trough we could see nothing but green water on all sides, and sometimes we had to use our bailing baskets. The traders were not alarmed by the sea, but were concerned only about the possibility of losing their trade goods. They informed me that they were excellent swimmers and had held swimming races between this island and the mainland.

In late afternoon we paddled into a protected cove where there was a fresh spring, and made camp. One of our party served as cook. Some gathered dry wood, and some filled seal bladders with fresh water. The cook searched along the beach for a specific variety of seaweed. He then rinsed the seaweed thoroughly in fresh water. He explained to me that he was leaching out the salt: many would omit this step since they were accustomed to digesting a great quantity of salt, but he contended that too much salt was unhealthy.

Next he placed the leached seaweed in a steatite pot and added a powder of dried fish, freshly ground in a rock mortar located next to our campsite. This mixture, together with some wild onions and red spice seeds, was boiled in the pot until it was a smooth soup of light orange color. A young sea lion was wrapped in large green leaves and buried in dull red cinders to roast. Our cook had a well deserved reputation for good food, and he was much appreciated.

After supper several sailors got out their panpipes, and others sang ballads about sea exploits.

I was up early the next morning to watch the cook at work. He asked one lad to go down to the bird rookery and get him fifteen (twenty less five) fresh eggs, admonishing him to select only fresh ones. I asked our cook how he could be sure that he had brought back only fresh eggs. "Ha," he exclaimed, "I will place the eggs in a pot of cold water. If they try to float—he will have to go back and get me better ones."

Next he opened his bag of leached acorn meal, and placed a steatite skillet on the coals to warm. He mixed the acorn meal with the eggs and a little soda powder [probably from Mohave dry lakes far to the east] to make a batter. A few drops of water on the hot skillet hissed and rolled about. He was ready to fry cakes: "Call those sleepy ones and tell them we are ready—and they can scrub the pots." I asked if he didn't want to add some oil to keep the cakes from sticking, and he informed me that acorns were loaded with oil. We ladled honey onto the cakes, and there were no complaints (Ocean, 1999).

From the southwestern part of this hilly island comes the steatite that is so sought after all along the California coast, because it is very good for carving. It is fashioned into all manner of useful items: cooking utensils, pipes for smoking and pipes for music, and sculptures of sea mammals and birds, some realistic and some imaginary. Some of the stone is carved by the people who live on the islands and some is traded as raw material. The folks who live here are very protective of their treasure. You can visit the quarry and even choose the blocks you wish to trade for, while the rocks are still in place—but don't try to sneak off with any.

We had specific instructions from the high chief of the Santa Barbara Chumash to trade for the largest, most flawless, most evenly colored stone available. The quarrymen knew what was ordered and had been setting aside prized pieces for this exchange.

> *California Indians used a great variety of rocks and minerals (Heizer and Treganza, 1944). Native Americans used all of these materials:*
> *Obsidian and flint, for tools and arrowheads;*
> *Steatite for utensils and art work;*
> *Hematite, manganese dioxide, calcite, and cinnabar for pigment;*
> *A variety of rocks for construction;*
> *Quartz crystals, turquoise, tourmaline, galena, mica,*
> *and graphite for decoration;*
> *Salt for preserving food and for cooking.*

In trade we had not only obsidian, the principal cutting tool, but also an elegant gown of feathers and fur, fit only for the bride of an indulgent chief. The Chumash used shell money, in several denominations: "ones" were the diameter of a fingernail, "twenties" were several times larger, and "eighties" were the size of your hand.

After resting, visiting the quarries, and trading, we turned our crafts north toward the coast of the island [Isla Santa Cruz]. This is a large island with thousands of inhabitants. We stayed there several days, since some of our young sailors fancied the Santa Cruz women.

Then the sailors rowed toward home, across the wide channel that separated the large islands from the mainland to the north. We saw many boats setting nets, and trapping lobster and turtle. I asked the oldest of the sailors if these wonderfully built craft were owned cooperatively, or individually, or how? He laughed and explained that all their boats belong to the high chief. The sailors are, shall we say, "share croppers." The chief leases the craft to an individual, or to a group, and they split the proceeds with him: fish, shells, steatite, whatever.

"Is that true for all the villages along this shoreline?" I asked.

"Well, many of the lesser chiefs work a similar economy, but they in turn purchase boats from the high chief, and he earns a share of all the profit of the several lesser chiefs."

I let out a big exclamation, and offered that the high chief must be a very wealthy man. "Indeed, indeed, and you shall soon see what a very wealthy man he is."

THE CHUMASH, 1263 BCE

As it seems always, news of our approach preceded us. Other boats joined our three, until we were a flotilla paddling toward the mainland shore and gliding across the calm water of an estuary, with many houses and people of all ages standing along the shore, anticipating our arrival.

We were to be the special guests of the high chief. He was a plump fellow whose dark and wrinkled skin looked like he had been enjoying the beach most of his life. His home was at the top of a rise, surrounded by meticulously cared for playing fields and parade grounds, with flowers blooming everywhere. The great hall was about 20 meters long, and served as an art gallery with examples of craftsmanship from much of California lining the walls: only the most marvelous treasures of stone, wood, and shell, furs, feathers, and weaving. The chief and his three wives came forward to greet me. I was the center of attention. The wives and children were introduced, and they bowed as would visitors in China (albeit that experience was still several years ahead). They were elegantly dressed in furs, woven cloth, precious stones and colorful feathers. The high chief called in an interpreter so that we could better converse. And I was impressed that the women and older children were included in the conversation (Miller, 1988).

The chief insisted that the success of these people was due to their penchant for hard work, and that his wealth was not his personal wealth, but the collective wealth of the people. A servant brought us tea and sweets, after which the wives and children excused themselves, and the high chief and his captains took us on a tour. It was impressed on me that the captains each had a very important role, and it was a position earned. Men outnumbered women in this hierarchy, but we were told that this was not essential. In some of the villages women were more equally recognized, for example with participation in the activities of the sweat houses, or ownership of shares in plank boats.

One captain was in charge of warfare, although it was not clear how much actual warfare took place. One captain was in charge of ceremonies and athletic contests. One was in charge of education. One was in charge of vital statistics: births, deaths, marriages: he traveled from village to village and recorded such events on notched sticks. One was in charge of gathering debts, and payment of bills. Then there were the guilds: boat building, stonework, basketry, coinage, and so on. The specialists in these crafts were very proud of their skill, and to be selected as an apprentice was a great honor. The artisan in charge of boat building was an essential and highly respected individual.

And of course there were the chief shaman and his assistants—more about them later.

It was time to participate in the sweat house activity, a new experience for me. We men all sat around sweating profusely, very hot, and then we ran out and jumped in cold water. I guess we got very clean. Many do it every day, at least those of high caste.

Finally, as it grew quite dark out we had to do a little gambling. I soon learned that these people are addicted to gambling, and this included the women. So that I would not be left out the high chief dipped into an ornate wooden chest and handed me a great pile of coins, the value of which was unknown to me. We were playing a guessing game, in which one person hides an object behind himself, and another person guesses which hand it is in. The high chief, having thousands and thousands of coins at his disposal, could raise the bet endlessly, and he seemed to think this very funny. The others ostensibly shared the merriment. One fellow, who is both a sailor and a boat builder, lost everything he owned, including his partnership interest (a leasehold) in a plank boat. He did not seem too distressed; he said he would start first thing in the morning to build a new plank canoe. That task might take most of a year to accomplish. I learned later that the high chief loaned the money he would need, with interest of course.

In the days I spent with the Santa Barbara Chumash, I learned many things. The artisans were extremely proud of their work, and were constantly comparing the detail with that of articles fashioned by other California people. Most of the work bore designs which were not just for beauty, but had serious connotations. In some cases the object itself held magic power, since the hand of the spirits had helped shape it. Many of these objects, of wood, shell, stone, cloth, and feathers, were considered too precious for common use, perhaps only for very special occasions. The chief paid high prices for the fabrication of special art, and then added the art objects to his collection.

One day I asked the high chief why he had only three wives. I had visited cultures where a man as wealthy as he would have many wives. It took him a moment to organize his reply. "My older children are by my first wife, the middle ones by my second wife, and my youngest by my youngest wife: thus we never had more than a few babies at a time, and she and I had the opportunity to care for each of them. I appreciate all of them, and each one is important. We use very few servants, and we are our children's principal mentors."

I noted that the village included teachers, and I wondered what they taught and whom they taught. He smiled and said, "Mostly we are democratic,"—they had a word for this!—"but the children of the chiefs and captains are the most often selected for school. But any child, even of slave or servant parents, can be recognized and included. We believe that for the strength of our community, giving opportunity to all children is important. Our rulers are not hereditary. The brightest children are taught the history of our people: the songs, the sagas, the rules of behavior. But everyone is taught skills, how to fabricate, to fish, hunt, do battle. No one is thrown aside. If an orphan child comes to me and says, 'I would like to study in the house of the teacher,' he will have his chance, and if my son wishes only to fish and gather mollusks I do not require him to be a scholar.

"There are no class restrictions on marriage—we want strong, intelligent kids, but not too many."

≋

The chief shaman lived by himself in a sandstone cave high above the village (Miller, 1988). He was a tall man with very long hair. He wore a single animal skin, probably that of deer, and no ornaments. It would be hard to say how old he was, and no one presumed to know. The high chief was proud of his station and wealth, but was personally humble. The shaman chose to eschew wealth, but clearly placed himself above mere humans. The villagers believed that he had magical powers, and it was clear that he believed this himself. He had the human fault of arrogance—he despised the wealth-based power held by many of the chiefs. He had his own assistants, but who they were was largely a secret (Grant, 1993; Patterson, 1992; Hudson and Underhay, 1978). This shaman did not hesitate to invoke the superhuman, the unseen, the all-powerful. To not believe was to inhibit the power of hypnotism, the power of knowledge, the power of speech.

I spent a great deal of time with the shaman, because he fascinated me. And I think that I fascinated him—he considered me his equal. He knew the name, age, and thoughts of everyone in the village. He was uncanny with language, and not only knew the languages of the several groups in coastal California, but could tell just where on the coast each person came from by their dialect, and he kidded me about my mixed dialect. He had talked with many visitors and traders, some from far distances.

The shaman showed me hidden rock surfaces, painted by himself and other shamans: they contained maps drawn in at least five dimensions. He pointed to a cross enclosed in a seven pointed star: this represented the four phases of the moon, each with seven days. People, like the moon, follow a 28-day cycle. He described a complex of symbols and cycles, some relating to the stars, telling the history and prophesying the future of the universe. He seemed pleased to talk about things that he felt unable to share with those for whom he had "spiritual responsibility."

He told me that far to the east were millions of giant animals, in herds numbering in the thousands. There were people who planted and irrigated seeds. In a forested land to the north people lived in giant plank houses and erected wooden monuments to their ancestors. And in an area many days travel to the south, mighty shamans had painted giant humanoid figures and animals on the walls and ceilings of caves and on cliff overhangs (Crosby, 1997). I asked him how he had learned these things and he explained that shamans had the power to transmit figures and knowledge to other shamans over great distances.

I admitted to him that I had not seen the great rock art on the cliffs and caves to the south, but that I had indeed observed both rock engravings and paintings in other parts of the world (Clottes, 2002).

I told him I had traveled for many years, always in the direction of the setting sun, and that I had met many races and cultures, plants and animals. I described for him in detail the animals which lived in my homeland, people who rode on horses and camels, vehicles which moved on wheels drawn by animals, boats which were propelled by sails, writing that portrayed speech, and writing on papyrus and wood and stone, and wise men who studied the stars and the rotation of the heavens. With some hesitation I told him that the earth we live on was a sphere, and to go away from its surface, from any place on the earth, would be to go "up."

He believed all that I said, even about the earth being a sphere, because, as he explained, he always knew "when truth was spoken." But he saw all these things as knowledge to be shared only among knowing persons like ourselves, not as something which would intellectually enrich humankind.

The shaman showed me how to cure illness with plants and ritual. I believe that he was the most intelligent human I have had the fortune to work with. But I never could understand why, when he was more than willing to apply a poultice and spend all night praying with a sufferer, he would not teach his people the wondrous knowledge of the outside world.

The Chumash were an enjoyable group. They appreciated beauty in all things, and rewarded those who provided it. But our world is a long ways around and it was time that I was on the go again.

≋

I joined a group of traders, some of whom had started in the eastern desert and traded not only obsidian, but turquoise, hematite and cinnabar. From the land of the Chumash they carried objects of steatite and serpentine, seashells, and the furs and skins of sea mammals.

The traders' community had some practices very similar to the Chumash, but in governance they were more of a theocracy. The office of high chief and high priest (or shaman) was held by the same individual.

In their home village, most of the men belonged to a secret brotherhood where they learned and practiced a life-ritual that was pervasive and rigid. The rules of life were handed down from a great teacher who one could calculate lived about 1,000 years earlier. The original teachings had been intended to produce a self-sustaining, healthy and clean society, but many of the strictures had been distorted, and others had been totally ignored.

Some of the rules were commendable: for example, the sanitary disposal of garbage and sewage. It has been my experience all around the world that the outer edge of most villages is a stinking, fly-infested mess, without any particular place for the disposal of sewage. Not so, in the California coastal ranges, where such was buried in a high dry place. Bodies were burned and in some cases the residences of the deceased were burned and the sick were banished from the village. There were complex rules concerning who could marry whom, and how many children they were allowed to have. Every child at birth was assigned to a caste, and marriage partners were in some cases also decided at birth.

The chief/shaman was superhuman, and he ate a special diet. (Some claim that on occasion this diet included small children.) He was waited on hand and foot by his assistants (mostly female), who acted as midwives, but also as the shaman's slaves and spies. The village people were terrified by his presence. Children would run and scream when they saw him or his assistants. There is no question but that this shaman ruled by threats and fear.

One of the responsibilities of the shaman was to make sure that there were deer and rabbits in the fields, fish and birds in the lakes, and that children were born healthy. When problems occurred the shaman was often blamed for not adequately protecting the people.

Initially, I was accepted by all, primarily because I had a working knowledge of several California languages and could work as a translator for the traders (trade being an important part of the economy).

Not long after I arrived several babies were born still or deformed. There were strange lights in the sky [aurora borealis, very unusual at this latitude], and I noticed that the shaman of this group was giving me the "evil eye."

There was in this village a young woman from a more northerly group who had become the bride of a man of this village, and as is the custom, she moved to the home of her husband. However, in some manner not clear to her, her young husband had been fatally injured. It seemed there was no available man wishing to take her as his wife, and so she had become more or less a slave of her husband's family.

One evening she came to me and reported, "The shaman has decided that your presence is the cause of these unfortunate events and that to placate the spirits you should be destroyed." She continued, "There was much discussion. Some argued to return you to the Chumash, as

63

they feared the soldiers of the Chumash might take revenge. But they may fear their own shaman more."

To the east of the Chumash realm is a great lake of tules. The young widow's people to the north were experts with reed boats, and she too was expert with these craft. On a recent fishing excursion she had hidden one of these boats with two paddles. And now she proposed to me that we slip away at the first light of dawn and paddle the reed boat north to her people. I agreed to go with her.

There was a full moon, and no one saw us leaving. We found the reed boat as planned, and paddled northward. Even if the villagers had pursued us, they could not have followed us through the myriad patchwork of tule reeds.

The woman's relatives were astonished at her return. They had no fear of the people with whom she had been living—she was simply returning home, and her husband's family had nothing against her. However, I was "wanted," and they might be resentful that I had foiled their "sacrifice." We agreed that I should move on. They equipped me with a sacred blanket with magic protective powers, and they delegated two young men to accompany me north to a friendly people who would recognize and honor the bearer of the blanket.

THE SACRED VALLEY, 1262 BCE

The tribe to which my fellow fugitive belonged was extremely friendly, and even offered to lead me to the Sacred Valley [Yosemite Valley] in the snowcapped Mountains to the east [Sierra Nevada]. To visit this Sacred Valley was deemed a special reward for noble deeds or a heroic life. Individuals (men and women of middle age) could come from any of the local tribes [northern California and adjacent Nevada], but they must come in peace. Members of the most antagonistic groups can enter without fear, and sit down to pass the pipe. Here all are brothers and sisters. Even the deer and bear are unafraid. We ate fish and piñon nuts cooked together with an abundance of savory greens. Some brought special dishes to share.

This deep canyon is enclosed on all sides by almost vertical, sheer walls of white crystalline rocks. Above the canyon the streams flow across a plateau of nearly barren rock, then plunge into the canyon, falling more than two hundred meters in a single leap. The noise created by the falling water is heard throughout the valley, and the spray keeps everything damp for a hundred meters around.

There are groves of trees that we called "the Red Woods." Roughly measured they are as much as 10 meters in diameter. Sighting over an improvised triangle, we decided some of the trees appeared to be almost 100 meters tall.

One of the giants, apparently weakened by fire, had fallen and broken open so that I could count what I assumed to be annual growth rings. My very crude count for this tree was about 3,000 years. Extrapolating the count to larger standing trees I estimated that there are trees at least 3,500 years old. That was hard to comprehend. Imagine planting a seedling today and coming back to see it in 3,500 years!

Brightly colored flowers grow in profusion, especially in the meadows near the steep canyon walls. One of these [California poppy, *Eschscholzia californica*] is bright orange, with four orange petals making a deep cup shape, and with fern-like leaves. Equally abundant, and often in the same field, is a tall stalk with multiple purple flowers [lupine, *Lupinus latifolius*]. Its leaves are arranged in a fan-like pattern. One could spend days in this valley, just studying the many beautiful flowers (L. Wilson, J. Wilson, and Nicholas, 1987).

We hiked around this beautiful valley and wondered how peoples who appeared so similar, producing very similar craftwork, singing similar songs, praying to similar gods, and in some cases speaking mutually understandable languages could appreciate the magic of this valley and leave to go about their not unusual practice of killing one another.

WE ALONE

ARE WE HERE
TO LET THE SAND FLOW PAST OUR FEET,
TO SPLASH IN CLEAR, COLD POOLS,
AND HAVE THE WARM SUN
DRENCH OUR BACKS?

To look up at the great blue arch
And watch the vaporous pillows march?
Is it enough to let the hourglass run,
The moon and sun,
The thunder storms?

To silhouette
The needled pine

Against the sky—
Or must we seek
Some satisfaction quite beyond:
To know the truth of what's to come,
And what is gone.
Must we look at these white walls of
    granite,
And wonder why?

Why we alone, of all the creatures
Look at them and ask a question
Of their cause
And think of endless eons past:
From pressured melt to crystal stone
And wonder, wonder—we alone.

CHAPTER NINE

LAND OF THE TOTEM

1261 BCE

Northern California

When the Europeans arrived in North America, in the part of the continent north of Mexico there were 23 language families divided into 90 languages and countless dialects. At least 15 languages and dialects were spoken along the northern California coast alone. Languages of the Hokan Stock were found in five separate regions of California, including the area along the Colorado River and southernmost California (6 languages, including the Kumeyaay and Yuman languages), the Santa Barbara area (Chumash languages), and northern California (Shasta and Karok languages). The Uto-Aztecan Family of languages were spoken in areas of both southern and northern California (Moratto, 1984; Brown and Douglas, 1969).

Many students are today learning the Hokan stock of languages, with help from remaining native speakers.

CROSSING THE GREAT VALLEY of California I noted that almost every village had its own language and it was difficult to understand the people, even when I started to learn the language of their village. But there were some similarities among the languages. I discovered that related languages [the Hokan stock of languages] were spoken in areas as far apart as northern California and western Mesoamerica.

For the past year I had been preparing to enter the land of scowling faces, the Totem folk. Among the people of northern California were some who knew the Totem language. One of these was a very bright young widow named Tohwa. She and I had an informal exchange: I represented her in doing manly chores, like deer hunting, and she taught me the Totem language. Before leaving for the north I also visited the Old One, who once lived in the land of the Totems. He still spoke several Totem dialects fluently, but he was crippled and nearly blind. He laughed at my pronunciation. I was glad to do chores for him also, and he too worked on my language skill.

Tarya, who is locally accepted as "chief" of the northern California groups, sent best wishes to his powerful neighbors to the north. He also sent presents of exotic shells and two young emissaries who were to accompany me to the southern boundary of Totem Land (Croes, 1995).

It was early spring and snow remained only on the high peaks. Nights were chilly, but the trail was clear and flowers were opening. The three of us carried several days' supply of dried food. We had walked three days when, from an overlook, we saw a small, vertical plume of smoke. We continued with some trepidation since we did not know whose fire this was, or whether the fire makers would be friendly. The trail widened to a clearing, and in the center of the clearing stood several warriors next to an ornate and colorful totem pole. My guides told me that the top figure on the totem was Raven, supported by Wolf and Bear. The totem was carved with stone tools and erected with ropes made of spruce root—in this thinly populated land, no small accomplishment (Allen, 1994).

After a considerable silence one of the warriors asked, "Who are you and why do you come?" They could see that we carried no weapons.

Being the one best able to speak the Totem language, I replied, "We come in peace with a present for the leader of the Totem people. These two Californians came to show me the way, and they now return to their home. I am the One Who Follows the Sun. I come as an emissary from all peoples of the south to all peoples of the north. I wish to learn some of the great knowledge of the peoples to the north and exchange good wishes in the name of the great spirits who guide us all."

Our "greeters" spoke briefly among themselves and accepted me. My two companions left me, and returned to northern California. I continued north with the Totem men. To me they said, "You are expected. We have several days to travel by trail and canoe to where you will be met by the chiefs and dignitaries of the Totem people. I was surprised that they knew of my coming, but they told me of a woman known as "The One Who Killed the Evil Bear," the eldest child of a powerful chief, who had seen my coming in a vision.

We crossed a great river and passed through magnificent forests of spruce, fir, hemlock and cedar. The mountains rose thousands of feet and were covered with snow fields and small bodies of perpetual ice. The melt water from this ice was so laden with rock powder that it looked like milk. For food there were abundant fish, bulbs, and sprouts. I was not sure if I was a prisoner or a guest.

Since I was a few years older than my guides, I thought they anticipated a slower pace. They were used to traveling by canoe and had very muscular arms, whereas in my life I had traveled predominantly with my legs. On the sixth day we camped just short of where we were to be formally greeted. Our "guides" carefully brushed their garments, applied paint to their faces and chests, and braided their hair. Only then, as the sun rose to the top of the sky, did we walk forth. In the background were many totems, in a variety of colors and styles. Behind the freshly decorated poles were more ancient ones that had withstood the weathering of many centuries. All of the totems were carved of red cedar, a very durable timber.

The most important chief and his wife were seated first, and then their eldest child followed by younger children. This, our guide explained, was very unusual, as tradition stipulated that the eldest son be seated first, but The One Who Killed the Evil Bear enjoyed a priority apart from tradition. In fact, when she strode forth and seated herself she did so in a regal fashion and there was a deferential lowering of eyes and a murmur from all present. Then came other distinguished elders, shamans, and invited guests, which included leaders from several days distant.

I was instructed when to appear, and I approached offering the gift of exotic shell jewelry to the chief (understanding that it would be shared). I extended the customary arm grasp to the chief and his family, and I showed no special deference to The One Who Slew the Evil Bear—an intentional gesture on my part toward an egalitarian status. It had been explained to me that her visions had lifted her to super-human respect, and I hoped that "He Who Followed the Sun," having been envisioned, might enjoy the same respect.

Next it was the chief's turn to present gifts to me. I felt very appreciative, as he presented customary clothing with embroidery signifying high status, a spear tipped with sharp splinters of quartz, a bow and arrows, a fur robe for wearing on cool nights, and a one or two person canoe. I knew full well the hours of labor required to craft these items.

Then it was time for music. Each family played and sang a piece of music recalling their tribal ancestry, valorous deeds, and in some cases hardships overcome. Several of the visiting emissaries presented a chant accompanied by drums and other instruments. Finally the host chief's family presented their traditional chant with drums, performed by elders and older children.

When the chanting was finished a message was passed from mouth to ear that a new piece of music, commemorating the slaying of the evil bear, was about to be performed, and the audience hushed and rested upon their knees. This was like no piece of music they had heard. It began quietly with drums positioned all around the forest opening. Gradually the beat became louder and more rapid, and then suddenly the drums ceased and the music of flutes was heard. She who slew the evil bear appeared midstage carrying a spear, moving deftly in dance steps toward the north, the south, the east, and the west. Now the drumbeat rose in a crescendo and The One Who cast her spear into the damp ground. The drums stopped abruptly and The One Who began to sing like no voice in these parts had ever sung—at least so I was told. Some said they heard the cry of a wolf, a lion, and many birds. I do not recall all the shrill words, but she concluded, "My spirit protected me; your spirits will protect you; our spirits will protect all of the people." Tears ran down the faces of both the ancient ones and the children. It was an experience such as few had shared before.

From the ceremonial area we walked to the house of the chief and his family. These were impressive buildings built of red cedar planks as much as 15 meters feet long, and 3 centimeters thick by 20 centimeters wide, overlapping and tied by thongs of animal hide. Nearly square, the spacious lodges were built about a depressed fireplace, and lighted softly by stone lanterns burning seal oil. Typically a lodge housed several related families: aristocrats, commoners, and servants (slaves). I was given a place in the chief's house, a place of considerable respect. Houses were permanent, at least for winter occupancy, but could be taken apart and moved quickly. They were decorated with the same colored figures as the totems. These were stylized birds, beasts, and people, and they told a story of a group or of an individual, and in this regard reminded me of the stories in stone that I had seen in southern Mexico and in Egypt.

That evening around the fire The One Who, her older brother, her parents, and a few others encouraged me to recount my exploits in distant lands. I told them that while I was willing to tell them all that I knew, I wanted to learn about their way of life, in particular their building and food gathering technologies. The older members decided that it should be the responsibility of the oldest brother to show me all of the arts used by the men. The One Who Slew the Evil Bear volunteered to show me the skills of the women, an offer which was not comprehended by the others. But she prevailed, arguing correctly that I could not get a comprehensive appreciation of their culture from a man alone (Croes, 1995).

Thus it was that through that spring and summer I took part in felling giant cedar trees to be hollowed for canoes, or split into planks for houses, and sometimes I went out with the men to spear sea mammals. On other days The One Who showed me which berries to harvest, and more importantly, which ones not to eat. "Be sure to cook the red elderberry," I was reminded. I learned how to smoke fish, how to make tailored clothing from animal skins, how to gather spruce roots and twist them into thread, cord, and rope. I am still a pretty clumsy carpenter and an even more clumsy tailor. Some of the skilled work is hard to comprehend, for example the precise cabinet work required to make water-tight cedar boxes, or to securely attach broken splinters of quartz to the point of a spear or arrow. [Translators' note: The artistic skills being used today, for construction of canoes and baskets, reflect those used 3,000 years ago (Chaussonet, 1995; Christopher, 1952; Neel, 1995).]

I have fished on three continents and observed skilled fishermen wherever I went. Much to my surprise the iron hook used in much of the eastern world is not the most effective. Without doubt the bent wood device used by the people of the Totem Land is superior. The bent wood is a spring, and when the fish swallows it, he rarely escapes.

One day when The One Who and I were alone I asked her why she was spoken of as the "One Who" rather than the "Woman Who" or the "Girl Who." She laughed, "That is gender prejudice. The others cannot comprehend that a female killed a bear, so they avoid the thought by

71

using a gender-neutral word." I was astonished that she would confide this. She went on to explain that by "playing along" with the elevation to semi-divine status she would be able to accomplish more for women, and indeed for the whole people. "I would not talk to any others as I talk to you," she said.

Then I requested, "Tell me the truth about your adventure with the bear."

"A couple of years ago when I was 16 I went out with my basket to gather berries in an area where a bear had been seen. I was foolishly fearless since I had always considered myself invulnerable. Sure enough the bear showed up. He stopped his berry eating and snarled at me. You must understand that we Totem people can speak with animals. This bear told me that these berries were his and that if he found me here again he would kill me.

"I told no one of this encounter and in a few days I returned with my basket, but this time I brought a spear, one edged with the flakes of quartz. When the bear saw me he was furious. 'You think that spear will stop me?'

"I called his bluff—for I am a human. I held the spear high over my head and the bear lunged. I cannot say exactly what happened then—the emotions welled up in me: hatred and fear, and superhuman strength. I think the bear may have tripped on a tree root, or a vine. I apparently thrust the spear into his throat and severed his spine. After that he never moved—it was an instant and merciful death."

"You were just lucky."

"No, nothing in this world is just luck. My protective spirit thrust that spear. As strong as my arms are from canoeing all my life, I alone could not have killed the bear."

"What did you do next?"

"Seeing that my deer hide garment was splattered with blood I hurried to a stream to rinse it before the stain set. I knew the work that went into making that skirt. It was only then that I realized that the claw of the bear had lacerated my right leg. By the time I reached the village it was stiffening up and painful. I told the villagers where to find the dead bear, and they brought it in.

"I did not want to tell the others about the lacerations. I guess that I thought the wound would just heal up. But the shamans—our village has both an elderly man and a younger woman—knew that it would get infected and they took me to the secret ceremonial lodge where difficult healing was done. They cleaned the wound and made a poultice of yarrow, and gave me medicine that only they know (Viereck, 1987). They chanted night and day, as did my family. Sometimes I would awaken sweating, in a fever. And sometimes I would be delirious. And I would dream of the husband I would someday have and the children I would someday bear. And yes, I dreamed of your coming—the kind stranger from the south. And it is because this prediction came true that you were welcome and I have been so respected. And yes, I regretted that it had been necessary to slay the bear."

One day I asked The One Who to tell me about the spiritual beliefs of her people. At first she was not sure what I was asking. "Well, for example," I said, "the other day you were describing to me how a spirit protected you from the evil bear. Can you ever touch or see these spirits?"

"No, but I speak to one spirit, and she speaks to me. She is always there when I need her. I depend on her."

"You should depend more on yourself. I believe the spirit is you."

"You do not understand. When I was still a child, several adults and I were out in the bay in dugout canoes. All of a sudden a terrible storm arose. There were lightning and thunder and the sea water turned to giant waves of foam. The sky turned black as night. We were all tossed into the ice-cold water. A while later I was found on the beach, terrified but alive. One of my uncles was never found. No one could imagine how I got back to the beach—least of all me.

"Then just three years ago," she went on, "I went hunting with several friends on the snow capped mountain to the west of the bay. It was an unseasonably warm day. Before I realized what was happening, the wet snow was detaching from the underlying rocks. It was on the move, slowly at first. But then more snow, ice and loose boulders, pounding against one another, became an avalanche. Fortunately the mass of sliding snow and ice stopped and I was able to walk away, with a few scratches. I lost my bow with arrows—but I could have been killed."

"I can't argue with those accounts," I replied. "Would it be proper to say that you are fortunate to have such a guardian spirit?"

"You are so devoted to the idea that everything in nature can be seen and touched," she observed. "You have experienced earthquakes, volcanic eruptions, tsunamis, and river floods. And I have witnessed tsunamis and great floods, thunder and lightning. And who do you believe has the strength to cause such phenomena? I do not believe that man or beast can effect such havoc. These feats can be attributed to nothing less than gods—and they cannot be touched or seen."

She went on to ask, "How about your people? What deities do they worship?"

"They believe in many spirits and in many local deities. I guess that I didn't pay much attention to those deities—I spent my time trying to find practical ways to escape damage from these god-given phenomena."

Feeling that she had bested me on the visibility question, she wanted to know what I knew about the organized religions that she had heard the shaman speak of.

I answered, "I generally avoid saying anything about someone's religion. But for your future information: these men of piety begin by burning good and valuable items as sacrifice to their gods. Then, needing more sacrifices, they butcher a goat—and waste the meat while some nearby people are starving. Finally they turn to sacrificing their fellow humans, the bravest and the brightest."

Soon it was fall. One day I complained that where I came from the water was not always cold and it was easy to bathe. The One Who fetched a small canoe and told me to bring clean clothing and a towel for drying. We walked several kilometers up the river to where the water was steaming—it was a warm spring. She dipped her foot in a pond and declared it just right. Then in one swift movement she lifted off her single garment and placed it on a bough, then plunged into the pool. When her face emerged she was smiling broadly, "Come on in." And I did. She had the most perfect body I have seen anywhere around the world. When we were drying off she looked at me and asked, "Did I embarrass you?"

"No, but you surprised me. You have always been so modest."

"Well, I guess I consider you family."

"You mean I am now a 'brother?' "

"No no, I have three brothers, and they are the sweetest. They are very special to me. You are not a brother."

"Then maybe you love me like a spouse?"

"No, I will someday have a spouse, my mother will arrange that, and I will be very loyal to him. As the wife of a powerful chief I will have great influence, and will be able to do a great deal of good for the people. I love you like a friend, a very special friend."

"Is it ever possible for a friend to be elevated to spouse?"

She thought on that one, I think a little long, and responded, "I will let you know."

Winter was a time to think. Both The One Who and I needed to learn the language of the related peoples to the north. We found a speaker of that language and spent many hours studying. The One Who was fascinated by my notations. I was marking on birch bark the vocal sounds, transcribing from what I heard. I explained what I knew about languages, and we discussed the degree to which the symbols of the totems constituted a hieroglyphic inscription, a kind of written language.

We toyed with the possibility of writing symbols to represent the sounds of our words for the bear, the wolf, and so on, and putting these symbols together to represent the words. For example, a circle (o) could stand for the sound "be", and a tooth (l) for the sound "rr." Then, written in order, "ol" would sound like "berr" (bear). If then all languages could be expressed by a single set of symbols, it would be easier to translate from one language to the next.

Having pushed our imaginations to this point I asked if it would not be beneficial if all people spoke the same language. She thought on this one and replied, "Each of us speaks a little differently, indeed each of us speaks differently to each person we speak to. Sometimes I speak and do not open my mouth. I can speak with my eyes, I can speak as I roll my shoulders. All the universe speaks: the whales in the sea have a complex vocabulary, and I can speak to you, to my mother and father, to my brothers, to the creatures, even to the trees and the clouds. I wish to speak in different languages, many different languages."

≋

One day The One Who summoned me to the lodge where serious councils met. Why I was included I am not sure, but I believe that it was at the request of The One Who. It seems that the Totem culture was matrilineal and the mothers arranged the marriages. Among the "aristocracy" marriages were not only the vehicle for inheritance of wealth and power, but of obtaining peace among related, and even sometimes distant peoples. Both The One Who and her oldest brother were to marry the oldest son and daughter of a powerful chief about two weeks boat travel to the north, the hope being that uniting the two most powerful groups among the Totem people would put an end to the frequent warring which plagued the area. This would be hard for the son and daughter who would be so separated from their families, but it was a part of the price of being rulers.

Several months ago a young hunter of the northern people had been found dead on a major trail not far from the boundary of this land, and we southern people were blamed. Although not officially sanctioned, such murders did happen, and no one could say for sure how or why it happened. In retaliation the hunters from the north had slipped into southern Totem territory and killed two young men who had nothing to do with the earlier death. The bodies of the dead were lashed to totems and a third youth was lashed but left alive to transmit the oral message that two southerners would be killed for every northerner.

The tribal council was convened to discuss the response. Invitations to the council were also sent to several adjacent groups who were not directly involved, but were loosely allied with the southern group. The tenor of the discussion was that only something very decisive would prevent this from occurring again and again. The feeling among the southerners was that ultimately they were stronger, and by using their strength they could pacify the northerners forever. The thoughts ran to slaughtering whole villages, appropriating their hunting and fishing grounds, taking them all as slaves, and so on. There was also an initiative to form a confederacy of adjacent peoples, to isolate and punish the northerners.

Finally, they looked to The One Who. She of course was directly involved as she had been promised to the son of the northern chief. There was a silence as she looked from one face to the next. At last, making eye contact with each one, she spoke, "You men are crazy. No wonder that every year some of our strongest and bravest are killed for no reason, upholding the 'honor' of our people. If anyone picks up a spear and goes forth to protect our honor I hope it is the wise elders, not my young brothers. Do you not see that perpetuation of the slaughter has no end, each side trying to be more vicious, each side believing that they can scare the opponent? Tell me, because they killed two young men are we scared of them? If they killed ten young men would we be scared of them? If they killed all of our men would we be scared of them? Scared yes, but the women would fight them on the shore and in the lodges, until we all lay dying. It has happened before. And who won? Both groups were decimated, both are known now only by the weathered totems who have no descendants. Their history is lost; their language is lost. Their spirits can only be heard in the forest on a windy night.

"We bury our young men with honor. Let us not dishonor them by killing others equally innocent. I am very angered." She reached for her spear. "The spear that slew the bear is angry. Outfit a fast canoe. Give me a crew of strong paddlers. And snow or wind I will take the message to these people. I will show our anger; I shall insist on a treaty. If they wish to kill or enslave me, the spirit which slew the bear will protect me."

Being one of the few who had learned the northern language I was encouraged to join the mission.

The weather was trying, but The One Who paddled as strongly as any, and seemed not to feel the cold. As we had expected, word of our coming preceded us. As we traveled by both day and night great fires were lighted on islands and high points to show us the way, and at first a few, and then many canoes paddled alongside of us. Some of the bonfires beckoned us to feast. And we slept in our fur blankets in an unexplained sense of security.

It was mid-day when our craft rolled over the round poles placed on the beach. Hundreds of people of all ages, and from several ethnic groups, assembled to greet us. The One Who, wearing her bear hood, strode majestically to the center of the clearing, holding her spear above her head. In her well-practiced northern dialect, she spoke with strength: "Greetings to all the people of the north, to your leaders, to your friends, to the elderly, to the tiny children. I greet you all, and I bring blessings from all the people in the south. I bring no material presents and I expect none. Except for this spear we bring no weapons, and we make no threats of war. I bring one gift, and expect to receive a gift far more valuable than any material goods: I come to offer peace.

"As you know, one of your hunters was found dead. We do not know how he died, but we regret it. In response, two of our young men, innocent young men, were slain. This angered us very much. It angered me just as if they were my brothers, and I felt like sending the spirit who helped me slay the bear to take revenge. But revenge only brings more revenge. It settles nothing; it rights no wrongs.

"The southern Totem people, through history, have not been a peaceful people. We have tried again and again to take revenge. But where has it brought us, and where has it brought you? Today we come to take no revenge. As we came along many shorelines, bonfires lighted our way, canoes of many people joined us. They knew that one canoe from the south was not coming in conquest or revenge. They hoped that we were bringing peace. Just as I saw in my dreams, The One Who Follows the Sun has come in peace, peace for us, for you, and for the people around the world."

In their own language, I thanked them for greeting us. Over the next week, we met with the elders of the north, and discussed making a treaty of peace and cooperation. As a token of peace, the northern son and daughter who were to marry the southerners accompanied us on the return trip south.

Spring was the time for The One Who Slew The Bear and her older brother to marry the son and daughter from the north. She would live in the north, he in the south. The giant red cedar canoes would be used to transport a large portion of the two groups.

An important part of Totem culture was what might be called traveling minstrels. These groups sang and danced, told stories of past events, and foretold the future.

The people of Totem land were so inspired by the singing and dancing of The One Who and her friends that they asked them to perform in many places. In addition to drums and flutes there was always the song of The One Who. In her song she sang to the spirit of change—keeping the good and ridding us of the evil. Speaking of the totems she asked to replace the scowls with smiles, to seek trade not battle, to perfect new arts, new skills, new attitudes toward women, toward servants, and toward the elderly, to judge wealth in spirit, rather than in material possessions. "Those men no longer strong enough to help fell a giant tree, or with eyesight keen enough to make the best baskets, still possess a guardian spirit which assists not only them, but strengthens all of us."

"When we give presents," she admonished," we should give to our brothers and sisters in need of help, rather than to those who already have plenty. We should never give to shame, we should never give in pride. The wily raven sees our false generosity and laughs."

The dance begins with a line of men and a line of women facing each other. They step toward each other, The One Who steps first to the chief, then her brother steps to their mother. Then each chooses a partner. The One Who chooses a ten year old boy, then an ancient man. Then for a woman who has difficulty rising to her feet, The One Who kneels in front of her and they slap hands together. Then a group of young people circle one another holding their hands high as the drum beat rises faster and louder. Suddenly the drums stop and all the dancers stand, applauding each other. The One Who and her brother walk among the group handing out token presents.

The minstrel trips completed, the several giant cedar boats were specially decorated for the traveling marriage party.

One night The One Who summoned me to follow her to the secret lodge where she had the vision. We kindled a small fire in the ashes and talked of many things, about the world, about our lives to come. "My mother," she related, "called me aside recently to tell me how much she appreciated my willingness to accept the traditional marriage for the benefit of our family and all of the people. She understood the degree to which I was a leader, and the degree to which I might be putting aside ambition. She also said that she understood how much I loved the One Who Follows the Sun. My mother then said, 'Take him by night to the secret lodge and for one night you will be his and he will be yours.'

"I responded that I had thought on all these things and that both of us had our missions: I to our people, you to circling the earth. While I seek to unite Totem land, you are bringing together people of the whole world."

On her wedding day I saw The One Who Slew the Bear for the last time, viewed from the edge of the crowd. I never heard of her again, except in dreams.

≋

CHAPTER TEN

THE COPPER MAN

1260 BCE

IN NORTHERN TOTEM LAND, I met a trader who was known as the Copper Man, because metallic copper was the most important item of his trade. The northern Totem people wanted caribou skins and native copper; the interior people wanted dried halibut, fine cedar woodwork and canoes. Copper Man was fascinated by geography and the prospects of traveling great distances to find exotic trade items. He spoke several languages. Thus our shared interests struck a friendship and I joined him in his homeward trip north from Totem land (Langdon, 1993).

> There were roughly three groups of ancient peoples in what is today known as Alaska, coastal British Columbia, and the State of Washington. The first groups are the Pacific Northwest people of the preceding chapter. The second groups are the Athapaskans, who lived in the interior, reaching the coast near Anchorage. Third are the "Eskimos," which include Aleuts in the southwest, Upiks in the west, and Inupiat in the northwest and north. Some of these people are traders, and adapted to a variety of environments and diets. Locally, the Athapaskans shared many cultural practices with the Eskimos and with the Pacific Northwest peoples. In general they lacked the large trees to make dugout canoes and plank houses. The traders typically spoke several languages and dialects.

Copper Man was almost two meters tall, had hair the color of burnished bronze, and eyes as blue as the glacial ice. His wife, who grew up in Totem land and spoke their language, enjoyed singing and dancing, and talked all the time.

The party of Copper Man consisted of six very strong young men, plus himself and me, traveling in three umiaks. The boats were loaded with the furs of sea mammals, fine wooden articles, and dried halibut. Carrying the umiaks from the coast, we climbed a steep and rough trail past the toe of a glacier. This was my first close-up view of these frozen monsters of blue ice. Further north the trail became less steep and was interrupted by lakes. We would paddle to the end of a lake and find the next trail. Copper Man knew just where to find the trails. Some of the lakes were clear of glacial powder, and provided us with abundant fish.

Having lived the past two years among giant trees I was astonished to find only short slender trees [spruce], and then still shorter, scattered trees, and in places no trees, just dwarf vegetation clinging to the ground. In a few places we walked across snow, and where we stepped we crushed cranberries, frozen from the previous year, leaving the snowy trail speckled with red cranberry juice.

In places the bare rock was exposed, presumably carved away by the movement of the ice. It was foliated rock laced with white mica, and cut by many small veins of quartz. In my homeland on the other side of the globe, miners sought out such veinlets and washed the related gravel in search of gold. If there is gold in these rocks no one seems to have discovered it, which perhaps is a good thing, since men lose all reason when they discover gold.

At last, after several weeks of canoeing and portage we reached the shores of the Tanana River and the encampment of Copper Man's people. They lived in temporary dome-shaped dwellings, partially below ground level. Local "merchants" from some distance around were anticipating our arrival and were there to barter for the trade items. Each of the bearers was paid for his service, and that included me. I was equipped with a complete outfit of light weight, warm and comfortable clothing made of animal intestines and decorated with feathers and porcupine quills. Copper Man did his best to get me to take on a handsome young widow who he explained was very lonely and needed my help. I told him that I was willing to "help out" in any way the group needed, but that I became sentimental when faced with women. So he brought me a fine young puppy and explained that it would be my task to raise a strong dog.

≋

One morning I asked Copper Man why the dogs were not hungry. He replied, "The dogs found a carcass [a mammoth] thawing out of the glacial ice." He went on to explain: "Many, many generations ago there were vast areas covered by permanent ice [glaciers]. These glaciers have moved slowly toward the sea. Some of them fractured, snow covered the fractures [crevasses], and giant creatures fell through the snow into the crevasses and were frozen hard. And sometimes people fell into the crevasses. Not that I have found any. Maybe someone was always there to pull them out."

Copper Man asked me, "Would you care to see one of these skeletons?"

"Yes," I replied, "Yes, if we can get the dogs to take us back to it." Copper Man hitched up six snow dogs, and we headed north across the featureless, snow covered terrain, made more obscure by a dusting of fresh snow and intermittent ground fog. But the dogs knew where we were headed and it was not too long before Copper Man pointed to the northeast and shouted, "Over there! Over there! Over there!" He turned to me and asked, "Is this a big one? What do you call such creatures in your country?"

I answered, "I have never seen such a monster. This creature does not resemble anything I have ever seen. In my home, Morocco, and in Egypt, there are huge beasts with trunks and tusks, and almost no tail. We call them elephants. But this is not an elephant."

Copper Man listened attentively, but when I told him that in other parts of the world we put elephants to work, he was incredulous. He told me a legend about the frozen mammoths. "Once one of our people was caught out in a storm, and could not see well enough to find his way home. He came upon a mammoth carcass, took out his knife, and cut his way into a cavity between the mammoth's ribs. By using this makeshift shelter, he was able to keep himself alive until the storm subsided, and he was able to find his way home."

We saw the bones of many creatures. Some were the Arctic cousins of familiar species, like the giant bear and giant bison, one was like a horse, and a few were totally foreign [giant ground sloth]. I asked Copper

Man, "Weren't there any large carnivores to feast on these herbivores?"

"Indeed so. The most impressive was the giant cat with fangs about 25 centimeters long" [saber toothed tiger].

"Did these giant cats eat people?"

"The people were very frightened, so they chose to live on the islands where they felt that they were safer. Some people attempted to hunt the mammoths with long flint points that could penetrate the hide of the giant creatures and cause them to stumble over cliffs," Copper Man informed me. "It is a much safer life on the islands, where large carnivores are rarely seen."

I asked him, "Do you know what the people on the islands eat?"

He replied that he had grown up on the Aleutian Islands and had at least visited most of them. "What did we eat? When a whale was beached, people came from all around to share the meat and blubber. We had walruses, elephant seals, shellfish, and other fish in abundance. On the shore we gathered birds' eggs and special varieties of kelp."

"Food appears to have been plentiful, but can you get along with just kelp for a vegetable?"

"The Island dwellers had a few secret sources of plant food that they brought along on long journeys."

I asked him, "What were these secret plants?"

"Some were lily bulbs. If you plant them, they produce lilies in a variety of colors in the springtime, showing themselves just as the snow is disappearing."

"Do you have any here in camp?"

"No, not unless someone has brought them from the coast. They don't seem to grow north of the Aleutian Peninsula."

The next day I was again thinking about my route to the west. The lilies [*Fritillaria camchatcensis*] grow on the Aleutian coast and yet they are named for Kamchatka, a mysterious land of volcanoes located far to the west. If this same lily blooms in Kamchatka there must be ocean currents that can take you there. So I asked Copper Man, "Have you ever been across the sea to Kamchatka?"

"No," he replied. Then without shaking his head he began to tell me of an old man who had traveled to Kamchatka and some years later returned to Alaska, with many stories to tell. "It is not a journey to plan alone. But you are in good fortune. Several fellow copper tradesmen and I are planning a trip down the great river to the coast, whence we have several choices. First, we can go north and cross on the land bridge, and reach Central Asia via the Sea of Okhotch. Or, second, we can travel down the great river, follow the current west from Alaska to Kamchatka, and thence via the Kuril Islands to the islands of Japan. A third route we could take would be to follow the Aleutians west to the south eastern coast of Kamchatka, whence we could continue south into Japan, or we could go directly to China, via Korea."

We resolved to postpone a decision until we had the information closer at hand.

≋

It was time to plan a trading venture down the big rivers to the west to meet traders from the other side of the eastern ocean. This to me was an important step. I should explain why. In retrospect, I distinguish the "western" ocean from the "eastern" ocean, since they in turn were both to the west of me when I began my travels. Starting from northwest Africa or the Mediterranean region, the first ocean to be crossed was that located immediately to the west of Morocco. If you travel to the east you encounter more ocean, thus, the "eastern" ocean. Whether the ocean, the eastern shore of which we had been following for several years, was indeed the "eastern" ocean, or possibly still another ocean, we did not know.

The native copper had been gathered as boulders and pebbles from the drainages near Mount Wrangell and brought to the Tanana River for trade. We could go down the river by raft and umiak during the warmth of summer, or we could wait until the rivers froze over and go by snowshoe. The problem with winter was that we would have to make camp frequently for food and warmth, and the perpetual darkness made traveling hazardous. We decided to pack and leave at once. Since the summer is short here, we needed to hurry, if we were to gain the advantage of the season. We devised a plan by which we could make the best use of our time. Copper Man and Tor, our companion from the far North, both knew the river route well and planned each stop along the way. One of them would travel ahead and make camp, and then the cargo boatmen would see the smoke and rejoin them. The umiaks would be traded and most of the crew would return by frozen river. Tor and I would continue, either by way of the Bering Strait, or by the Aleutian Islands.

It was an interesting group: Alou was part northern Eskimo, part Chukchi from the other side of the Bering Strait. He had traded in many lands and he told many tales. Tor was a giant man of red hair and enormous strength. He spoke Athapaskan and Eskimo. But his native language was totally foreign to the other members of the party. Knowing Greek, I had a sense that it was a language at least distantly related—but how did he get here? All he knew was that he and a party of kinfolk had traveled across the northern ice, totally lost. I showed him some Greek letters but they meant nothing to him. He carried with him a knife made of brown metal and which easily cut copper [bronze]. This certainly suggested he had come from the continent east of the western ocean. We puzzled over the inscription on the handle of the knife. Copper Man confided that when he was across the Bering Strait he encountered traders who were using symbols to "count" and to "talk." For example, a mark like this 𐤙 means "man", and like this 𐤙 means ten men. It kind of looks like a "man," doesn't it?

There was always plenty of fresh food and we had little difficulty keeping to our projected schedule. So we sat around the fire and related stories from at least four different heritages. People on both sides of the strait relate to the story of Raven. Why? Not only are the exploits rather silly and contradictory, but why a raven? Why not an eagle or a sea gull? I proposed that these tales were allegories with a secret meaning. Perhaps the inventor of the story feared to tell the truth and so told something preposterous, with hope that the listener would perceive the true meaning. Copper Man repeated the Athapaskan account by which the earth is multi-layered, with a "heaven" layer above, an underworld, and then further below a repetition of a land like ours in which their summer is our winter and their winter is our summer.

I responded that I believe the earth is a sphere and that indeed the reversal of seasons on the opposite side is correct. This account is fascinating because it implies that someone creating this story either knew or suspected the truth.

Among the many fables that Copper Man could relate from his journeys into Asia was that of four-legged creatures with the torso and head of a man. I told him that on the other side of the world there were many of these large hoofed creatures, and that men had learned to ride them. I surmised that someone in the east had seen horsemen at a distance and imagined that man and horse were all one creature.

I went to sleep marveling that among this small group there were at least three of us who had made some contact with other continents, and we heard a creation story that implied that someone was aware of the southern hemisphere (Oman, 1995). Perhaps we are not as isolated as we had thought.

We traveled the Tanana River to the Yukon River, and down the Yukon to where it flows south toward Katsukwim Bay. At this point there is a village of traders and bearers who take the goods either overland to the Seward Peninsula and across the Bering Strait to Eurasia, or along the chain of Aleutian Islands, to Kamchatka. Traders had their goods on display, and there were men looking for wives. Most of the traders buying here would transport the goods to inland Siberia, and many were native to those areas.

Copper Man loaded his packs with sea mammal fur and walrus tusks. He was waiting for the river to freeze over. Tor and I were waiting for a good snow so that we could begin snow-shoeing. We were just about to leave when Copper Man appeared with his wife, who was all smiles.

"One Who Follows the Sun, I am loaning you my wife. She speaks excellent Eskimo and you need her help." Tall and strong, she threw her arms around me and said, "Copper Man must think a great deal of you, as I am his number one wife and he loves me very much."

Native copper was highly prized, even more so in eastern Asia than in Alaska. The plan was for the three of us and several porters to see the copper safely to mainland Asia, from whence Tor and Copper Man's wife would return with other trade items, and arrangements would be made with Asian traders to accompany me traveling west and southwest into Asia.

CHAPTER ELEVEN

STEPPING STONES TO ASIA
1259 BCE

A LASKA IS A LARGE LAND, a cold land, in winter a cold, barren and windy land. And winter lasts much of the year. If I had known the geography of Alaska I would have followed the southern coast westward, and never visited the interior. But we had lots of fun, and I learned a lot by working with Copper Man and Tor.

THE BERING STRAIT

Prior to the present open water of the Bering Strait, there was a succession of withdrawals of water from the sea to ice on the continent, leaving the Bering Strait dry. At the time of the most recent withdrawal, perhaps about 24,000 BCE, the sea level all around the world was about 100 meters below present sea level, exposing more dry land along the coastlines all around the earth, and allowing some plants and animals to migrate across from Asia to North America or the reverse. By 10,000 BCE the seaway had again opened and the land bridge had been submerged.

We were on the southern coast of Alaska, and we had to make a decision. We could follow the chain of the Aleutian Islands west, and then cross the open water to Kamchatka. Alternatively, we could paddle along the coast, with the current, north to the Bering Strait, with land almost always in sight. But along the coast the total distance is greater, it would take us longer, and it would be colder.

At this time, my first objective was to avoid another winter like the last one on the frozen Yukon River. I was thinking that if our party could make it to Kamchatka by fall, we might find comfortable shelter where we could study the languages that lie ahead.

Fortunately, we encountered a group of migrants, traders, and adventurers who had recently come from Kamchatka by way of the Aleutians. This group of about 24 men and women, most of them 20 to 30 years old, had left their home in the Kuril Islands in search of a temperate climate where they could plant seeds, breed animals, fish and hunt. They appeared to belong to more than one ethnic group. They were traveling in two giant dugout canoes brought by traders from far to the east, where the giant cedars grow. They had covered their boats with skins and giant animal intestines to keep themselves dry and warm. They were carrying a cage with six chickens. They had two large puppies, cold weather dogs (to protect them). There were three ewes and one ram, of a breed praised for their long-fiber wool. They also carried a variety of seeds for planting, principally rice and other grains.

Early agriculture in Asia spread from at least two regions. The cultivation of rice, native grains, and other seeds began in the south of China about 8000 BCE, and progressed northward to Hokkaido and the Kurils.

The ancestors of the sheep tending people that Follow the Sun and Tor had encountered in Alaska lived thousands of years ago in Xinjiang province of China. When their homeland became too dry for sheep they migrated to coastal East Asia, where they flourished on sea food. However, they never forgot their sheep-raising skills.

The more ancient ancestors of these people may have been those that occupied the center of the Black Sea depression, which filled with water about 7,000 years ago. The survivors of the flood migrated up the valleys of the Danube, Volga, and other rivers, into the headwaters of the Rhine, and ultimately to the British Isles. Those that followed up the rivers east of the Black Sea occupied the area of Xinjiang about 5,000 years ago (Ryan and Pitman, 1998).

The migrants who occupied the area of Xinjiang in northwestern China left their mummies there about 3,200 years ago (Barber, 1999; Mallory and Mair, 2000). These people collectively have been called the Celts and they share the Altaic language group. By the 13th century BCE, the Jomon people in the Kuril Islands also spoke an Altaic language, and they were known for their excellent ceramics and their keeping of sheep. It is possible that the Jomon people who lived in northern Japan in 1300 BCE arrived in Japan sometime after 3000 BCE and are represented today by the small group of people known as Ainu.

ALEUTIANS

An old man among them had traversed both the Bering Strait and the Aleutian routes and declared that the Aleutian route was both safer and faster. That settled it: we were off to the Aleutian Islands.

The Aleutians and the Kurils are two volcanic island chains connecting Alaska to Kamchatka, and Kamchatka to Hokkaido, respectively. The Aleutians consist of a peninsula followed by a string of about 25 islands, about 900 kilometers long. The Kurils are a group of about 50 islands, extending a distance of about 300 kilometers (B. Fitzhugh, University of Washington, 2000).

A few plants and animals extend across the straits to easternmost Asia. One plant that persists both in Alaska, and from Kamchatka to the Japanese islands, is the purple-brown lily [*Fritillaria camschatcensis*], with bells hanging down from its slender stem, and with shiny green leaves that are bigger at the stem than at the ends.

The people in this environs have migrated here from the northwest [Eskimos], from the east [Athapaskans], and from the southeast. A mixture of Jomon and more distant people migrated here to avoid predatory beasts. In the mountains there was an abundance of deer, wild sheep and goats, and moose. Rabbits were an easy catch. On the salty side there were large fish, seals, walrus, sharks, and for those who preferred the near-beach there was ample shell food, even giant crabs and lobsters. The weather was cold, damp and windy, but less harsh than where some of the migrants came from.

Most of the Aleutian Islands have sources of fresh water. Some have several hundred inhabitants and practice a kind of agriculture that selects plants useful to man. These include several lilies, especially varieties of *Fritillaria and Allium*. We observed the genus *Fritillaria*, blooming along our trail, again and again. Dried *Fritillaria* bulbs were always a must in packing for a seagoing journey.

We planned to travel about 20 kilometers a day toward Kamchatka. We would be passing about 25 islands, while we covered about 600 kilometers by sea. This seemed very strange to the people living on the islands, because they seldom visit another island except in choosing mates. The language spoken was slightly different on each island.

These people were divided into clans, each with its own clan elders, and each with its own recognized hunting and gathering range. But they had no formal government, no taxes, and no king.

One evening just before the autumn equinox I heard a rushing of bare feet past my shelter. Men and boys were shouting, women and girls were unfolding sturdy baskets, and sharpening their biggest knives (made of walrus tusk). A twelve-meter whale was beached and lay helplessly dying. The local shaman stood by the animal's head and reminded the gathering crowd that this was a child of the Great Spirits, a present to us from the gods of nature, and woe to anyone who raised his knife before the great creature expired. The shaman faced the sky, the dying whale gave a final shudder, and the people began carving. They had done this before and knew exactly how to strip the meat and blubber from the bones. Every family on the island was represented. How did they hear about the beached whale in the middle of the night? Why was there not the slightest disagreement over which family deserves which part of the carcass?

We left the scraps for the gulls.

≋

CHAPTER TWELVE

JAPAN

1258 BCE

From Kamchatka to Hokkaido the islands are small and forested, there are mariners for hire, and fresh water is not a problem.

Hokkaido

Japan had the largest concentration of people I had encountered so far on my journey. Looking down the coastline at dusk, I could distinguish dozens of villages, each with its many oven fires and stone lanterns. This land was host to a vigorous forest of hard and soft wood trees [maple and pine]. One day I was walking through the forest with my new Japanese friend, whom we knew as Keiji. I commented on the fact that all the lower and small limbs of the trees had been trimmed. Further, the trimmed branches were set up like teepee poles under the cover of trees.

"Why are the branches stacked like this?" I asked.

The answer came, "Because that is where the mushrooms grow. We do not want to waste the space under the trees."

Indeed, no space was wasted. Each pit house was home to more people, as the population grew.

Wild game was no longer a large part of their diet. Shoreline crops had become scarce, due to the advent of diving.

The people of northern Japan at this time (1300 BCE) were the Jomon people, probably ancestors of the Ainu who live in northern Japan today (Imamura, 1996). They cultivated millet, and then rice, which became essential foods for them. By the end of the Jomon period, Japanese farmers were growing rice in wet fields.

The Jomon people of Japan became deep water fishermen, professional artists and potters, pearl divers, and traders. There was a demand for jewelry, ceramics of all types, precious metals, and anything made of bronze. The market for these objects came from a growing elite class.

Archaeological studies show that the first significant production of ceramic pottery was by these Jomon people of northern Japan (Imamura, 1996). They made a great number of varied, decorated, ceramic articles, including some that are true art by modern standards. The Jomon people made many different patterns on their pottery, by pressing cords into the pottery while its surface was still soft. The word "Jomon" in Japanese refers to the marking of pottery by cords.

The use of parallel lines and repetitive patterns for decoration is seen throughout southeast Asia, China, and Egypt.

The Jomon period in Japan is dated from about 10,000 BCE until the second century BCE.

"Tomorrow we will rise early, for I am taking you to the market," explained Keiji, my new Japanese friend. "You will see with your own eyes many wonderful things."

And he was correct. There were wild deer, goats, moose, and boars. There were also rabbits, squirrels, rats and large lizards. My friend said that in the fall there were ducks, geese, chickens and pigeons. For seafood the offerings ranged from small shrimp, clams, oysters, and barnacles, to abalone and lobster. Fish ranged from those no larger than your finger to swordfish bigger than a man, and sharks nearly as large.

I asked the fishmonger, "Do you sell the meat of the whale?"

"Sorry, we are all out of whale meat, but maybe we'll have some next week. How about some manitou?" Like any good salesman, he offered me a substitute.

These were all fresh, on the hoof, salted, or bedded in the ice. If you wished, you could have your dog or turtle butchered while you watched.

The sea also produces a variety of nourishing plants, some of which are for sale here.

This market also had a variety of fruits and vegetables: cranberries, blueberries and more. There are several types of lily bulbs, especially the brown bells.

In addition there were several types of eggs, goat cheeses, honey, and many types of herbs for medicine.

There were tables displaying farming and dairy supplies and equipment, blacksmithing, fishhooks, beekeeping equipment, ceramic wares, precious metals, pearls and valuable stones. Particularly interesting to me were the displays of painting and statuary.

I asked my friend, "What is the role of the large fellows with shaved heads?"

"They are the security staff. All this merchandise is really expensive."

"How do they find buyers who can afford the exorbitant prices?"

"Well, if you can put several hundred serfs to work, growing fruit trees for food and mulberry trees for silk manufacture, and also men growing millet and wet rice, then you will make a profit. And you will need to have a place to use that profit.

"You have at least two ways to use it. You can invest it and make more money. Or you can spend it on favors for your lady friends, bringing them long silk gowns sequined with gold and pearls, or cottages trimmed with ebony and artistic tile. And some gamble away their fortune, in effect leaving it for others to spend."

"How did the hundreds of serfs get in this condition?"

"We have in this land torrential storms, tsunamis, earthquakes, and volcanic eruptions, not to mention warfare and disease. A young family struck by one of these disasters may be left with nothing but their hands and their strong backs. To support the family, they will sign on with an elite land owner, but then they cannot leave."

The group of faithful traders and adventurers who joined me on the Aleutian Peninsula nine months ago were now beyond their language limit and were ready to turn around and return home. I thanked them, every one. Tor and Copper Man's wife bade us farewell, and we parted.

We had been practicing Japanese and Korean with the crew members for several months. Apparently the traders of northern Japan needed to be fluent in Korean, Japanese and Chinese to handle the large volume of sea-borne trade plying the strait that separates Honshu (the major island of Japan) from China.

> *The Jomon people spoke a language that belonged to a language group that existed all across northern Asia and west to Turkey and the lands between the Black and Baltic Seas. (Descendants of the Jomon people today are found only in the Island of Hokkaido and northernmost Japan.) The Jomon language is distantly related to the wide-spread Altaic language group which included Japanese and Korean. The geographic range of any language today is unlike its range in the 13th century BCE.*
>
> *Early agriculture in Asia spread from at least two regions. The cultivation of rice, native grains, and other seeds began in the south of China about 8000 BCE, and progressed northward to Hokkaido and the Kurils.*

I was very fortunate to gain the friendship of a young adventurer named Keiji. He was somewhere between a rich playboy and a serious student of geography, and he had all the answers. He taught me the Jomon language, and he was my contact with the local people.

One of my new friends asked about the acquisition of tradable goods. "You seem able to barter for all kinds of supplies, including large boats. How do you do it?"

"I have traveled many years, and I am fortunate to have met people who were genuinely interested in the earth beyond their own horizons. They may be fearful of me, as a stranger, but they are soon impressed by my knowledge. Rulers will always listen when I speak of distant places, perhaps from an interest in subjugating more people and territory. Scholars are intrigued by my accounts of very different plants, animals, and geography. Traders are eager to learn of distant lands where their trade goods would be appreciated. Most of these people are willing to barter with me, for the things I need to continue my travels.

"But getting back to the economics of this archipelago . . . So, it is easy to become a serf, but difficult to leave?"

Keiji responded, "If you leave, you are an outlaw. Most don't leave, because they can't take their family with them. But a few do leave, and they subsist by marauding the countryside. The elite counter this by hiring soldiers."

Then a local crew member asked me, "What are you, an outlaw, an elite, or a soldier?"

"I am a sort of scholar, far from home. I am also a trader."

Keijii commented, "To be a successful trader in our group, you need to speak or write at least three languages, calculate prices in your head, be able to recognize gold and jade when you see them, and much more.

"So we belong to a guild, and we travel in groups for safety. We hire soldiers, and we are respected. The elite cannot disregard us because they seek our goods, and we can guarantee authenticity."

Then one of my crew asked, "Is there widespread unrest in Japan, which might turn into hostility between soldiers of different loyalties?"

Keiji replied, "I don't know. I hope not to get mixed up in a war."

We had traveled down the west coast of Hokkaido. The shoreline of this large island at this time of year is populated by thousands, perhaps millions, of large water fowl, predominantly geese.

Honshu

Now we were traveling down the west coast of the largest of the Japanese islands [Honshu]. Small homes were everywhere, grasping the rocky mountainside. Some homes were elegant. Each house was surrounded by tiny fields of rice and millet. But the population density! Never in my travels have I seen such population in such steep and rocky terrain. It's no wonder that the effort has changed from gathering and hunting to intensive agriculture, diving for mollusks and pearls, and harvesting kelp.

In the villages men, women and girls worked at fabrication, producing items of wood, leather, ceramics, and fiber. But people attached greater value to any product that was made in China.

One bright summer day we were on the beach repacking our load of trade goods, when we saw a plume of red smoke rising from behind the coastal hills. Keiji told us, "We must prepare for disaster. The hills are very dry, because there has been a drought here. Let's get our boats away from the shore."

We lashed our boats to piers well out in the bay, and posted guards to watch them.

The wildfire was moving closer, it had reached the crest of the hill, and its base with bright white smoke appeared to be creeping down toward the hillside homes. Smoke, with its acrid odor, started drifting our way, and quickly became more dense. It was like being in a fog, except that fog is not hot, fog is not tinged with red, and fog does not carry ashes in suspension. The smoke stung our eyes and made us cough. The sun hung like a big red disc, high in the sky. People were now pouring down from the hills. Two girls were carrying an old woman, and a cat too. They needed help.

I turned to Keiji, my local authority on all things, and asked him, "How do we fight it?"

He looked at me gravely, and exclaimed, "Heaven help them! You cannot fight it. You can fight a bear, and you can fight a tiger, but no one can fight a forest fire when the weather is dry and windy. There is no way."

"But what about the people and livestock? And their houses? And their gardens?"

"We will do what little we can, to help the people escape. But we can do nothing against the fury of the fire."

We all scrambled out of our boats and ran back along the pier to the shore, to help however we could. We saw people carrying their possessions on their backs, carrying heirlooms of their ancestors. Men were trying to carry the ancient ones, and the infants, all desperately struggling toward the beach.

The smoke was choking us. I tied a piece of cloth over my nose and mouth, but I was still coughing a lot. No one had shoes or clothing suitable to wear around a fire. Our crew carried some of the children to our boat, with their parents laboring along behind us, carrying still more small children.

Trees as tall as 20 meters crashed and fell across the narrow walkways. In a few places where the steep hillside was covered with underbrush and ancient maples, the fire consumed everything in giant explosions, sending showers of black and gray ashes over all of us. The wildfire reminded me of a great storm at sea, blowing fiercely and taking everything in its path.

We somehow managed to get back to our boats, where we were safe from the raging firestorm. The children were so frightened, and so choked up on the smoke, that they did not cry. The boats were crowded, with all the people we had dared to bring on board. We tried to sleep, but for the adults that was a useless effort.

The next morning we went back to the shore. The pier was not burned. Charcoal blackened all. Most of the houses were destroyed. Again and again we heard the loud crash of a blackened tree falling.

When we walked on the shore, Keiji pointed out to me how the trunks of the stoutest trees were still burning on the inside. "They will be burning, inside, for several weeks," he informed me. "When they have finished burning, small mounds of white ash will almost fill the hole left behind after their roots have burned. Be careful where you walk around the burned area, because you could step on the ground above a tree root that is still burning, and fall down into the burning root below the ground."

≋

This was a turning point in my journey. Until now a handful of faithful teammates and I have dared to match our wits against the elements, the oceans, and the mountains, sometimes navigating without a star to guide us. But from now on, our party would travel with comparative ease. Thanks to the Honshu Trading Guild, we were outfitted with a ship that had a deck, sail, deep water keel and space for twenty people. It took us just two days to cross the Korea Strait, and after eight more days on the Yellow Sea we expected to reach Shandong province, China. Keiji and I were accompanied by two master sailors, six soldiers, a general crew of five strong men, and five traders who were headed for China. Everyone except me would be returning to Japan with the ship.

This was progress. I was not accustomed to such speed, not since we traveled across the great western ocean, and that was many years ago. What had changed about me, despite my continual exercise: I was a little heavier and my hairline was retreating from my forehead. Also, I dare to hope, I was a little wiser.

Our voyage across the Korea Strait began with an easy breeze and a placid sea. Everyone had just settled down for a pleasant ride under a clear sky. Suddenly the trader on watch hollered out as loud as he could: "Pirate ship approaching from south of west." All became chaos. Soldiers were running about brandishing their bronze weapons and shouting menacing dares to and from the pirate ship. Our first master sailor suggested that we out-maneuver them, leaving them adrift in still water. We tried. It did not work. The local crew knew well this bunch of thugs. They plied these waters to intercept the flow of prized goods to the elite of Honshu and Hokkaido. I was thinking, "They probably know just what we are carrying. We have been betrayed!"

The men of the Honshu Trading Guild had presented me with a marvelous steel sword, that they insisted had been made in a village many days travel west of China. Little did I suspect that I would need it the very next day!

At this time soldiers were equipped with bronze swords and spears, of widely variable quality. The pirate ship was gaudy in shades of red and gold. As the pirate ship drew alongside our boat we could see that the pirates were clothed and body-painted with designs to represent dragons, tigers, bears, and serpents. Their champion pranced about, gesturing as to his victory and our fate, intending to scare us.

"Bring me your champion!" he screamed, alternately in Korean and Japanese. "Bring me your champion!"

It was only now that I realized that I was the champion of the traders. "Wow!" I thought, "It has been decades since I had handled a sword, and that was not for real."

The pirates' champion stomped the deck and swore at me for some time, implying that I was a merciless servant of all the elite in the realm.

He was as tall as me, and at least twice my weight. His head was shaven, and his long, curled moustache encircled his foul mouth. The heavy one made several tentative lunges, testing my reflexes. With each lunge the group of pirates cheered and waved their bronze swords in the air. Then suddenly their champion charged low and ferociously. It was my chance. I summoned all my weight and determination into one downward blow, aimed at his extended bronze sword. It bent perceptibly. Later examination showed that my steel blade had nearly severed his bronze one.

The old pirate was on his knees, holding up his mutilated sword and pleading for mercy. None of the pirates chose to be a new champion to retest my steel. So the fight was over.

What was to be done with the criminals? This was a problem. We took the three youngest on our boat. The erstwhile champion of the pirates and his unsavory cohorts had political ties to the insurgents on the island of Honshu. We took over their boat, and searched it for weapons and stolen goods, which we removed. Our crew sailed their craft to the closest small island. We took their sail and oars onto our own boat. Then we left the pirates and their boat. They may have deserved hanging but none of us wished the task.

≈≋

CHAPTER THIRTEEN

CHINA

1257 BCE

IN THE SEVENTEENTH YEAR of my travels I began to hear of a giant and powerful empire to the southwest [China], and from hearing a little about their technology and art I became very curious. I traveled from the cold and scantily forested northeast of Asia to the lush and densely populated land to the southwest. China is a vast land. In its eastern extent it consists of a series of steep and rugged mountain ranges trending more or less east-west. In the north there is ample rainfall for spruce forests and dry-farming agriculture. The northern ridges are densely forested with coniferous trees, but further south the dominant vegetation of the mountains is bamboo.

Everywhere in the east the exposures of bedded rock are limestone [in many places displaying classic karst topography]. The valleys that lie between the ridges are narrow in their upstream portions, widening to deltas as they approach the east coast of China. Most available space is planted to rice and other grains. Along these valleys are hundreds of villages, usually built adjacent to the river. Homes are made of sun-dried brick, plastered over with mud. There are trees for shade and trees for spice, some of them reputedly thousands of years old. There are shelters for livestock and waterfowl. The sizes of fields vary, according to the overall slope of the stream. Where the valley is wide the fields are large and are tended by a group of families; where the valley is narrow a single family may cultivate several small fields. Wild goats and giant pandas graze the steep mountainsides, where they are hunted by tigers and wolves.

The important domestic animals are horses, donkeys, water buffalo, camels (mostly two hump), goats, sheep, and in the far south, elephants. The Chinese grow a wide variety of vegetables and fruit. In a good year there is a great surplus. As a result fruit such as apricots and grapes are dried. Fish and other flesh are salted, and then they are traded over great distances.

But there are years when the rivers are too low for irrigation or great floods destroy the canals, villages, and crops, sometimes with great loss of life and livestock through famine. It is these periods of famine that result in a stable population.

Since there are more able hands than fields in need of tilling, there is a significant segment of the population engaged in other activities. Artisans make ceramic ware, glass, castings of copper and bronze, and weavings of various animal and plant fibers. Perhaps the most important textile is silk, which is gathered from the silkworm cocoons found on the leaves of the mulberry tree. The "secret" process of harvesting silk consists of soaking the cocoons in warm water and then "working" the unraveling fibers with a large comb. How did the people learn to make silk? The story is that the queen was sitting under a mulberry tree when a cocoon from the tree fell into her cup of tea. When it fell, the fibers began to fall apart into very fine threads.

Other important occupations are the military, and the bureaucracy, which collects taxes and records population growth and crop yield. The role of the imperial military is small compared to that of other large, organized societies that I have visited. The roles of scientist, teacher, and philosopher overlap and are not clearly defined. For example, a common figure of Chinese mythology shows two entangled "human" figures, one holding aloft a draftsman's compass, and the other a T-square. What are the meaning and the use of these drafting instruments? Were engineers using these since the dawn of civil engineering?

Most of the teachers in this land are middle-aged men, but their veneration is based on "higher knowledge" regardless of age or gender. As in other lands, the king or "emperor" was anxious to hear of those from whom he could learn, and so he sent out couriers to bring these people to him. At the emperor's court there were people from far parts of the world, with unusual visages and exotic tongues. There were also animals and plants from foreign lands, some of which had to be protected in winter from freezing temperatures.

The emperor, who it turned out had a fascination for exotic objects and cultures, sent emissaries to meet us. He was relieved to learn that I was not the leader of a military force!

The emperor, a tall man with a soft voice, was very open and genuinely interested. He was a collector of art of all types, priceless treasures. He understood the importance of these works, not just to boast among his peers, but to upgrade the technology of the nation, to place Chinese products on a trading par with any of their neighbors, and to train technicians. Far from using his position to acquire these objects he dipped deep into the treasury to pay unheralded prices, thus elevating the price for art throughout the known world (Hodges, 1992).

For another example, he encouraged the spread of written language throughout his realm. The people of China speak a myriad of local languages and dialects, but the few who are truly literate share a common set of written symbols.

China was more than I had hoped for: a written language, a literature, a history, polite, and genteel. They built palaces, prized works of art, and constructed irrigation canals to foster agriculture. As with other leaders I encountered, the elite were hungry for information about the "outside world." Through the silk traders they had heard of civilized lands far to the west and to the south, but they had discounted most of what they had been told as myth.

Because of my interest and knowledge in geography and geology the emperor introduced me to his "chief engineer," a tall, muscular young woman who I was soon to learn was the emperor's daughter. The doting father provided her with a staff of artisans and soldiers, and I was to be her chief assistant.

She immediately took an interest in me and taught me how to ride one of the royal ponies. She was as tall as me and no push-over at arm wrestling. Because of her engineering skill and my facility with languages, she and I were assigned the task of visiting the various provinces of greater China. We were to reassure the bordering states, and see to the progress of canal and dike construction. This undertaking took several years, during which time she and I probably became more familiar with greater China and its ethnic groups than anyone, including the emperor.

We set out to create topographic maps of critical irrigation areas, a maze of small and large irrigation ditches. My boss was known simply as Li, and she generally addressed me as "my friend." She rode so hard on horseback, and worked with such diligence, that I found it difficult to keep up. We soon realized that we needed a device that would allow us to determine a level line over long distances and determine the relative elevations of distant points. This was accomplished by mounting a spirit level on a tripod.

≋

In many places water was being transported long distances by open ditches in order to pass around small canyons, whereas in fact this was not necessary. Instead we could build closed, "U-shaped" tubes, made of fired brick. The water from the ditch could enter the tube at the top, go to the bottom, and rise again on the other side, almost as high as the level of the open ditch from which it had come. The water could thus pass under a ravine, and come up to another open ditch on the other side, saving a great deal of construction [Figure 5]. This worked for ravines as deep as ten meters.

I generally enjoyed China. Its function and success were based on ability: a farmer with a valuable idea was justly rewarded. Some of the

FIGURE 5. TUBES FOR CROSSING A RAVINE [A REVERSE SIPHON]

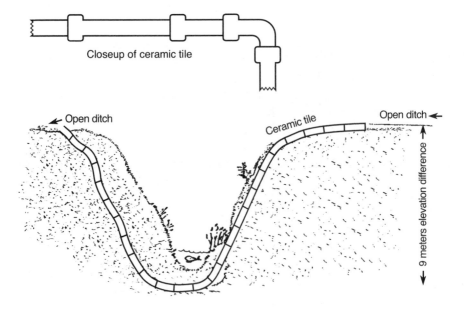

elderly gentlemen with their little white beards were still venerated, although they brought little to the discussion.

≋

One day Li and I were studying Chinese art when I asked her, "Why do artists draw such monstrous dragons? Surely they have not seen such beasts. Are there any such creatures in China?"

"Well, I have not seen any, and I suspect neither have they. But I have seen their bones. Every day I see huge bones coming south from the northern desert [Gobi Desert]. The apothecaries grind them, and distribute the powder as medicine."

"So you believe that these giant bones were left by enormous creatures that no longer exist?"

"The traders employ people to extract the giant bones from the sedimentary stone. The matrix is so solid that it has to be broken out with huge stone chisels. But I understood that they are paid well for them in the south. At one excavation the workmen had uncovered a giant backbone at least 30 meters long. What a shame to destroy it! I wonder how long ago these giants lived. Or are they still living somewhere?"

I suspected that the artists had never seen the creatures from whence these disarticulated bones had come. But with their imagination, they had given them the scaly skin of a crocodile, the teeth of a tiger, and the hind legs of a grasshopper.

Li suggested, "If these creatures ever lived in my neighborhood, I'm just as glad they're extinct. And I'll not be needing that powdered medicine."

≋

The Chinese definition of a garden is a place with water, rock, vegetation and "room," meaning a place for humans to sit and enjoy. One bright morning, atypically, Li chose not to saddle up the horses. Instead she said that she wanted to show me some sacred gardens. In one cascading, rock-strewn channel was a school of golden fish. Li stopped and asked, "Have you ever heard about the philosophers and the golden fish?" No, I had not. "Well," continued Li, "the first philosopher, viewing the fish, proclaimed, 'The fish are happy, swimming freely.' The second philosopher responded, 'How can you know that the fish are happy? You can't know.' The first philosopher replied, 'How can you be sure that I don't know?'"

After sitting an appropriate time on the bench by the pond, and having been served tea, I said, "This is a wonderful land where people can be concerned with what fish feel. But I am concerned that enough fish are caught to ensure that no one goes hungry. I guess that to be a teacher I must learn so much more."

Hours after leaving the gardens, we finally reached the top of a steep, forested hill where we had a view of the country far about. Here we found a poem about the land of silk, inscribed on a slab of polished marble.

THE LAND OF SILK

SOFT FOLDS THE FABRIC,
TIGHT IS THE WEAVE.
MOUNTAINS AND VALLEYS,
AND I BELIEVE
THAT WHEN ALL IS WRITTEN,
AND LESSONS TAUGHT
HERE IS SWEET SLUMBER
WATCHING AND SOUGHT.
FOR INSTEAD OF TEACHING
WE SHOULD LEARN,
FOREVER LEARN.
MY BRUSH PLACES STROKES
ON SMOOTH BAMBOO
I PAINT A PICTURE – IS IT YOU?
I WRITE A VERSE
OF HUMAN VISION
CAN I FAIL?
YES,
IF I FAIL TO ASK
FOR THEE.

I was stumbling over the archaic characters, when Li interrupted, "We learn these lines as small children. They are inscribed in many places." Then she looked me in the eye and said, "Would you like to marry me? You know—father, mother, two kids?"

I did not hesitate to agree, but I added, "You are the daughter of the emperor, and all marriages in China are complicated. Surely the marriage of the emperor's daughter would be very complicated. And I am not a Chinese nobleman! I am not a nobleman of anywhere."

"It will be simple," she replied. "I will ask my father." When Li asks her father, she gets what she asks for.

I was torn between my pledge to travel around the earth and my love of Li and China. I concluded that I had traveled about half way—and surely that was proof enough that the earth is a sphere.

≋

The emperor set aside a special residence for us, including a warm spring. When the emperor learned that Li was pregnant he sent a team of medical specialists, to be available on short notice. As with many other facets of life, the Chinese were advanced in medicine.

When other peoples would call upon ritual and magic to cure diseases and to protect good health, the Chinese experimented and applied whatever appeared to work. The Chinese did not adhere to a widely held and powerful religion, like the Egyptians. Instead, they followed the teaching of revered scholars. [Their philosophical works were collected and organized about 700 years later under the name of Confucius.]

The chief doctor assured us that because Li was in such great physical condition it would be an easy birth. It was some months before we knew that we were expecting twins. Apparently twins are an auspicious omen in China—and the word spread throughout the realm. We soon had our twins: Lui, a boy, and Chi, a girl, both looking like they would grow tall like their mother.

≋

About this time the emperor, in discussion with some of his council, decided that China was so large and had such a large population, that a concentration of learning in the imperial court staff was no longer sufficient as the source of knowledge for the whole country. The emperor decided that China needed a formalized system of higher learning and research designed to strengthen and advance the entire nation. He therefore brought together a large group of teachers and students dedicated to the diffusion of knowledge. There were to be studies in language, medicine, physics, and—because of my interests—the study of rocks, minerals, and land forms.

Eventually the university developed an extensive library including collections of minerals, rocks, and fossils. One of the displays showed the native metals: gold, silver, and copper, and how combinations of the minerals copper and sulfur found in the rock could be heated to drive off the volatile sulfur to yield pure metallic copper. It also showed how other minerals such as tin oxide could be heated together with copper to yield a stronger metal known as bronze. [At this time the Chinese had not developed the use of iron for making steel.]

Agriculture and stock breeding were key topics at the new university. Stockmen discovered that they could develop strains that were particularly adapted to differences in climate, soil, and resistance to disease. This upgrading of agriculture reminded me of the work of the Olmecs in Mesoamerica.

Putting in place a university system was a daunting undertaking which required constant travel. We were on the road much of the time, and the kids were always along. It was customary for these erstwhile nomadic people to bring family along, which we enjoyed. Our son and daughter were riding ponies before they were competent at walking. The kids, now barely six years old, were picking up a polyglot of languages, saying "My mommy and daddy are engineers," and hearing in reply from another child, "My daddy is a warrior."

Life was so pleasant in China, and my skills and knowledge so prized, that I was agreeable to spending all my days there. I seldom thought about my intended journey around the globe. But my wife had not forgotten. She said that this was my destiny, and an important step in the achievement of a "global society." Of course she and the children would go too.

But there were other reasons for continuing the journey.

We were in inland south China when the word arrived that the emperor had died. Amazingly, due to a system of towers and smoke signals, the news took only a few days to reach us. His death was unexpected. Li's father had been in good health. Was there treachery? Was this the end of the Shang dynasty (Fairbank and Reischauer, 1989)?

On our return to the capital, it was some relief to learn that the death resulted from a hunting accident. The emperor was chasing antelope in a chariot and a horse had fallen, tossing the chariot into the air and cutting a deep gash in the emperor's arm. He allowed the surgeon to wash and wrap it, but being overly proud, he insisted on continuing in the hunt. The family doctor assured Li that if her father had allowed treatment there would have been no blood poisoning. The lesson Li drew for me, from this, was: "Don't be a fool! If you or I or one of the kids is injured, let the doctors do their best. Life is too precious to waste on pride."

The question of succession was complicated. There were brothers of the emperor. Li herself, as the oldest living child of the emperor, could conceivably be selected, albeit female rulers were the exception in China. There was even the possibility that our son would succeed the emperor. None of these potential successors was anxious to be emperor, but each had advocates who saw one of the possible candidates as beneficial to themselves.

Considering these questions, Li told me that it was time to renew the journey west, and I agreed. One of her uncles was acting sovereign. He appointed Li ambassador to the states bounding China on the west, and provided a loyal military guard. We were provided with a retinue of horses, livestock, supply carts drawn by oxen, camp orderlies and soldiers. Fortunately we had a guide who was conversant with the varied ethnic groups, and we carried appropriate gifts. We would also be traveling with a camel caravan, with traders bringing silk and other goods for trade. We carried items of art, gifts to the adjacent sovereigns.

From Xian, the capital of China, we traveled west to Lanzhou, Kashgar, Bukhara, Nishgur, taking a route south of the great inland seas, then north of the Caucasus Mountains. We were not alone. The trail was well trodden by trader caravans going both ways between China and Anatolia. From China came cast bronzes, silk, and other textiles. From Afghanistan came lapis lazuli. From the steppes of Central Asia came horses and other animals, being delivered both to the west and to the east. To China came precious metals, and breeding stock for a variety of domesticated animals and birds.

Western China and the lands immediately to the west and north consist of deep, hot, dry basins bounded by high mountains that are capped with snow and ice even in summer. Winter is extremely cold; summer, extremely hot. Because there is almost no rain in the basins, agriculture is limited to a few interior drainages, springs, and a marvelous system of man-made tunnels [karez] that have been dug under the foot of the mountains. The melting ice feeds into the fractured rock of the mountains. The man-made tunnels intersect these fractures and drain toward the intermountain basins.

Apparently the climate has been changing such that there is less snow in the mountains today. Springs and rivers that once provided natural irrigation have dried up, or terminate in saline lakes that grow ever smaller. The man-made tunnel systems require ever more work to maintain the needed water supply. In some places the farmers and stockmen have given up and wind-blown dunes mark the place where prosperous villages once stood. The oasis villages that survive grow rice and a variety of grains, vegetables, melons, and above all grapes and apricots, which they dry for trade.

Today the city of Turpan is still famous for its grapes and the region around Kashgar for its apricots.

The people of central Asia are very different in appearance from the Chinese and Mongols. They are lighter skinned and tall. They speak languages related to those of Persia, the Caucasus and other lands further to the west [Indo-European]. [These are the Celtic people that archaeologists have recently discovered, occupying the oases as early as 2600 BCE (Mallory and Mair, 2000; Barber, 1999)].

Our caravan followed the northern edge of the great desert [Tarim basin] and enjoyed the industrious culture of the semi-nomadic peoples. There were many small children, and ours picked up the language so different from that spoken by their parents.

The chiefs enjoyed evaporative coolers to protect themselves from the punishing heat of mid-summer. Intrepid horsemen packed ice from the mountains to the oases to stock specially built underground ice houses. Using the crushed ice, melted by salt, we could create frozen desserts, which made the extreme temperatures more bearable for all of us.

A JUNCTION OF TRADE AND LANGUAGES, 1246 BCE

At the western end of the Tarim basin the various trade routes coalesced. There were traders from China, India, Afghanistan, Persia, Mesopotamia, eastern Europe, Anatolia and northern Africa. There you could hear and read almost all of the languages of the civilized world.

Despite my conviction about the spherical shape of the earth, I was startled when I spied several cargo boxes labeled in cuneiform letters. You cannot imagine my excitement! I had last seen this form of writing along the shores of the eastern Mediterranean, before I began my journey. Today here it was, stenciled on boxes from the west, coming from that part of the world to which I was headed, and going to China, from which I had just come. Li shared my exhilaration, but most of the travelers just did not understand our excitement. Here was proof, that by going west I would find people who were to the east of me when I began! How many years ahead was my goal? The traders told of great land-locked seas, more snow-capped mountains, and more deserts. I thought, "I really shall return to my first home, by traveling west—by following the sun!"

We bade farewell to our Chinese guard, and distributed gifts and promises of peace to the local sovereigns, who provided us their own mounted guards.

My camel reached down and wrapped his tongue around a mouthful of camel bush, a small spiny plant with red blossoms. But it was the only digestible morsel he was likely to see for several days. A last swig of water, the sun was setting in the west, the moon was nearly full, and we were on our way again.

GOLD AND JADE

Two of the most sought after commodities in the ancient world were gold and jade. Not only could they be crafted into beautiful works of art, but they were virtually indestructible. They represented great value relative to their weight, and thus could be easily transported all about the known world, at minimum expense.

The ability of rulers to accumulate indestructible wealth that could be stored and exchanged for material and services made possible the rise of empires, indeed the rise of what has become known as civilizations. Both gold and jade were and are mined from many parts of the world, in some cases far from the centers of power and craftsmanship. Not only were gold and jade laboriously gleaned from northern Africa, the middle east, and many parts of eastern Asia, but from two of the civilized centers of the new world: Mesoamerica and Peru.

Ironically both gold and jade occur in relative abundance in California and southern Alaska, but the gold hungry conquistadors failed to see it. Jade is relatively abundant in California, Washington, and British

Columbia, and while utilized to a limited extent by native people, for axes, there is no evidence that it was treated as a commodity of great value.

Gold occurs with quartz veins in schistose rocks. Through time, the schist and quartz veins weather and disintegrate to sand and clay, leaving the particles of gold behind in a "lag" deposit. After a torrential rain you may find little "nuggets" that have been scoured out and left behind on the dry streambed.

Jade is found as resistant "nodules" in terranes of serpentine, talc, and mafic rock, in a sense parallel to the occurrence of gold. The "tough" blocks or nodules are excavated by river or sea cliff erosion, and "left behind," again, as a lag deposit. Some of the blocks of jade were so large that the local people had difficulty cutting them up.

There is much more to the study of the earth [geology] than telling folks how to find gold and jade, but how to find gold and jade is what they wish to know. The mountains of northwest China, the Tianshan and Altaishan are in places underlain by a variety of schistose and veined rocks. They have been eroded by ice, wind, and sediment-laden flash floods, ripping up the schists and scattering them across the alluvial plain.

The particles of gold and the boulder-like blocks of jade are distributed across the plane of alluviation very unevenly, and the task for the prospector is to find where they are concentrated. There is an old saying: "Gold, and we could add jade, is where you find it." This is a very erroneous conclusion. One method that I used is to "pan." I carried a small copper pan: copper is best, but not necessary. I knelt down by a stream and filled the pan with water and sediment. As I swirled the pan around, the heavier particles worked their way down to the bottom of the pan, and the lighter particles came to the top. I threw out the pebbles and the lighter particles. Soon I would have a concentration of black grains and little else in my pan. If I was in a favorable locality, there would be a few shiny grains of gold bringing up the rear of the concentrate of black grains. Knowing that I was on the right track, I walked upstream to the first fork, where I sampled both branches with my pan. If one fork showed grains of gold and the other did not, I kept testing upstream, always following the richer fork. When no gold was in my pan, I had passed the source. Then I needed to test again, immediately upstream from the last positive test point.

China Today

It is difficult to visit 1.2 billion people in three weeks—but we tried.

We visited the camps of herdsmen riding their shaggy Siberian ponies through verdant fields in the view of glaciers and ice-fed lakes, in the mountains above Urumqi. We visited a class of pre-schoolers in Beijing. They sing and play and act like happy pre-schoolers everywhere.

In Kashgar, the westernmost city of Xingjiang Province, we elbowed our way through the bazaar where the cattle are noisily traded, where scoops of saffron are weighed, and the farmers spread out their melons and litchi nuts for sale.

In the produce market of Jauregui, the city at the western end of the Great Wall, two young ladies, ages 13 and 15, with very broad smiles, motioned to us to come to their fruit table. Pulling their school books out from under the fruit, they excitedly talked to us, in English.

"Our parents are workers, and we are students. You speak English? This is our textbook. Would you like to see?"

"We think your English is remarkably good. Your textbook must be good. Your teacher must be excellent. Your parents must be very proud of you."

"Oh thank you" (bowing). "Our teacher is the best teacher in the world. Here is our address. We would like it very much, if you would write to us from America."

CHAPTER FOURTEEN

CENTRAL ASIA

1246 BCE

UZBEKISTAN

W E WERE NOW WELL WEST of China, west of Tibet, north of India, south of Mongolia, and still far to the east of the Mediterranean Sea. Yet most of the caravan leaders had at least a vague idea of where these places were (Macleod and Mayhew, 1999).

THE ANCIENT TRAIL

HIGHER THAN THE HILLS OF CHINA,
FARTHER THAN A THOUSAND SWITCHBACK
    TURNS,
THE RIVERS CUT DEEP CANYONS
FROM GLACIER TO FLOWERING FOREST.

I SEE A NARROW VALLEY SO FAR BELOW
IT'S ALMOST OUT OF SIGHT. CARVED BY ICE,
CARPETED BY MOSSY TURF—ABOVE,
BY FLOWERING TREES AND VINES BELOW.

I SEE A VILLAGE—THATCH AND STONE—ALONE
NESTLED IN THE SHADE OF ICE-CLAD PEAKS,
BY TORRENTS OF MILK-WHITE WATER—
DWELLINGS OF STONE, BUILT IN A CLUSTER,
WITH CHICKENS AND GOATS.

I SEE THE PEOPLE: WOMEN IN BRIGHTLY
    COLORED SKIRTS,
WASHING GARMENTS BY THE STREAM.
CHILDREN PLAYING,
A BOY WITH SLING IN HAND, BRINGING
    IN A CARAVAN
OF BURROS LADEN WITH FIREWOOD.
OLD PEOPLE, MOTHERS ARRANGING.

I SEE A TRAIL WORN DEEPLY IN THE MOUNTAIN.
WHO WENT HERE? A COURIER OF THE KHAN?
SOLDIERS FRAUGHT WITH FEAR?
A THOUSAND THOUSAND BURDEN BEARERS—
PASSING VERY NEAR.

THREE THOUSAND YEARS AGO,
FIELD ON FIELD IN TERRACED STONE,
ONE ABOVE THE OTHER TILL I PEER THROUGH
BROKEN CLOUDS OF ICY MIST.

THE TRAIL MOVES BACK AND FORTH—STILL
    HIGHER,
A HOE TO BREAK THE MOSS-BOUND TURF,
A FIRE TO BURN; AND PLANT AND PLANT,
AND PLANT AGAIN.

AND WHAT STRONG HEARTS MUST CLIMB
    EACH DAY
WITH HEAVY HOE
FROM THE VILLAGE—FAR BELOW?

We were now well beyond the influence of China and our contingent of helpful soldiers had to return. With the help of a local sovereign we attached ourselves to a large caravan destined for the Hittite capital of Hattusas.

On all sides are high mountains where the snow rests year-round. The Pamirs and Tian Shan Mountains are separated by narrow valleys with rich soil and isolated settlements, idyllic agricultural communities

116

[reminiscent of the legend of Shangrila]. To the west is the landlocked Sea of Aral. The snow-melt of the mountains flows westward to the sea down two great rivers, the Amu Darya to the south and the Syr Darya to the north. In places the rivers are more than a kilometer in width, with many large irrigation canals, providing flood or subsurface irrigation to vast areas.

Surprisingly the barren, steep, snow-capped mountains are terraced, nearly to the summer snow-line. Why? Why should steep mountains be terraced for planting, where there are vast, almost level areas far more amenable to growing crops?

Giant caravans travel through these passes and we met one every few days: hundreds of travelers, and thousands of animals: camels, horses and donkeys. These comprise a virtual city on hooves: artisans of many kinds, medical staff, clergy, and of course a contingent of soldiers on horseback.

Caravaning is a very dangerous occupation. Isolated amidst desert mountains, rolling pastureland, or featureless plains, we were threatened daily by everything from small groups of mounted bandits, to organized armies. We were supposedly under the protection of the local sovereigns, but most of these were suspected of collusion with the thieves.

As one might suspect, there were a few professional gamblers and a few money lenders riding with the caravan and charging outlandish usury.

A round trip for caravan employees is seldom less than a year, and oft-times they never return. Thus, families commonly come along. There are groups of women with small children, riding on bumping wagons, often engaged in needlework while the wagons are halted. There are groups of teenagers circulating the length of the caravan. We were fortunate, since our children fell in with some from India who were learning algebra and the use of the abacus. Then the children were trying to teach me—another generation gap. Li and I were serving as interpreters, an essential part of the caravan operation. And of course we were adding to our store of languages.

What were these caravans carrying, that people would risk their lives to make this journey? From China come silk and other textiles, bronze castings, art work, objects of gold, glazed ceramics, and jade. From Afghanistan comes lapis-lazuli, a semi-precious blue stone. From the steppes of central Asia come domesticated animals, particularly horses, two-humped camels, goats, sheep, and pigs. From the area around the Sea of Aral come cotton, grain, and dried fruit. From the area between the Sea of Aral, the Caspian Sea, and the Black Sea come iron and wheeled vehicles.

An essential part of the load, traveling both ways, is food for both man and beast. Most of the food is dried: fish, meat, vegetables, and grain. The animals get cottonseed and almost anything they can chew, but the native animal food has to be gathered or grazed at some distance from the trail, because everything near the trail has long ago been eaten. There are springs, and a few small torrents of water, but for fuel every bush has long ago been used, leaving only dung. The principal need for fuel is to boil water for tea. Unless the water is boiled the caravaneers get sick.

The plume of dust generated by the caravan can be seen for many kilometers, and the smell is overpowering. The caravaneers are careful to load animals so that from the outside a shipment of silk looks like a load of dried fruits and vegetables. Where the river becomes navigable, the animals are placed on barges: the camels kneel down facing one another, and the horses and burros stand upright in teams.

One morning our scouts reported that on the road ahead were the remains of a small caravan which had recently been way-laid by bandits. There must have been quite a battle. None were left alive, except for a dog that crouched near his dead master and growled at anyone who approached. We stopped long enough to bury the bodies. Our leader, who I believe was entirely reliable, said that we should take up a defensible position and seek support from the local sovereign before proceeding. Our leader organized us in a rock shelter and sent two fast horsemen to reach the local king. One thing to our advantage—we were prepared to pay royally for protection. Our kids brandished spears and thought it all very exciting, but Li and I were petrified. Before long, our two horsemen returned safely, with a local protective escort.

When our caravan reached the wide, smooth Amu Darya, we found a rough village constructed entirely for servicing caravans. When we reached the barge-loading area most of our drivers got drunk and we could not have departed in a hurry if we had wanted to.

Once out of the mountains, we traveled across broad valleys that are sub-irrigated, or irrigated by flooding from canals. In some places, rivers entering the sea form deltas, with mixed marshes and tules, subject to abrupt changes in water depth. The area around the Sea of Aral is particularly dangerous. The Sea itself is very shallow and varies appreciably in size and depth from year to year. Bandit groups and paramilitary organizations thrive in this area, collecting tribute from both farmers and caravans. The latter are typically chased onto islands from which they are unable to escape. Fortunately our caravan leaders were very experienced at avoiding the deep water, the quicksand, and the watery cul-de-sacs.

UZBEKISTAN TODAY

Three millennia ago trade and travel passed through the heart of continental landmasses, like the silk road from China to Europe. With the advent of large sea-going ships commerce and travel became centered on sea ports and the great inland cities like Samarqand were largely forgotten. Today, with commerce primarily by air, urban Uzbekistan has joined the modern world.

To the west grow giant fields of cotton, too much cotton. To the east we can see the snowclad Tian Shan, Kum Loon and Palmier Mountains.

One day we employed a young professor to drive us from Samarqand to the mountains. We drove through a variety of mud brick villages to "the place of four ancient trees." A small Uzbek lady in her late 70s showed us around the grove and mosque. She told us that during the years of Soviet rule, when the practice of Islam was prohibited, the devout villagers carved out a room beneath the enormous roots of an ancient sycamore, and she led us down to a small room under the roots of the tree.

The oldest of the trees reportedly had been dated at 1,014 years old. When we saw them we assumed they were not the same variety of sycamores that grow in western North America. But I later read in a travel guide that the trees are really sycamores. So here is a mystery. If the trees are truly sycamores, is the sycamore endemic to central Asia, or was someone carrying sycamore seeds to central Asia more than a thousand years ago? Perhaps the sycamore is native to more than one continent. We have also read that sycamore lumber was used for short timbers, in boat construction by the Egyptians, over 3,000 years ago.

WEST OF THE SEA OF ARAL, 1245 BCE

On the west bank of the Sea of Aral was a sophisticated city that had grown wealthy on the caravan trade. At last we were coming in contact with the "mid-eastern" world: a variety of markets, elaborate rugs, different religions, imperial government, and centers of scholarship. [Aside from the trade, this had been a pathway for intruding peoples and armies, unrecorded and forgotten. The streets and buildings of this once proud city have been lost to history.]

Diversity is the parent of advancement. In this region we encountered varied topography, varied climate, a variety of cultures, and the chemistry for new ideas (Hodges, 1992).

≋

I was asked to present lectures and experiments on the natural world. I found that the students here were steeped in astronomy and the relation between man and the cosmos. They were excited about the property of magnetism as revealed by lodestones [magnetite]. The existence of these black stones was not a new discovery. The curious had discovered that a small splinter of lodestone, when placed on a chip of wood and floated on oil or water, always pointed in the same direction: toward the "north star," the star around which all of the other stars in the northern hemisphere appear to rotate. This relationship demonstrated to them a kinship between material objects, part of the earth, and the objects seen in the sky.

Sometimes the students discussed the nature of and the relation between air, fire, and solid substances. For example, if you pulverize the mineral calcite (a seashell will do) and mix the powder with vinegar, it emits bubbles, and thus part of what was solid material becomes part of the air. If you do not believe this, take a jeweler's balance and weigh the remaining calcite. It weighs less because part of the solid material is now gone as bubbles. Where did it go? Apparently it became part of the air. This experiment shows that the air has weight.

One of the students objected, saying that some of the shell had been totally destroyed, and therefore had no weight. "All right," I said, "I can show you that you can measure the weight of air. We can take a chip of black lodestone, powder it, and heat the powder over a flame. The lodestone not only loses its magnetic property, it also increases in weight and turns red. Where did the extra weight come from? Did it come out of the air? Some of the air has combined with the lodestone to produce a new substance called hematite [red iron oxide].

"Let us try the experiment differently. We place the lodestone powder in a clear glass vase. We chose clear glass so that we can watch what happens inside. Now we place a lighted candle in the vase and we seal the top of the vase. First we notice that the candle promptly goes out. Could this be because there is not enough air to keep the candle burning? Then we notice that the black powder does not change color. Could this be because there is no air left in the jar to combine with the black powder and make the hematite?"

The air experiments led to a discussion of the atmosphere. Everyone agreed that apparently "empty" space is filled with an invisible material, and that creatures like us cannot survive without it. Most of us had heard from those who enjoyed climbing high mountains that there is difficulty breathing enough air at higher elevations. And so we formed a small group of scientists and adventurers, to plan a trip up the southern mountains to carry out breathing experiments at different elevations. The kids insisted on being included. In fact they proposed that they measure the elevation differences, using a tripod with a sight, and a carpenter's level. This became their part of the project. And we believe this was one of the first high mountains to be measured for elevation [Figure 6]. Our conclusion was that the air ingredients important to the life of breathing creatures are enriched in the lower elevations.

To measure the height of a mountain, one needs a level, to obtain a level line of sight. There are several ways to construct a level. One is to put a bubble in a slightly bent tube, and then adjust the tube to the position where the bubble records zero slope. We found that you can make a fine level from a stalk of well seasoned bamboo. You can hold the level in your hand, for rapid work, or hold it on a tripod for more precise measurement. To use the level, the surveyor holds it in a horizontal position, and sights a level line to the ground ahead. An assistant marks the spot where the level line touches the ground, at which point that assistant places a mark on the ground, and the surveyor comes forward and sets up again, over the mark. Measuring the elevation change over a moderate slope, an experienced team can tabulate about 20 stations an hour. Each station measures an elevation change of about one and a half meters, so a team can measure about 30 meters in one hour, or 200 meters in a day.

FIGURE 6. HOW HIGH IS THE MOUNTAIN?

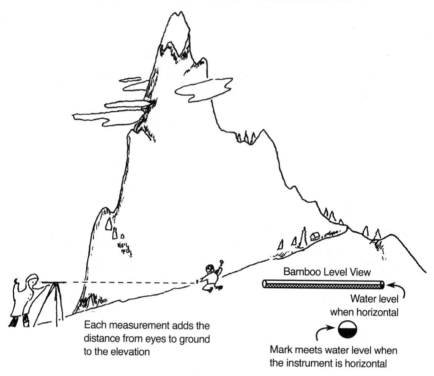

Bamboo Level View

Water level
when horizontal

Each measurement adds the
distance from eyes to ground
to the elevation

Mark meets water level when
the instrument is horizontal

Assuming that the Black Sea is close to "sea level," we estimated the crest of the Caucasus at between 5,000 and 7,000 meters of altitude. Most of us did not actually scale the peak, because of ice and avalanches.

New developments in metallurgy around the world had inspired an economic interest in locating valuable earth materials, and we were sent students from a wide spectrum of localities and nationalities. My lectures were actually written down in cuneiform, and later used as texts in Mesopotamia.

We tried to explain geologic phenomena by field examples. That sometimes required a good deal of traveling and hiking, which my family and I certainly enjoyed. One day we visited some cross-bedded sandstones and agreed on their ancient direction of wind transport. But we disagreed on the environment of deposition. I found a clincher, preserved in sandstone: animal tracks. But what animals made such tracks? Our second field puzzle was "carbonate rocks," in some places bearing fossils. We could not agree on the depositional habitat of the unfossiliferous limestone [micrite]. Perhaps it was deposited under deep water?

Having visited active volcanism at several localities around the Mediterranean and in the Canary Islands, I was not surprised by cold and deeply buried volcanic rocks. Some of these had sharp "intrusive" boundaries. It was hard to convince my students of the concept that these rocks had actually been liquid. They asked, "How could the rock get hot enough to actually melt?"

Another type of rock, in some places the most prominent, I call "basement rock," by which I mean a hard, crystalline rock which seems to underlie all sedimentary and volcanic rocks.

We had not gotten far in our discussion when some of the students raised the question of age and relative age of the different rocks. There was general acceptance that sequence of deposition meant sequence of age, and that the upper strata were younger than the lower strata. But what about the beds of seashells which we found more than a thousand meters above sea level? And what about the beds that are tilted? They must have been near level at the time of deposition. How did these strata become deformed and elevated?

≋

CHAPTER FIFTEEN

ANATOLIA

1244 BCE

NOT LONG BEFORE WE VISITED the southern shores of the Black Sea, the inhabitants had suffered a devastating earthquake. The earth had shaken so violently that many villages had been destroyed, and thousands of people had been killed or injured. When we visited the area of destruction we could see the actual surface along which the opposite sides had moved: the side toward the Black Sea had moved to the right; the side away from the Black Sea had moved to the left. The most recent motion, of about three meters, had been almost horizontal. The intense disturbance in the soft sedimentary rocks on both sides of the most recent plane of movement strongly suggested that there had been repeated intervals of movement, perhaps over a long period of time.

Indeed, the oldest citizens gave graphic accounts of similar disasters that had occurred when they were young, and other similar events recalled by their parents and grandparents. Their language contained several words relating to this phenomenon: land-shift, tsunami, sea-quake, earthquake, soil liquefaction.

What was the age of these geologic events? How long did it take for seashores to be uplifted many hundreds of meters, for erosion to gradually carve down the mountains, for increments of earth movement to tilt and bend the rock strata? Perhaps a small amount of time in the history of this earth, but an unimaginably long time in the memory of the people who live here.

THE GREAT FLOOD

I believe that we humans are the first creatures on earth with an awareness of time. And only in the past several millennia has any history been written down. How faithful are the verbal records passed from generation to generation? People after people throughout this part of the world repeat sagas telling of a great flood, so violent that it changed the course of history. This event or events are now so distant in the past that the best we can decipher is that the account is common to much of the then civilized world from India to Mesopotamia, to all of the peoples surrounding the Black Sea, extending into southeastern Europe (Ryan and Pitman, 1998).

One theory is that the people who farmed and herded in the Black Sea basin before the great flood were surrounded by fresh water lakes and streams, which were ultimately drowned by salt water when the Holocene ice melt caused a rise in sea level throughout the world. Indo-European speakers may have carried the tale with them from the Black Sea basin into lands far beyond the area of the flooding. Thus the weavers of China's Xinjiang Province were the same stock of people as the modern weavers of Austria and Scotland (Barber, 1999; Mallory and Mair, 2000). The account of Noah's Flood may have become common tradition, through a commonality of language rather than a geographic extent. When the water of the Mediterranean poured through the Bosporus Strait to flood the Black Sea basin the occupants were forced to leave—just how quickly we do not know. We can imagine that they retreated up the river valleys, for example: the Volga and the Danube, taking with them their culture and little more. Probably they took seed and livestock (as did Noah). In some areas their language and culture prevailed; in others they were absorbed. What great cities and temples lie submerged beneath the Black Sea? We do not know (Ryan and Pitman, 1998).

Some students of the Black Sea have seriously questioned the conclusions of Ryan and Pitman. They see evidence that far from flooding the Black Sea with saline water from the Mediterranean Sea, the flow has been from the Black Sea into the Mediterranean, for several million years. This would preclude this origin for the Great Flood.

Archaeologists and oceanographers place the flooding at about 5500 BCE, or perhaps one millennium before the civilization of Egypt and Mesopotamia. Did the struggle to overcome disaster kindle civilization? (Aksu, Hiscott, and others, 2002)

THE CIRCLE

The awakening of civilization as we know it took place abruptly about three centuries before the end of the second millennium BCE. It can be related to the discovery and application of the circle and the discovery of the wheel, coordinated with the ability to use iron and to domesticate horses (Hodges, 1992; Kaplan, 1999).

To those seeking perfection, the circle is about as close as you can get. It relates the finite and the infinite. It has no size; it has no limit; it includes all. The path of the heavens is a circle. And at the center of that astronomic circle is the direction north. And what disappears each night reappears again the next morning, having traversed an unseen circle overnight. It is no accident that among the first accomplishments of civilized man in each of the disparate centers of civilization was a calendar. And that calendar was a circle. Once inspired by the circle concept it was adopted nearly overnight.

Geometric figures were achieved by tying a string to a point, and drawing a circle, then crossing circles, turning angles and repeating measurements. Nothing was too simple or too complex to be created by the circle: wagons, chariots, potter's wheel, the millstone, the rotation of oars aboard ships, the motion of a saw, a drill. How many applications have I omitted? It was no accident that the discovery of the circle occurred close in time to the first use of zero in mathematics (Kaplan, 1999). Indeed the compass is a tool of geometry; thus the circle describes distances and angles as well as spheres. The circle relates to rectangles by the magic number 3.14.

CARVING STONE

I KNOW A MAN WHO CARVES IN STONE
BOTH DAY AND NIGHT, AND ALL ALONE.
A LIFETIME HE HAS LABORED THUS
AND STRIVE RELENTLESSLY, HE MUST

BECAUSE THE GODS ARE WATCHING HIM.
HE WILL NOT FAIL.
HE SMILES AT ME
AND I SMILE TOO
THOUGH NEVER WILL HIS WORK BE THROUGH.

THE HITTITE EMPIRE

Anatolia is a beautiful land of green meadows crossed by cold rushing streams, with fish, deer and other game. Ancient timber, sometimes a meter in diameter, both coniferous and hard wood, lines the streams.

The temples and fortifications, walls, and cities were built of stone and timber. The lower story was stone, marble and gabbroic rock. The upper floors were timber. Timbers were pinned together with pegs fitted into drilled holes, and attached to the underlying stone by wooden pins seven inches in diameter.

What happened to all the timber? Was it a change in climate, insects or viruses? Was it men using timber for fuel, or men clearing fields for pasture, or men building forts and cities, or even roads for wheeled vehicles? (Macqueen, 1986)

What occurred during the 13th century BCE? The base metal deposits of Cyprus and nearby Syria, the far off deposits of tin in Cornwall, the wheeled vehicles, especially those with spoked wheels, and brass halters for horses, spread from China to Egypt in one generation. Written language produced an explosion of scribes, literate traders and literate technicians. It also advanced the rise of entrepreneurial commerce and craftsmanship. And above all came the rise of long distance travel, trade, and the diffusion of knowledge.

The timbers of the Hittite temples have long since returned to dust, but we can still see the drill holes in their foundation stones. The saws and drills used by the Hittites were of bronze, but iron weapons were beginning to appear (Macqueen, 1986).

Inside the temple the Hittites had many clay pots, almost as tall as a man, and about a meter in diameter, smaller at the top and bottom. When these were filled, the people had a large store of grain and other foods, for use in hard times.

My family and I arrived in Anatolia at a critical time in the evolution of the Hittite empire. Through metallurgy and burgeoning agriculture they were a wealthy nation with imperial ambition: an ambition to be like Egypt, to be as skilled as Egypt's artisans, as free as their middle class, as educated and as sophisticated as their rulers. Our family traveled the length of Anatolia, to Cyprus, the Levant and Crete. We spoke their several languages, and understood their written languages. We were what the Hittites wanted to be, and they welcomed the arrival of our family with a world view of mankind, with an appreciation of literacy, a thirst for knowledge, and a merchant wealth that made empires viable. We had the ear of royalty for the asking. We lived and were served with the members of the royal family. Evenings were replete with dance and music, in halls decorated with flowers and tapestries. We would have enjoyed less incense, but one cannot argue with culture. We spent our days learning geography and ethnology, and ultimately setting the groundwork for the 30 years of peace between Egypt and Khatte.

One day I overheard my son, Lui, ask his twin sister, "I see you and our mother sneaking off twice a week with towels in hand—what are you doing?"

"Oh, we are getting our exercise. You are tuning up your brain, and we are tuning up our bodies."

"Steam and oil and perfumes—I should visit you."

"I think not. This is just for us girls. But we are serious. I bet you guys can't tell your trapezius from your medial deltoid."

≋

Another day my daughter and I were visiting a stone quarry. We marveled at how easily the quarrymen were able to "cut out" huge blocks of hard rock.

Where they wished to break the rock, they would drill a row of holes with a bronze drill. Then they would drive wooden pegs into the holes, fitting very tightly. Then when we were back a safe distance from the pegs, they would pour water over them. The dry pegs would swell up, and "bang!" The expanding pegs would cause the hard rock to crack, neatly breaking out the huge blocks just where the quarrymen had intended. How marvelous! We agreed that the force applied by the swollen pegs was greater than that of a giant man with wedge and hammer.

Chi asked me, "Where does the energy come from?"

I was able to answer her, "A dry porous material will always suck up liquid from a wet material—look at the wick in an oil lamp. Apparently the force to fill porosity is amazingly strong."

"But how do you suppose such a bright idea for splitting rocks was discovered? Do you suppose it was an accident? Maybe there was a dry, dead root filling a joint in the stone. And unsuspectingly, the quarrymen had poured water on it."

I told her, "So far I think your hypothesis is explicable. The next part is more difficult—the quarrymen would have been startled. But they did not realize what had happened. They did not realize that the phenomenon could be repeated in a purposeful way.

"Or did a philosopher view the event, and contemplate the idea of wet pegs? Discovery is a marvelous event. And do you know, people are not the only discoverers, really?"

"You mean that animals discover?" My daughter was not so sure.

"Certainly. Put a rabbit in a fenced enclosure, and it will quickly discover that it can dig a tunnel under the fence, and regain its freedom."

Chi thought about this for a moment, and then responded, "I think the endangered rabbit is operating on instinct. It is instinctive for rabbits to dig. They don't really think about why they are doing it. But tell me, what do you think are the most important discoveries made by people?"

"Language, both spoken and written. Fire, for warmth and cooking. Domestication of animals, for many purposes, in particular for transportation. Shelters, for protection from storms and heat, and also from large animals and from other people. Weapons and tools. Fibers to weave. The use of metals. First copper, then bronze, and most recently, iron. Ships to cross the deep water" (Hodges, 1992).

On another occasion my daughter exclaimed, "Well, Father, look at the leaves at the top of that tall tree. There is water in those leaves, which has risen from the roots, in some places a hundred meters below. This water, or in some cases syrup, has run uphill!

"Tell me—is every tree and flower stem an example of water running uphill?
So what happens then?"

"Water evaporates from the leaves of trees requiring more water to be sucked up from the roots below." How much we do not understand!

Within the century of our traveler, great advances were achieved, or were in the making: the use of horses and wheels with spokes. And perhaps most important: the use of iron, and with this, the ability to do battle on a grand scale (Hodges, 1992; Drews, 1993).

TURKEY TODAY

I have heard that there are fewer than a dozen major nations in the world that produce enough food to feed themselves, and Turkey is one of them. Ankara, the capital, is a truly modern city. We traveled by excellent bus 200 kilometers east from Ankara. Small towns are tucked in among the hills, each with its mosque and minaret. Shiny green tractors are moving before dawn. The soil is black and rich. It is time to gather the sugar beets. In the town of Bo azkale, next to the ancient Hittite capital, the students and young professors will soon be walking to school. Boys age eleven and older wear a shirt with tie. The girls wear a blue jumper over a white blouse. The geese walk up the center of the cobblestone street. And yes, there are turkeys in Turkey.

We hired a young man to drive us to a nearby town to see another Hittite ruin. This was the time and place for the weekly market. Our attention was drawn to a truck filled with ice and small fish. Our driver said, "You buy some and Mama will cook them up. Very good." So on our return we got to see the whole family from grandmother to the smallest.

We took their picture, which they were later very happy to receive.

On two separate occasions middle-aged gentlemen extended their gnarled farmer hands to me, saying, "You are Americans. America has been very good to us—we want to thank you."

Intense interest by many people around the world in the correspondence of historic record and religious tradition has fostered numerous archaeological examinations over the past two centuries. The translation of this travel account is not intended to address the biblical record.

≋

CHAPTER SIXTEEN

EGYPT

1242 BCE

At this time what is now known as the "near east" was dominated by two empires: Egypt and Khatte. Egypt ruled the lands along the Nile, Palestine, Lebanon, and a small part of Syria. Khatte (the Hittites) ruled much of Anatolia, the Caucasus, Assyria, Babylonia, and most of Syria. For generations the two empires had battled over the head-waters of the Euphrates and the land between Egypt and Anatolia.

FINALLY, AFTER COSTLY AND inconclusive battles, wherein the leaders of both sides claimed victory, the emperor of the Hittites delivered a plaque of solid silver on which was proposed a treaty of peace between Khatte and Egypt. Ramesses II accepted it, saying to the Hittite king, "We are now brothers." Using runners, a message could be transported between the respective capitals of Hattusus and Memphis (or Pi-Ramesses) in about one month, so the messages flew back and forth. The emperor of the Hittites, Attusil III, proposed to send one of his daughters as a wife for Ramesses II.

Ramesses II already had several wives, beautiful, educated, and skilled. But if he thought the Hittite emperor was sending him a young, bashful damsel for his harem he was sorely mistaken. The new wife was an experienced diplomat, was fluent in several languages, and was no stranger to intrigue. In fact some have suggested that she might have been a spy.

My wife and I had been working with Ramesses II's new wife-to-be, Matt-Her-Nefenuur. We were translating what we knew of world geography for the Hittite court, and wondering just how we were going to continue our travels, when Matt-Her-Nefenuur invited us to join the royal retinue headed for Egypt.

THE PROCESSION FROM KHATTE TO EGYPT, 1242 BCE

It was an amazing procession. The principal representatives rode horseback. The supplies were transported in ox carts. There was not only food of every imaginable variety, but cooks and bakers, spare horses, a variety of livestock for fresh meat. And in case we should get bored on this two-month sojourn, there were magicians, musicians, chess boards, and a variety of contests. When we arrived at a camp for the night the tents and rugs were already laid out with care, and there was even a vanity table for the princess. Then, while most of us were slumbering, those in charge of camp preparation would guide the slow ox carts to the breakfast camp, so that all would be ready for us when we arrived.

We passed Aleppo and Ebia, and, on reaching the Orontes River we were at the boundary between the Khatte and Egyptian empires.

WIND-WORN IMAGE

WIND WORN IMAGE CARVED IN STONE,
FACING TO THE SEA ALONE,
WHAT GREAT GOD DID YOU BESEECH?
WHAT WAS THE EMPIRE OF YOUR REACH?
GONE, ALL GONE IN BLOOD STAINED DUST.
SILENT NOW—AND YET WE MUST
REMEMBER: IT HAS E'ER BEEN THUS.

TODAY, SOME WATCH IN DREAD
OF A FUTURE NEAR AHEAD.
OH ROCK, YOU'VE WATCHED THE VILLAGE BURN,
PILLAGE, PLUNDER, PLAGUE IN TURN.   •
WERE THERE ANY THERE WHO CARED?

WERE THERE ANY THERE WHO DARED
TO ASK IF KNIGHTLY PURPOSE
WAS INSANE, OR PRIESTLY DOINGS COULD
   EXPLAIN
THE REASON FOR IT ALL?

NAY, NOBLE DEEDS ARE BRAVE, BUT VAIN.
THEY RISE ABOVE THE FILTH AND PAIN,
TRANSCEND REALITY AND GAIN—
THE RICHES OF THE WORLD—AND REIGN
BLINDLY TILL THE IGNORANT END;

AND TAKE THEIR PLACE
THERE BY THE STONE:
DUST AND ASHES, CHIPS OF BONE.

One day we encountered teams of oxen dragging giant logs of cedar. Some were headed for the Phoenician ports, some ultimately for Crete, and some for the Nile and Egypt.

Here we bade farewell to the contingent of Hittite soldiers, and their duty was taken by a similar contingent from Egypt. Here Queen Rudukhepa bade farewell to her daughter, but royalty sheds no tears.

My daughter Chi spent some time inspecting the giant cedar timbers from Lebanon. She asked, "Dad, are there many of these giant timbers remaining?"

"No, Chi, there are only a few left."

And so she complained that at the rate they were being hauled away, there would soon be none remaining. "But that is terrible," she concluded.

I replied that we might wish to travel by giant ships and these cedars are the best for building the ships.

Chi continued, "These trees are as tall as 70 meters, and some are 400 years old. The least we could do is plant thousands of little trees, and hundreds of years from now there would be a forest again."

"Not many people are concerned about what this world will be like 400 years from now. They'd soon be in there, cutting down the saplings for firewood. But you are right to think about the future. If enough of us thought about the future, we might have a part in design-ing it."

And I believe that she will.

PALESTINE

One morning we were camped at the north end of a fresh water lake [Sea of Galilee]. At this point thermal springs run into the lake and cause a bloom of algae. The algae attract an abundance of fish that can be easily gathered with a seining net. It was fish for breakfast.

Further down the valley the stream [Jordan] runs into a saline lake [Dead Sea] from which there is no outlet. I was told that the level of this lake is considerably below sea level. On our route westward from the Dead Sea we encountered cliffs, hundreds of feet high, composed mostly of salt. Because salt is so soluble rain water has cut deep ravines and tunnels through it. Salt merchants were busy loading salt into carts, and the local sovereign was exacting a tax.

As we passed villages, the people, and especially the children, brought flowers and music to please the princess: she was a celebrity. But look at your feet. The very dust we step on has been the path of ancient hosts: Egyptians, Hykos, Persians, Hittites, Assyrians and oth-ers. And if you look carefully you can find bits of pottery, bits of glass, a worn out horseshoe. See them with their banners flying, their proud voices predicting triumph—and how many of them did not return?

It was a warm day when at last we reached the Mediterranean. The kids who had seldom seen an ocean had to stop and splash in the water. Come to think of it, the princess joined them. And they came back with their hands full of seashells.

EGYPT, 1241 BCE

Soon we were in Egypt proper and there was a royal reception awaiting us. Representing Egypt was the royal mother Nefertari who delivered a spellbinding oration. "Peace," she said, "is the victory of the future. With peace we all obtain divinity. At sunset we see the blood of a million brave soldiers, and in the mountains the clouds deliver rain, the tears of a million proud mothers who will never see their sons again."

The Hittite princess, speaking flawless Egyptian, praised the two emperors, their families, their people, and the gods of both lands.

Night was falling as the party reached the boats of the Nile. The sunset was indeed dramatic and rain clouds capped the mountains to the east. Banners of papyrus or linen decked the pathway and decorated the royal yachts. Each banner showed the faces of both Ramesses II and Nefertari. "Welcome," they read, "to the land of Egypt, Ramesses II and Nefertari, the greatest empire and the greatest rulers on this earth." The princess took no offense for she was a royal diplomat and understood that the boasting was for the eyes and ears of the Egyptian people, not intended as an insult to herself.

The full moon rose over the Nile and a gentle breeze pushed the giant yachts upstream. Sparkling fires lined both shores of the river. At intervals hundreds of archers let fly burning arrows so that they described an archway of light across the river.

Now Ramesses and his wives and children climbed aboard specially prepared chariots, and reviewed the multitude, estimated at near one million. The next day the princess was introduced to all of the family members, and also to the warm baths and showers. The palace was profusely decorated with flowers, some of which had been transported for hundreds of kilometers. To further impress the new arrivals there were lions, elephants, cheetahs, giraffes, and zebras, and I probably have omitted some. Indeed, in all I have seen there is no comparison. Later we were introduced to the vast library, which unquestionably is the greatest storehouse of knowledge known to man. There were hundreds, if not thousands, of scholars, artists, and scientists. But I am skipping ahead.

The second day after our arrival was a feast in a columned room seating nearly a thousand, with acoustics so perfect that a speaker could easily be heard. Ramesses II presented his new wife with a solid gold life-size head and shoulders of himself, and his new wife presented Ramesses II with a head and shoulders of her father in solid burnished iron. The not-so-subtle messages were: Egypt has immeasurable wealth and Khatte is the foremost fabricator of iron. There was much to be learned.

For example, the several wives of Ramesses II were not idle playthings; they were consciously the brightest and most accomplished women in the realm, and worked long hours in the school for advanced students. Education, in some manner for all, was the policy of the pharaoh. In these advanced schools were young scholars from around the

Mediterranean, Ethiopia, Arabia, and deep into Africa—better that they appreciate that Egypt and Ramesses II are the greatest.

RAMESSES II AND NEFERTARI

I had met Ramesses II almost 35 years earlier, and I had begun to hear about him and other members of his family as soon as we reached the Hittite empire, so their magnificence was not a total surprise. But the reality of it is so much greater than any description, that it takes considerable time to come to grips with what you encounter. In all humility I should remember that Ramesses II had been informed about us some while before we arrived. He prides himself on knowing everything transpiring in the world, at least in his own world (Kitchen, 1982; White, 1970; Hutchinson, 1978; Manley, 1996; Wolinski, 1995).

Some short while after our arrival in Egypt, Ramesses II invited us to meet with a distinguished group of geographers, astronomers, and adventurers who had visited far places. I wondered at first if he was really interested. If so, why was he not meeting with us himself? We found the answer: it seems that even before our arrival some of his advisors had offered their opinion that I was a hoax. They questioned the sphericity of the earth, and the existence of many of the places I reported visiting. It had even been suggested that I might be an assassin.

Obviously there was jealousy here. Which of his prophets could compete with someone who claims to have traveled around the earth? And if his most prestigious advisers had such limited knowledge, why?

Meanwhile Nefertari was gently interrogating my wife and children. This questioning was abruptly concluded when Ramesses II's chief biographer reminded him that in the third year of his reign, he had outfitted a young man from Morocco who was intent on traveling around the earth. That boat was never heard from again. That was almost 35 years ago.

From that time on, my family and I were indeed honored guests. Ramesses II had his scribe take down every thought. He was torn between boasting of his newly acquired knowledge, or keeping it secret. He insisted that the scribe keep the information protected. He liked to think of himself as emperor of the world, even if only vicariously.

And now Ramesses wanted to show us his accomplishments. We went fifteen hundred kilometers up the Nile, climbing around the cataracts, visiting many temples, including the magnificent giant statues of himself and Nefertari at Abu Simbel (James, 2002). We also saw ancient pyramids, some larger than any other man-made structures. Amazingly, the Egyptians have kept a record of the last several millennia.

Temples have been built of stone, some of granite so tough it is hard to believe that they could carve it. In some places the temples are 30 meters high and completely adorned with carved and painted figures. The figures are almost entirely stylized, and the same scenes are portrayed over and over, some identical to scenes drawn fifteen hundred years earlier. I was so fascinated by this art form that I spent days observing the artisans, the architects, and the engineers. It was clear that they took great pride in being able to reproduce art that was first created millennia earlier.

There are three faces of Ramesses II, embodied in one person. One commands thousands of artisans to carve multiple figures of himself, up to 100 cubits high. He commands the construction of temples greater than anywhere on earth of such stone that they will be here many millennia from now. He boasts irrepressibly of being the greatest of all, declares himself a god, boasts of having fathered at least 100 children, and even, it is rumored, takes credit for temples built by others.

The second Ramesses II works indefatigably, develops water on the desert where others have failed, works to improve the irrigation system and the quality of farm animals, creates a school for women as well as men, and upgrades the general life of the ordinary people of the land.

And a third Ramesses II, who is humble in all things, regularly sits down to supper with a few wives and children, occasionally joined by an honored scholar or artist, even interesting folks like us.

Occasionally my wife was not above making fun at the expense of Ramesses II. "Everywhere," she probed, "carved on walls I see women who have bodies that all look alike. Some are goddesses, some are royal wives, and some I guess are servants. But uniformly they have very large eyes, broad shoulders, small breasts, very narrow waists, tall sleek stature, and long fingers. You can hardly tell some of them from the men, who seem to wear false beards. Now some of these women have reportedly borne twelve children. What are we to believe?"

Ramesses II was obviously amused, but up to the defense. He replied, "Most, but not all, of the carvers and painters are men. Most of them worship their mothers, but also hold their sisters and wives in high esteem. Where these ideal, surely not realistic, figures come from I do not know, but in the minds of the sculptors, they are ideal. So rather than depict a goddess whom they have never seen, mothers, sisters and wives with different bodies, some less ideal than others, they draw them all the same. Now they are all beautiful, not only in mind and devotion, but in body as well. I cannot fault the artists for this."

I brought up another topic. "In the history of Egypt, and indeed to the present time, we read of many instances of royal men marrying their sisters or other close members of the family. I have observed cultures all around the world, and no others make a practice of such inter-family marriage. In fact some people go to great lengths to prevent this. Granted, Egypt is far ahead in the practice of medicine, but the practitioners of medicine elsewhere generally warn of unhealthy offspring from such marriages."

Ramesses II replied, "I am aware that our neighbors around the Mediterranean are shocked by our marriages, and indeed there is some disagreement about this practice in regard to livestock as well as people.

"It certainly is not necessary. There are plenty of highly intelligent mates available. I think that it arises from the belief of at least the early royalty, that they were so much better than the 'common' people, that they assumed marrying within the family would intensify the royal attributes. My ancestors were not all royalty, and most of my children are not. With a little encouragement I think the practice will gradually die out."

One evening when Ramesses II had us foreigners alone, I asked him what he considered his primary accomplishment as pharaoh. He replied, "It is improving the daily lives of the common people: better diet, better medicine, more education, more local rule. But it is not easy. There is a continual struggle between the Pharaoh and the priesthood. The priests have an easy life, and they have tremendous influence, but they contribute little to the general good. Because of general ignorance the priests keep the people in perpetual fear of disaster. You may think us a very superstitious people, because we have a god for everything and every place. The only way to avoid domination by the priests (that is, the gods) is to accomplish things they cannot. They cannot re-route the Nile. But the pharaoh, with engineers and lots of strong backs, can dig ditches that re-route the water. The idle are given a job, the farmers increase their yield, and the priests are quiet. All the prayer you like, and all the priests, cannot create great temples and statues. But Ramesses II can, and the people chant, 'Ramesses II is great.' Whatever I put my name to, whatever foreign adventure I undertake, adds to the belief that I can create miracles, and enhances the power of the Pharaoh versus that of the priests."

Ramesses II went on, "You hear of the prowess of Egyptian medicine. Yet you may ask the life expectancy of the average Egyptian. The great potion for good health is prevention. Here in the palace, we do not drink from the Nile. We do not wash our clothes and ourselves in the irrigation ditches. And we could teach the average farmer. But no, the priests (that is, the gods) say that our water is sacred. Here in the palace we use clean spring water, and we clean and cook everything we eat. Maybe someday there will be a pharaoh or a queen so powerful that he or she will be believed by the multitude.

"You wonder how I can spend Egypt's wealth to create enormous statues of myself. I can sit down with you and talk about these things. If I really believed that I were a god, if I really believed that by being mummified I would last forever, I would lose my sanity—as many pharaohs have. There is nothing of greater importance than to maintain sanity, and keep in touch with the real world."

≋

Our children quickly became conversant in Egyptian and attended classes in a variety of subjects along with the sons and daughters of the elite. One of their best young friends was the daughter of a very well to do family. When her father died, her mother had taken charge of the family nursery business and turned it into a smashing success, although business women were not common in Egypt.

To understand the florist business during the reign of Ramesses II, you must understand that Egypt is a very hot, dry, windy habitat during much of the year, with a small number of native plants. Water lilies are among the very few native flowers. Customers came from a sizable upper middle class, the families of scribes, distinguished artists, scientists and bureaucrats.

In Egypt, art and color, in any form, are at a premium. And most precious of all is the color provided by flowers and living plants of all types. These include succulents, shrubs, and trees. You can imagine how difficult it is to transport these tender plants across hundreds of kilometers to the palaces and elegant estates of those who can afford them. The resources required to provide such living color are hard to imagine. Needless to explain, only the very wealthy can afford them—

and price seems to be no object. Most plants are brought rooted in boxes, some from as far away as 1,500 kilometers to the south in tropical Africa. To accomplish this requires maintaining sheltered humidity.

Potted flowering succulents are a favorite gift. And there is competition to give presents of previously unseen or hybrid varieties. Begonias are a favorite. Gardeners who specialize in the discovery and propagation of exotic varieties are highly sought after.

The florist friends invited all our family to visit their estate on the lower Nile. This estate was a self-contained enterprise. Aside from the floral plant activity there was livestock: cattle, goats, sheep, swine, donkeys, buffalo, horses, ducks, geese, and pigeons. The elite did not eat fish from the river, but they did have ponds stocked with superior varieties of fish. The fields grew not only wheat and barley for bread and beer, but flax for linen and clover to feed the animals. The milk from the buffalo was prized above that of cattle because of its higher butterfat content.

The estate vegetable garden grew a variety of root crops, vines, leaf crops, onions, squash, and herbs. Among the employees were butchers, bakers, brewers, vintners, specialists in weaving and leather work, ceramic work, and metallurgy, not to mention scribes and religious functionaries.

The elite Egyptians of the time of Ramesses II placed great importance on appearance. They retained barbers and hair stylists, those working with oils and perfumes, body painting for both men and women, not to forget children. There were those providing stylish garments including highly prized silk from far to the east [Lubec and others, 1993], and jewelry from all the known world. But perhaps the most sought after artisan was the chief cook. Cooks developed reputations that were empire-wide. And if asked, the estate owner was honored to loan his or her chief cook to the emperor.

An important activity for the elite was providing events to which hundreds, or even thousands, were invited. These events were held to celebrate the anniversaries of specific gods, or perhaps a jubilee of the emperor. Organizing events was a profession in its own right. Decorated barges were contracted to bring the guests, sometimes for hundreds of kilometers. Many people were employed: musicians, poets, artists, extra scribes to provide embellished invitations, messengers to deliver the invitations. Elaborate gifts were presented to specific individuals to commemorate accomplishment, door prizes, and winners of contests.

≋

My daughter, Chi, was astonished to learn that the local agronomists had no system for selection of superior plants and animals, to ensure the best possible reproduction. In fact they commonly chose the poorest animals and seed plants for propagation.

"Father, I recall your telling me how the Olmec farmers far across the sea selected seeds from the best plants, for the next planting.

"Let's suppose we have some radish seeds, and we plant these seeds in our garden. In a few weeks the roots of these radishes are swelling large and plump, and we gather some for the table. Which ones do we gather? Why, we gather the ones that have grown best—the most healthy, the biggest, the prettiest, the juiciest. And the only ones left to gather later are the runts, the ones we did not select for the table.

"Because of this, the seeds of the poorest plants are gathered and planted, and they produce runts for the next generation. And so on, generation after generation, the crop becomes less valuable.

"With less productive plants the people will go hungry. And hungry nations fail. Thus we see that this simple action could bring the destruction of populations and nations."

ECONOMICS ALONG THE NILE RIVER:
THE RICH AND THE POOR

In traveling through the empire we observed the humble circumstances of the average Nile dweller and became curious concerning the social and economic relationships. One might suspect that with the great majority of people living in what we could easily describe as abject poverty, there would be an uneasy crown upon the emperor's head.

One warm afternoon, after returning from the fields, talking with the hard working farmers, the Pharaoh and I sat in the shade sipping delightful fruit juice. I posed a question: "The Nile provides such agricultural wealth for Egypt that there are surpluses in nearly every crop. This surplus makes it possible to send ships and caravans to all corners of the known world, to bring back tapestries, precious metals, gems and silk. This wealth makes it possible for the pharaoh to build a navy and to hire a mercenary army. This wealth makes it possible to put to work hundreds of thousands quarrying and carving stone, to make the world's most magnificent structures. But this surplus provides no bounty for the barefoot farmer, who struggles to feed his family, dies at a relatively young age, and sees many of his children die in the first few years of life. I have heard you proclaim that you consider that the greatest monument to your reign is the well being of your subjects. How do you explain this?"

He answered, "You dare to ask the pharaoh such questions? Should I allow a subject to ask such a question? Have you heard such questions raised? Have you seen me punish anyone for such criticism? The economics of the Nile are not as simple as you suppose. There have been years when the river did not flood, when there were no crops, and there was widespread starvation. That will not happen while I am pharaoh, for we set aside reserves every year, and if those are exhausted we have gold enough to purchase grain and meat from other nations. Perhaps you do not understand the system of hiring mercenaries? The mercenaries come to the Nile prepared for war. Their mothers and sisters, wives and children are starving on all sides of us. We can defeat them in battle, but they have a choice: they can die fighting to take our Nile, and their families back home die of starvation, or they can make peace, eat with us, serve in our armies, and thereby support their families.

"Now, I have a choice about how to spend the wealth of the Nile. I could raise the price of grain and livestock. Maybe the farmers would earn more and provide for themselves better homes, better dowries, or maybe they would grow less and live the same. We try to provide school for every child whose parents are interested. We try to provide medical care for all, but if we tried to spend the surplus across the board, if we tried to provide the life enjoyed by the elite, it would not go very far. The emperor of the Hittites also generates a surplus. He has a well trained army with thousands of the best chariots equipped with iron weapons. But he builds few temples, and he lives in a "palace" built partly of mud bricks. Do his subjects live better? And a thousand years from now, three thousand years from now—will anyone remember the Empire of the Hittites? Will his mud brick palace still stand? No, but the pyramids of Egypt will still be standing. Three millennia from now, they shall read from our temple walls about the nation of Egypt, the pharaohs of Egypt, indeed the people of Egypt. Remember the barefoot farmer cutting clover for his livestock helped make the surplus which allowed the pharaoh to build. Every farmer deserves part of the credit. I hope that three millennia from now they will remember Ramesses II, but that they also remember the poor farmers who made the glory of Egypt possible."

"I have listened to such excuses around the world," I protested. "Every nation has its elite and its poor, and the rulers all rationalize the necessity for this. I doubt that many of the poor families are concerned about what temples are standing three millennia hence, or whether anyone gives them credit."

Siwa, 1240 BCE

One day the pharaoh came to invite my whole family to go on a royal outing. Ostensibly it was a hunting party with chariots to follow and shoot down the wild beasts that live near the giant oasis. But actually the pharaoh was suffering from arthritis, and he wished to bathe in the magic warm spring located several days' journey to the west of the Nile.

We all went, along with some of the pharaoh's wives and children. And what a magic place it is! First we traveled to the northwestern corner of the great delta and followed west along the coast of the Mediterranean to a small port [Mersa Matrouh], where the water was clear and bright blue, and long sandy beaches lined the sea cliffs. Thence we struck out southwest across a desert so flat that you could turn around in a complete circle and not notice a single topographic irregularity on the horizon. Finally we descended into a long depression named Qattara, which is as much as 130 meters below sea level. Our destination [Siwa] had more than 200 springs, mostly fresh water, some warm and some cold. There were miles and miles of lakes and tens of thousands of date palms. The people who live there grow a variety of fruits and vegetables, but their only exports are olive oil and dates.

We visited under truce, because the people who live there speak Berber and the vicinity is claimed by both Egypt and Libya. This was very interesting to me, as my native tongue is Berber, and it reminded me that I was on my way "home."

Some Egyptian engineers have proposed flooding the Qattara depression, which is over a hundred meters below the level of the Mediterranean. This would involve a diversion ditch capturing the westernmost tributary of the Nile and releasing it into the depression. It would only remain fresh if the depression were filled to just above the level of the

Mediterranean so that it could overflow into that great sea. Calculations had been made to determine how much of the Nile would be required to overcome evaporation. Actually, Nile water could be used to irrigate the higher parts of the depression, leaving a saline lake in the deepest part of the depression. This could be done without inundating oases such as Siwa.

THREE POEMS OF EGYPT

I. THE EYES OF EGYPT

THE EYES OF EGYPT WATCH US,
THE BURROS BEAR THEIR LOAD;
MILLENNIA, THEY PASS US
ON A NARROW DUSTY ROAD.

MILLENNIA ARE PASSING.
THE WALLS OF MUD AND STONE,
THE SMILES OF CHILDREN GREET US;
TO EGYPT, IT IS HOME.

THE EYES OF EGYPT WATCH US;
THE VENDORS HAWK THEIR WARE:
GENERATIONS RISE AND FALL
CAN WE NOT WATCH, AND CARE?

THE CALLS TO WORSHIP ECHO;
THE TEMPLES, SHADOWS CAST;
THE GLYPHS OF ANCIENT EGYPT
INSCRIBE THE EPOCH PAST.

II. IMAGINE IF YOU CAN

MIGHTY IS THE RIVER
WHICH NOURISHES THE LAND.
ENCOMPASSED BY THE DESERT,
A WASTE OF REDDISH SAND.
MIGHTY WERE THE SCHOLARS

WHO MEASURED FOR THE PLAN.
MIGHTY WERE THE SCULPTORS
WHO EXALT THE MIND OF MAN.
IMAGINE IF YOU CAN,
THE HANDS OF ANCIENT EGYPT.
IMAGINE IF YOU CAN.

III. RAMESSES THE GREAT

YOUNG WAS THE PHARAOH,
BRAVE WERE HIS DEEDS,
CONQUERING ALL,
BUILDER OF GRANDEUR.

GLORY TO THE EMPIRE,
GLORY TO RAMESSES II,
GLORY TO RAMESSES THE GREAT.

MID-RULE HE VIEWS HIS TEMPLES,
HIS WIVES, HIS CHILDREN,
HIS VISORS, HIS GENERALS,
HIS SCRIBES, HIS MEN OF GREAT KNOWLEDGE.

ARE THERE DISTANT LANDS UNHUMBLED?
IS HE EQUAL TO A GOD?

ARE THERE ANY WHO CAN DOUBT
THAT HE, RAMESSES THE SECOND,
IS RAMESSES THE GREAT?

HE RULED TO AN ANCIENT AGE.
STILL STAND HIS TEMPLES STRONG.
STILL HONOR HIM THE PEOPLE.
BUT WHERE HAS HIS FAMILY GONE?
WHO FOLLOWS ON HIS PATH?
OH GODS WHAT IS MY FATE?
SHALL I BE KNOWN FOREVER AS
RAMESSES THE GREAT?

Maps

The pharaoh asked me to construct a map of the world. A map of the whole earth...wow! I thought about this for several days, and then began to work (Wilford, 1982).

The concept of a map, a two dimensional picture, can be compared to the layout for a building, a city, a plantation, a whole nation. When my father and I explored for gold we sometimes laid out a grid map which showed the distribution of different kinds of rock, and the gold content, at each intercept as determined from assay, showed where to dig for gold and where to dispose of the barren overburden.

The best part of constructing a map of the earth is that it tells us where our greatest ignorance remains. In Mesoamerica, I was told of the giant mountains, and of the great Amazon and Orinoco Rivers, which are located to the south, part of a whole continent on which I had never stepped. But how do I make a map, on a sphere?

One afternoon in the imperial gardens I was pondering how best to display the map of the earth when my daughter walked up carrying a couple of oranges.

"Oh, Father, these are the best oranges. They are sweet, and almost devoid of seeds. So peel me one. You know, Father, this orange is so easy to peel that maybe I could take off the whole peel in one piece."

Chi then scored the upper hemisphere just deep enough to cut through the orange skin, which came off in one piece. Flattened against the table, the pieces of peeling spread apart and looked like the petals of a flower [Figure 7].

"Now, look at this, Father. Take each petal of the flattened orange peel and hold them all up in the position where they were originally. We have converted a spherical surface to a flat surface, and back again.

"Surely Father, this is fundamental. This is the difference between living in a three dimensional and a two dimensional universe."

"But," I interjected, "as soon as people see the open spaces on my flat drawing of the round earth, they say it is nonsense. They reject all explanations of how those spaces are like the wide openings between the "petals" of the flattened orange peel. They say that the empty zones on my chart are impossible, because the earth does not consist of alternate zones of hard rock and empty space."

"But Dad, I thought this simple experiment would demonstrate the concept to everyone."

FIGURE 7. THE WORLD IS LIKE AN ORANGE

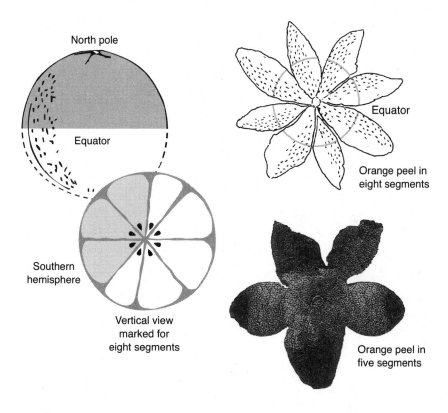

North pole

Equator

Southern hemisphere

Equator

Orange peel in eight segments

Vertical view marked for eight segments

Orange peel in five segments

"No, Chi. It will be a long time before many of our neighbors comprehend what we are talking about."

Taking Chi's ideas to heart, I began work.

To make this map, I first fashioned a sphere. Well, actually a half-sphere. The base of the half sphere was the latitude of the equator. The uppermost point on my half sphere I named the north pole. The closer one gets to the north pole the colder it gets; the closer one gets to the equator, the warmer. To make the map I chose as a starting place Morocco, located part way between the north pole and the equator, and an arbitrary line of longitude. From this start I drew in the west coast of Africa, extending it far to the south and to the east. To the west of Morocco I drew the Atlantic Ocean; to the north I drew Europe. To the east I drew the Mediterranean, the Black Sea, Arabia, and still further east, places like China and India, and an eastern ocean. I drew a range of mountains running east from Morocco: the Atlas Mountains east to Tunisia, then submerged mountains east to Anatolia, then the mountains of the Caucasus and yet more mountains all the way east to China. Glacial melt-water from the mountains flows both to the north and to the south. The steppes grow green with wild grain, so that herds of animals prosper, and both hunting and farming people multiply.

What are the directions and distances to these far-away places? The approximate direction can be seen by facing the sun at noon on the solstice and plotting the direction of your hands. The distances to these places are more difficult to measure.

The map I drew was a combination of the geography I had learned on my trip, fit together with reports from many other geographers.

Many of the places I visited are numbered on the map. I have also written names of places I have heard about, but not visited. Number 1 on the map is Morocco, my first home; number 2 is the Canary Islands. While in Cuba (number 3) and Yucatan (4), I heard many stories about the great land to the south [South America], but I never saw it for myself. Numbers 4 through 15 plot my trip to the Aleutian Islands. From Yucatan (4), we traveled through Mesoamerica (5), to Sinaloa (6), and

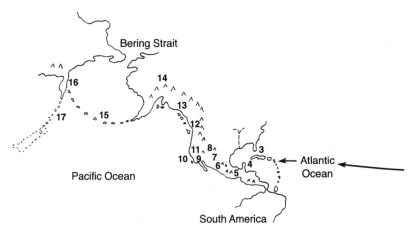

FIGURE 8. THE TRAVELER'S MAP OF THE WORLD

north to the Delta people (7). We visited the Great Canyon (8) and returned to Southern California (9). We lived with the Chumash people (10), visited the Sacred Valley (11), and traveled north to live with the Totem people (12). We continued north with Copper Man (13) and to the Yukon River (14). Not choosing to cross the Bering Strait, we traveled from the Aleutians (15), to Kamchatka (16), then followed the Kuril Islands (17) to Hokkaido (18) and Honshu, Japan (19). We crossed the Korean Strait and southern tip of Korea (20). Moving southwest, we reached Xi'an, the capital of China (21). When the emperor died, my family and I were in south China (22). I had the opportunity to view the maps made by the Chinese geographers, which are very well drawn.

When leaving China via Kashgar (23), we traveled through central Asia, Uzbekistan (24), saw the Sea of Aral (25), and visited the Hittite capital in Anatolia (26). We traveled through Palestine (27), and on to Egypt (28). Returning to Morocco, we crossed Libya (29) and the Sahara Desert (30). (Number 31 stands for Mali, which I had visited as a boy, with my father.)

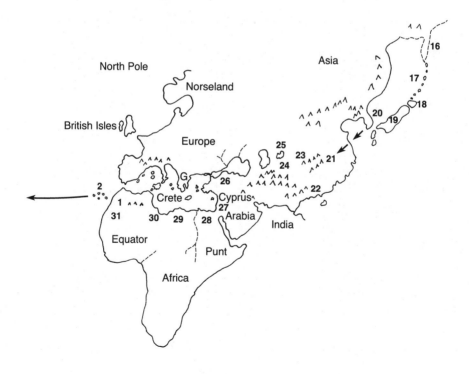

Everywhere we went I investigated the adjacent geography, by talking with traders, who had been to such places as Burma, India, and Arabia. I never stepped onto Europe, but I heard many stories about the British Isles and Norseland. I also heard about cold and distant lands at the top of the earth, far to the north. Other accounts described a trip by an Egyptian craft, which sailed all the way around Africa.

I quickly concluded that producing a reasonably detailed map of the earth would require many journeys. Since there is a limit to how much of this world one or several people can survey in a lifetime, what we know of the earth today is a combination of the accounts of many travelers. Even the best of these accounts can be misleading: some are misleading due to ignorance or confusion, but some others are intentionally misleading (Wilford, 1982).

[Translator's note: No remnant of this world map has been found. It was probably the most extensive and most accurate map drawn at that time. Figure 8 shows how the traveler's map of the earth might have appeared.]

Our children had been meeting with a circle of young people who appeared little employed except that they could predict the future and help plan for it. Some could predict the outcome of stock breeding. There were astronomers who could foretell with accuracy the next eclipse. There were agronomists who could estimate next year's crops. There were spies who could tell the pharaoh who his enemies were, and who his friends.

Since I had traveled so far, many supposed that my family and I knew the answers to the questions raised by these young people. We could not answer all their questions in detail, but we all benefited from the sharing of ideas and experiences. Their questions, and their manner of asking them, revealed their way of thinking.

When our children learned that I, a native of Morocco, could not recognize all the fruits and vegetables being cultivated in Upper Egypt, they devised a plan to educate me. Our horticultural friend selected a package of seeds and some cuttings and tubers, along with instructions on how to preserve and plant them when we returned to Morocco. They gave us nothing but the best. We took seeds of several large beans, eggplants, and melons.

≋

When did mankind discover irrigation, bronze, wheeled vehicles, wind-driven boats, and the art of horseback riding? The time and place of some of these discoveries are documented in stone engravings, so the discovery is at least as old as the engraving. On the other hand, the discoverer of the wheeled vehicle may have had no interest in informing the world about his discovery. So, the first scribe to illustrate the discovery may have been assigned the task centuries after the discovery. Any reference to a historical discovery should read "at least as early as."

In ancient times discoveries were by individuals rather than by a team or a segment of society. One man builds an irrigation ditch for his plants. Maybe his neighbor follows his example, or maybe he does not. In the case that no one does follow, how can we be sure when irrigation was "started," or how many times it was independently discovered? Of course if the first irrigator does not pass the discovery on to his children or his neighbors, it may be discovered and then lost. There were few libraries, and no journals.

The pharaoh was particularly interested in constructive ideas: developments in agriculture, woodcraft, metal craft, battle gear, and architecture. He would work with a draftsman until he had a clear working drawing of each new idea.

It disturbed the pharaoh that men's imagination could design such marvelous equipment and products, and yet if undocumented, the discovery could be lost.

When Was the Exodus?

In the time of Ramesses II there were many non-Egyptian people living in Egypt. Generally their occupation was limited to the more strenuous activities such as work in the brickyards. But they were not necessarily slaves. Some rose to high positions in the bureaucracy, at least one to the rank of general.

Most scholars of Egyptology would agree that there are no historical documents that clearly refer to the enslavement or deportation of the Hebrew people. Such deportations, however, are not inconsistent with accounts in the Book of Exodus. The Pharaoh, as referred to in The Old

Testament, was probably Ramesses II, who took the throne in 1279 BCE (Kitchen, 1982), or his successor, Merceptah. The exodus was a major event in Hebrew history, but it was a relatively minor loss, in Egyptian history (Kitchen, 1982).

The accepted chronology is a combination of radiocarbon dating, inscriptions, and papyrus documents. The carbon dating is subject to a plus or minus factor, and the inscriptions are dated from the year in which the successive pharaohs ascended to the throne. When there is a discovery requiring a change in succession of leadership, all subsequent dates must be adjusted. Ramesses II was enthroned as sole Pharaoh in 1279 BCE (James, 2002). But some Egyptologists claim that Ramesses II became pharaoh in 1290 BCE. If that date is accepted, then all subsequent dates must be changed to correspond to it.

K.A. Kitchen (1982) says that the exodus may have taken place in the first 30 years, likely after the 15th year, of the long reign of Ramesses II. The Trojan war is dated in the same decade, 1250–1240 BCE (Wood, 1988).

Intense interest by many people around the world in the correspondence of historic record and religious tradition has fostered numerous archaeological examinations over the past two centuries. The translation of this travel account is not intended to address the biblical record.

EGYPT TODAY

If you have never visited ancient Egypt, make a promise to do so. The enormity of the human endeavor, tracing back over five millennia, is stupendous. And the effort which the whole world has contributed to the unearthing and preservation of Egyptian relics is impressive. Alas, all is not perfect: the best view of the great pyramid of Giza is from the second floor of the Pizza Hut in Cairo.

One morning our van stopped to take pictures—and we were angrily told, "No!" We were not photographing military secrets. Our companions wanted to take a photo of a group of young people beating out their laundry on the rocky margin of an irrigation canal. The point is that Egypt is not a third world country—and don't you forget it!

≋

CHAPTER SEVENTEEN

MOROCCO

1239 BCE

In the years 1279 to 1269 BCE, Egypt had succeeded in throwing back the mysterious Sea People, who had ravaged the civilizations of the eastern Mediterranean. The Egyptian rulers were devising ways to permanently crush the power of the invaders from the sea.

One idea was to ally with the Berbers of northwest Africa, essentially outflanking the marauders from the sea. The Berbers are a nomadic, pastoral people. They share little of the culture of the Egyptians, their neighbors to the east, or other contemporary eastern Mediterranean peoples. Typically the Berbers wear long untrimmed beards, and many have a western European complexion.

The ancient Berbers built few monuments and temples. What we know of their history is limited to engravings, written in a language of which modern scholars have only fragmentary knowledge. Some archaeologists today recognize a phonetic alphabet of 24 phonemes, written from the top down and from right to left. These are similar to the undated engravings found in the Canary Islands, in particular, on Gran Canaria. The spirals and ring-in-ring glyphs resemble very ancient inscriptions found in western Europe and large parts of northern Africa.

In the High Atlas Mountains of Morocco there are several ancient rock art sites, such as Yagour (Searight and Hourbette, 1992).

THE PHARAOH, RAMESSES II, planned to send a sizable force, including horses and chariots, across the Sahara Desert and the Atlas Mountains. The Sahara is a wasteland of wind-eroded rocks and dune fields, extending deep into Africa. North from the Sahara are the sparsely inhabited Atlas Mountains. Between the deserts and the mountains are deep gorges, where cliffs more than a hundred meters high keep the streams below continually in shadow. Streams through these gorges flow to the south, where they disappear into the sand.

North of the Atlas Mountains the hills are forested and the soil is ideal for agriculture. The coastal lands are planted to olives, dates, and other useful trees and plants. The land is very productive and the people who live here are relatively prosperous (Rauzier, Tréal, and Ruiz, 1998).

ACROSS THE SAHARA

I was by now 60 years of age, and suffering from pain in my joints [arthritis]. Riding a camel many hours a day had taken its toll.

It was probably an unwise decision on my part, but I decided to take only a small force and push ahead with a minimum of organized preparation. The local sovereigns were in communication with Egypt, and their loyalty was rewarded with royal presents. After about a month's journey from Egypt, we were into some of the most barren desert that I have ever seen, where sandstorms beat the rocks until they are smooth and polished. There is usually enough rain to send up a few blades of grass, but this year those few blades had wilted and as a consequence herders and animals were camped near the few wells and springs, overgrazing the surrounding areas. Since there was no green food for animals, they were being slaughtered, and their meat was being dried.

After eating their dried meat and roots the herdsmen ate the edible bud of the date palm. The starving people stopped travelers by the road and pleaded with them for food. They were a pitiful group, showing all the symptoms of starvation. Young women held up their emaciated babies. "No milk, no milk!" they cried.

We were given refuge in the mud-walled castles of sovereigns, who maintained their own safety with a force of archers and mounted horsemen. These castle dwellers guarded a supply of grain and other foodstuffs, enough to last at least a year. Within the castle walls there was a marginal source of water. Even in the castle compounds, only the best livestock was being kept. Those who were maintaining the strongholds had planned for survival. There were very few elderly or disabled persons. Most frightening of all, no alms were being supplied to those outside the walls. Fear of disease required keeping the starving at a safe distance. Children, young women, and able soldiers were given priority.

We discussed this strategy with the rulers. They insisted that it was best for their society as a whole. The starving people outside the walls had already eaten their seeds for the next year's crop. Most of the artisans had been left unprotected. And many of the young children were gone. The local rulers seemed to be able to separate what was practical from what was just. The nights were cold and there was no wood for fuel.

We could only make a moralistic response. Living in protected seclusion inside the walls while the starving camped outside the walls was intolerable to us. We finally convinced the leadership that our continued presence within the walls was of no benefit to their overall scheme for survival. The sovereigns told us of an area where there had been adequate rain, and the people were surviving. When we departed, the starving were either too weak to pursue us, or had simply headed away in search of a mirage. We traveled by night, and we misled any who might follow us by walking up streambeds and crossing bare stone divides.

In the mountains, the people had great stores of dried figs, dates, almonds, olives, grain, and some livestock. They lived in one-story buildings of mud and straw, and survived on the produce from small, irrigated fields. Every member of the family had a task. Women were married at 15, and bore many children. Twelve to 13 year old girls gathered dry brush from cliff sides that appeared to be impossible to climb. They came down from the cliffs, bearing loads that bent them double.

The cliff sides are so steep that they appear to overhang, and indeed, so the story goes, one billy goat got up to a place from which he could not return. The children worked at getting him down, to no avail. Apparently there was enough grass so that he survived there for several years. No one could tell us what finally became of the goat. But anyway, it made a good story.

Morocco, 1238 BCE

North of the snow-capped mountains are irrigated fields with varied crops. How good it was to see my old home country again! I had almost forgotten it. Yes, indeed—home.

From a rise I could see the villages of home: fields of grain, vineyards, date palms, and small fishing boats pulled up on the beach. As we approached the village the people, especially the children, rushed out to greet us. Some brought sweets, the richness of which our kids had never tasted. Drummers beat out a familiar rhythm, and people along the roadside chanted in unison: "Follow the Sun, Follow the Sun. Greetings, Family Sun."

We were puzzled. How did they know who we were? And how did they know when we would arrive? We learned much later that the pharaoh had tried to keep track of our mission by sending emissaries to points where he thought we would pass, without success. Finally an Egyptian spy ship, ostensibly on its way to Cornwall for tin ore, stopped to re-stock at a village along the coast of Tunisia. While in port, the crew picked up a garbled account of a party on its way toward the capital of Morocco. By this time we were so close to home that little time remained to spread the news that we were to be welcomed on our arrival. This required prompt action, so the king quickly stationed lookouts at each mountain pass, and sent couriers with horses to spread the news.

I had decided to walk the final 50 kilometers, to assure those greeting us that I was no super-being, and to be able to shake their hands and grasp their shoulders. Though the fields of the villages I passed were heavy with grain, these people were poor and many were afflicted with illnesses—of what kind, who knows? So often when I shake a villager's hand, his first thought is to ask a favor, if not for himself, then for his poor wife or child. I stopped at each village, of perhaps 100 people. The village elders gathered about us to voice the needs of the community.

For the final kilometer we were accompanied by the Royal Guard, to the steps of the palace. I was knighted, using my own steel sword, and my wife and two children also received titles. I was titled "Prince of the Realm." My son was given the title, "Knight of the Realm," and my wife and daughter became "Ladies of the Realm." With our exalted new station came shelter, clean water, excellent food, and a maid.

Those who had been children when I left were now grown adults.

So good, so rewarding, so encouraging—they remembered who I was, and they were eager to hear my story.

What I had to tell was so improbable that most listeners tended to believe I was making it up, or at least exaggerating. Several would-be explorers and adventurers came to Morocco, looking for me, to hear first hand about the great earth I had discovered. But to me the wonder was not the immensity of the earth, but the ability of one of us humans to travel around it.

I asked many times, what had become of the ship and shipmates we had parted from, 36 years ago, on the opposite shore of the Atlantic? Were they stranded in a land from which they could not return? We never heard a word about what had become of them.

At last I had returned to my extended family, the place of my birth.

On my journeys I had made no attempt to take notes, determined that my memory would suffice—and it has.

We resolved to relate the story of my travels in a form that would not be lost. So with help from eager nieces and nephews, we wrote an account in our Berber script, pressed on thousands of numbered tiles. We fired the tiles, then placed them in a deep pit with cedar lining—a vault—and buried them.

According to one account the pit was covered by a stone block so large that four teams of oxen could not budge it. According to another account the giant stone was a ruse, and the tiles were actually placed beneath the floor of a building under construction. Over the centuries, thieves searching for gold and other valuables moved the great stone several times. But the tiles kept their secrets for millennia, and were not discovered until recent wind erosion exposed parts of the long abandoned village beneath which they had been hidden.

As soon as we were established in Morocco, we unpacked the seeds, cuttings, and tubers which the young Egyptians had given us. The melons grew large and juicy; and the beans produced many good meals for us. The eggplants grew long, curved and sleek, yellow with purple trimming. From all of them, we saved seeds for future planting. The cuttings failed to grow at all. We thought that our trek across the deserts had left them so dried that they would not grow.

Our children became leaders in the kingdom of Morocco. They married and they now have children of their own. Li and I took our children and grandchildren to visit the snow-capped Atlas Mountains, where we hunted for fossils [trilobites in the lower strata, and ammonites in the higher strata]. The larger ammonites were curled like the horns of a sheep. Local purveyors of medicine powdered these "horns" and claimed that they would cure almost anything.

On the day after our fossil hunt in the mountains, the children wanted to do something special for me. Li took them for a walk along the banks of a mountain stream, where they found flowers of many kinds. They returned with a bouquet of red poppies, little blue flowers that grow only about 2 or 3 centimeters above the ground, and wild irises. But their most remarkable find was the lily related to those I had found in California [*Fritillaria biflora*], in southern Alaska [*Fritillaria camchatcensis*], in Japan [also *Fritillaria camchatcensis*], in China, in Central Asia and in the land of the Hittites [many *Fritillaria* species]. How exciting it was to me! Here was a flower that once again proved to me how migration was a fact of life on this earth. The gift of this bouquet brought me delight and a renewed sense of wonder.

One day when my children and grandchildren were all together, my family packed a lunch and hiked to the coast. Here we could gather fresh seashells on the beach. There were many clams and mussels, tapered snails, and some flat forms with five symmetrical sections [echinoids].

"Hey kids, how goes the shell gathering? Have you noticed that there are also shells in the cliffs behind the beach?"

My oldest grandchild asked, "How can they live up there? They need salty water to survive."

"They lived a long time ago, when those stones up there were the beach, and the ground where we stand today was under water."

Then Li commented, "In the Atlas Mountains where the sedimentary rocks are tilted and folded, there was a noticeable difference between the creatures in the oldest and youngest strata."

"Grandma, don't you see why he brought us here? Grandfather wants us to compare the animals that live on the beach today with the creatures in those old bent-up rocks we saw last year in the mountains."

"So, can any of you state the principle that is demonstrated?"

"Yes," called out the youngest, "It's time for lunch."

Our kids were discovering the relationship between life today, and life from an earlier time. They were understanding the relative age of the rocks and the shells, as if this were something everyone could recognize.

Some day the people will understand a great deal more about this earth, and the sea life that changes from the way it used to be long ago.

There was so much to observe, so much to learn. What a wonderful world we live on! Someday people will explore every corner of it. I wonder if there are other worlds for people to explore.

My robust health has been restored, thanks in part to my being treated with the herbs of my home country (Sijelmassi, 2000). I am planning a variety of expeditions. I want to communicate with the people of all the world, in all the languages, even with the people of other times, as related in the magnificent accounts left for us in stone and papyrus. I dream of returning to China, the beautiful land of my wife and children. But it is too far away. Egypt, by sea, is a more realistic destination.

There is a saying, "None are honored in their own land." But that is not true here. The king, the whole nation, knows that "their boy" has been the first person known to have traveled around the world. They wished to share the glory—and well they should. There were a few old folks who knew me well before I left. Then I was a "dreamer." Now I am a "hero." Of course I had hair on the top of my head when they knew me before.

MOROCCO TODAY

Today the cities of Morocco house millions of people. Large jet aircraft bring visitors from distant continents. But out in the countryside the people still herd the goats, search for water, and irrigate their tiny fields, much as their ancestors did, millennia ago. The unyielding wind blows across the Sahara and the unkempt gravestones remain unmarked and barely noticed.

The Sahara Desert extends across northern Africa from the Red Sea to the Atlantic Ocean. We have visited the portions of the Sahara in Egypt and Morocco, but not those of Libya, Tunisia, and Algeria. Several millennia ago this was a fertile pasture for hoofed creatures, for the carnivores that stalked them, and for the human beings, who seem able to adapt to all environments. But with a drying climate, survival became ever more difficult. Thus people who live there today subsist on the ever-present edge of survival. Locally we can visit the palaces of Romans, Carthaginians, the beautifully tiled castles of recent potentates, and of course the Foreign Legion (Gordon, Talbot, and Simonis, 1998).

The people of Morocco write in French, pray in Arabic, and dream in Berber.

Most of the fruits and vegetables that grow in coastal Morocco were introduced at least by Roman times, but we do not know exactly when. There are in the Atlas Mountains cedars that grow 70 meters tall and live for 400 years. Clearly, great ships could have been built here, as well as in Lebanon. In 1300 BCE Morocco was a pastoral land. Mediterranean influences, likely Phoenician, arrived at least by 400 BCE, and possibly much earlier.

Today crops include coriander, thyme, parsley, bay leaves, mint, persimmons, pomegranates, oranges of many varieties, apples, cherries, tomatoes, eggplant, peppers, and zucchini. Two hundred thousand acres are planted to date palms (a native of Arabia). The upwelling cold water along the Moroccan coast had surely been a source of fish and other sea life, from ancient times. Today, 160,000 tons of sardines are harvested annually. Fishermen also catch octopus, squid, prawns, shrimp, several varieties of tuna, dorado, red mallet, and lobster. (Fouré and others, 1998).

Morocco is a kingdom. In the cities, we see the castles, the mosques, the mausoleums, everywhere the smiling face and splendid uniform. In the country, the dust blows across the barren ground and across the leaning grave markers of the poor. Life goes on. The people in the small farming villages greet us as friends. The foreign tourists ride in four-wheel-drive Land Rovers and enjoy the bazaar. The merchants hawk their wares.

Casablanca is the largest city in Morocco. The city rises up from the sea. Set on the seaside, surrounded by a giant square, is Morocco's large King Hassan II mosque, built in 1993, with a tower rising 200 meters. Morocco is truly a land of contrasts (Gorio, 1997).

POSTSCRIPT

EXACTLY WHERE OUR TRAVELER went in his last years, and how he got there, is unknown. It was his nature to leave messages in places where they could be found. Probably somewhere in the archives of the great nation of Egypt, a scholar studying the ancient papyrus scrolls will discover the last testimonial of the first geologist and world explorer.

But does this answer the question? Can we be sure that a still earlier traveler did not complete the journey—and the record has not yet been found?

THE TEXT AS PRESERVED

The text was originally written in an ancient Berber script. The traveler had also learned the cuneiform script, in Mesopotamia, but he used this only occasionally. The language used was mostly ancient Berber, incorporating a few words that appear to be ancient Egyptian, Hittite, and Greek.

With the passage of many centuries, some of the tiles had been discovered and used in local construction, as tiling for walls and floors of new buildings. Thus there are probably unintentional gaps in the story. A few of the tiles lead us to believe that the text was complete at the time it was buried.

More exciting is the fact that there are sequences of tiles found outside of Morocco, that were written in the same style, but appear unrelated to any known part of the journey described here. Perhaps in his later travels Follow the Sun reached western Europe, or his grandchildren carried on a family tradition of travel and discovery.

CONCLUSIONS

When we undertook the task of recovering the journal of a determined traveler encircling the earth in the 13th century BCE, I assumed that his problems would be human relations, linguistics, inadequate technology, and perhaps long term fatigue. I did not consider the fundamental problem to be that humans possessed less of "the right stuff" in such near antiquity.

But when we proposed that people of that age might not have the curiosity to measure the height of a mountain, I feared that I might be neglecting a critical shortcoming. What might the people of 1300 BCE be short on? Imagination? Curiosity? Mental flexibility?

When I look at the varied art work of ancient man, pieces created 20,000 to 40,000 years ago, I conclude that these artists were more than rote copiers. Ancient man created many things, not only because they were useful, but also because he saw them as beautiful or powerful. For example, he appreciated the colorful stones he strung around his neck.

Necessity is said to be the mother of invention. The ancient farmer selected the best breeding animals and the best seed corn, to produce better quality livestock and grain. Today few of us are faced with such day to day decisions.

Ancient farmers had to select properly, or their families might go hungry. Thus if ancient man did not possess imagination, curiosity, and perseverance, he might be the one falling off the evolutionary wagon.

The engineers who experimented with the number of spokes on a chariot wheel were inventors no less than the bicycle builders of the 19th century CE. If there is an evolutionary difference between the people of the 13th century BCE and today, it is probably that the common man of ancient times more successfully responded to the need for invention.

HOW DID ANCIENT MAN THINK?

Before learning about the ancient tiles, and preparing to write this account, I might have accepted the theory that Neanderthals thought differently from modern man—but surely not people of the thirteenth century BCE.

Modern archaeologists have found that Neanderthal people living as long as 50,000 years ago were placing flowers in a child's grave, and that they were providing day and night nursing care to a fallen warrior who lived on for years while his serious skull wound healed. If

Neanderthals showed these "modern" sentiments, why not the people of a mere 3,000 years ago?

Many cave artists of France and Spain, and the builders of astrological temples and palaces on each of the inhabited continents, also lived thousands of years earlier than our traveler. What evidence is there that at least a few "leaders" thought about the world they lived in, no differently than we ourselves do?

I have been told that it never would have occurred to ancient man to wonder about the elevation of a mountain, that he was frightened by the world around him, and was looking toward unseen spirits to protect him. Of course I could have included a few monsters, divine personages, and allegorical legends, in this account. Perhaps then the account would seem more " realistic" for bronze age people. We recognize that in past eras, most of the people (largely uneducated, by our standards) lived in fear of their surroundings and were indifferent to features of the natural environment that are interesting to you and to me. But this is the very essence of our adventure: we suspect that a few, or perhaps more than a few, ancient travelers shared our curiosity and questioned supernatural explanations.

What does it mean to "think differently" from modern man? I aver that the human beings that inhabit this planet today differ among themselves more widely than Follow the Sun differed from you or from me. The scholars of the 13th century BCE had their prototype of the abacus, the astronomical calendar, and a language that allowed them to exchange complex ideas. The modern scholar has available the total accumulated knowledge of mankind, and can locate his exact position on this globe at any moment, not to mention having knowledge of the heavenly bodies separating from each other at nearly the speed of light. The advance of science and technology is indisputable. But is the basic process of human thought, discovery, and invention so different (Gastil, 1993)?

Meanwhile, verbal narratives on the lips of storytellers have been transported to many places, as far away as China. And parts of our narrative can be heard even today, in isolated societies. Generally the account heard among many peoples is that of a master navigator, linguist, and scientist, always loyal to his wife and children, through decades of work and travel in foreign lands.

Some time after the traveler's account was deciphered from the tiles someone recalled that there was, at some distance, an enigmatic inscription on stone. The language and style were similar to that on the tiles. The translation follows.

WE FOLLOWED THE SUN

WE TRAVELED AROUND AN EARTHEN SPHERE
AND FOUND OUR WAY FROM THERE TO HERE.
THE PEOPLE WE MET HAD NOT TRAVELED FAR
BUT TOLD US OF CREATURES QUITE BIZARRE
AND OF CITIES PAVED WITH GOLD –
BETTER TO HAVE SHARED A SHELTER
WHEN THE WIND WAS VERY COLD.

WHO WILL FOLLOW, WHO WILL SEE
THE FOOTPRINTS OF ANTIQUITY?
AND WHO WILL SAY,
"THEY WERE THE FIRST, THEY LED THE WAY."

References

The references listed below are grouped first by chapter, region or subject, and then by author. A few references appear in more than one section.

Preface

Ambrose, Stephen, 1996, Undaunted Courage: Meriwether Lewis, Thomas Jefferson, and the Opening of the American West: New York, Simon & Schuster, 511 p.

Columbus, Christopher, 1492, Journal of the first voyage: Warminster, England, Aris and Phillips Ltd., 259 p., B.W. Ife, editor and translator, with text in Spanish and English, published 1990.

Cordell, Linda S., 1984, Pre-history of the southwest, Orlando, Florida, Academic Press, Inc., 409 p.

Gough, Barry, 1997, First across the continent: Sir Alexander Mackenzie: The Oklahoma western biographies, vol. 14: Norman, Oklahoma, University of Oklahoma Press, 240 p.

Heyerdahl, Thor, 1971, The Ra Expeditions: Garden City, New York, Doubleday and Company, Inc., 341 p., translated by Patricia Crampton.

Lo, Lawrence K., 2003. Ancient scripts are available at www.ancientscripts.com [accessed 3/10/2003]. We have used Lawrence Lo's symbols of ancient Berber script in Figure 1. We thank him for his permission to use his work in this manuscript.

Lubec, G., et al, 1993, "Use of Silk in Ancient Egypt," Nature, Vol. 362, #6415, 4 March 1993, p. 25. (Cited by Wolinski, 1995, p74.)

Macqueen, J. G., 1986 (revised and enlarged edition), The Hittites and their contemporaries in Asia Minor: London, Thames and Hudson, 176 p. (first edition, 1975).

Murden, Victoria, athlete. Discussion of her race from the Canary Islands to Barbados is available at http://www.adept.net/AmericanPearl/ [accessed 12/05/2004].

Regatta Magazine, 1997. Available at http://www.regatta.rowing.org.uk/ atlantic.html [accessed 12/06/2004}.

The Ocean Rowing Society, details of Canary Islands race to Barbados available at http://www.oceanregatta.com/intro.htm and http://www.oceanregatta.com/media_2004/South_devon_May26.htm [accessed 12/04/2004].

MOROCCO

Fouré, Catherine, and others, editors, 1998 (fourth edition), Morocco: New York, Alfred A. Knopf, Inc., 384p.

Gordon, Frances L., Dorinda Talbot, and Damien Simonis, 1998, Morocco, Lonely Planet Publications, 533 p.

Gorio, Nino, 1997, Morocco: Twickenham, England, Tiger Books International, 128 p.

Rauzier, Marie-Pascale, with photos by Cécile Tréal and Jean-Michel Ruiz, 1998, Tableaux du haut Marocain: Paris, Les Editions Arthaud, 199 p.

Searight, Susan, and Danièle Hourbette, 1992, Gravures rupestres du Haut Atlas: Casablanca, Idéale-Casablanca-Février, 103 p.

Sijelmassi, Abdelhäi. 2000, Les plantes médicinales du Maroc: Casablanca, Editions Le Fennec, 285 p. (not cited).

CANARY ISLANDS

Araña, Vicente, and Juan C. Carracedo, 1978, Los volcanes de las Islas Canarias: I, Tenerife: Madrid, Editorial Rueda, 151 p.

Bethencourt, Emiliano E., Francisco P. De Luca, and Francisco E. Perera, 1996, Las Pirámides de Canarias y el valle sagrado de Güi mar: Santa Cruz de Tenerife: Santa Cruz, Tenerife, Imprenta Reyes S. L., 266 p.

Bramwell, David, 1997, Flora of the Canary Islands: Madrid, Editorial Rueda, 220 p.

Castellano-Gil, José M. and J. Macías-Martín, 1993, History of the Canary Islands: Santa Cruz de Tenerife, Centro de la Cultura Popular Canaria, Litografía A. Romero, S. A., 152 p.

Martín-Rodríguez, Ernesto, 1998, La Zarza: Entre el cielo y la tierra: Madrid, V. A. Impresores, S. A., 110 p.

Navarro-Mederos, Juan Francisco, and Maria del Carmen del Arco Aguilar, 1996 (third edition), Los Aborígenes: Santa Cruz de Tenerife, Historia Popular de Canarias, Litografi a A. Romero, S. A., 118 p.

Simonis, Damien, 1998 (first edition), Canary Islands: Hawthorn, Vic., Australia, Lonely Planet Publications, 274 p.

CUBA AND MESOAMERICA

Aveni, Anthony, 1997, Stairways to the stars: Skywatching in three great ancient cultures: New York, John Wiley and sons, 230 p.

Bernal, Ignacio, 1968, Three thousand years of art and life in Mexico, as seen in the National Museum of Anthropology, Mexico City: New York, H. N. Abrams, 216 p.

Breiner, Sheldon, and Michael D. Coe, September-October, 1972, "Magnetic exploration of the Olmec civilization," American Scientist, vol. 60, no. 5, pp 566–575.

Carlson, John. B., 1975, Lodestone compass: Chinese or Olmec primacy? Multidisciplinary analysis of an Olmec hematite artifact form San Lorenzo, Veracruz, Mexico: Science, 5 September 1975, Vol 189, Number 4205, pp 753–760.

Clark, John E., coordinator, 1994, Los Olmecas en Mesoame rica: Mexico, El Equilibrista, 298 p.

Covarrubias, Miguel, 1986 (first published, 1946), Mexico south: The isthmus of Tehuantepec: London, KPI, Limited, distributed by Routledge and Kegan Paul, 443 p.

Dacal Moure, Ramon, and Manuel Rivero de la Calle, 1997, Art and Architecture of Pre-Columbian Cuba: Pittsburgh, University of Pittsburgh Press, 134 p.

Dirzo, Rodolfo, 1994, Diversidad de Flora Mexicana: Singapore, Toppan Printing Company, 191 p., CEMEX series.

Escalante-Rebolledo, Sigfredo, 1993, Jardín Bota nico Regional Guía General: Merida, Yucatan, Centro de investigacio n científico de Yucatan, 92 p.

Hunter, C. Bruce, 1977, A guide to ancient Mexican ruins: Norman, Oklahoma, University of Oklahoma Press, 261 p.

Leonard, Jonathan Norton et al, 1967, Ancient America: New York, TIME Incorporated, 192 p.

Ríos Meneses, Miriam Beatriz, [no date], The equinox and other knowledges of the Mayans: Yucatán, México, INAH, Instituto Nacional de Antropología e Historia, Centro INAH Yucatán, 20 p.

Stuart, Gene S., and George E. Stuart, 1993, Lost Kingdoms of the Maya: Washington, D. C., The National Geographic Society, 248 p.

Urrutia-Fucugauchi, Jaime, 1975, Investigaciones paleomagnéticas y arqueo-magnéticas en México: Anales Inst. Geof., 21, 127–134.

Urrutia-Fucugauchi, Jaime, L. Maupome, and P. J. Brosche, 1985, El compass magnético en China y Mesoamérica: Geos. Gol., 26, 1–5.

von Hagen, Victor W., 1960, World of the Maya: New York, New American Library, Mentor Books, 224 p.

SONORA TO DELTA

Cordell, Linda S., 1984, Prehistory of the southwest: Orlando, Florida, Academic Press, Inc., 409 p.

Cornett, James W., 1995, Indian uses of desert plants: Palm Springs, California, Palm Springs Desert Museum, 38 p.

Fisher, Richard D., 1992, National parks of northern Mexico: Tucson, Arizona, Sunracer Publications, 130 p.

CALIFORNIA

Barona Cultural Center and Museum, on the Barona Indian Reservation, Lakeside, California (San Diego County). Their website is http://www.angelfire.com/falcon/bccm (accessed October, 2004).

Brown, Vinson, and Andrew Douglas, 1969, The Pomo Indians of California coast and their neighbors, Nature Graph Publishers Inc.

Christopher, F. J., 1952, Basketry: New York, Dover Publications, Inc., 110 p.

Clottes, Jean, 2002, World Rock Art: Los Angeles, California, Getty Publications, 140 p., translated from the French by Guy Bennett.

Crosby, Harry W., 1997 (second edition), Cave paintings of Baja California: San Diego, California, Sunbelt Publications, 255 p.

Erlandson, Jon M. and Michael A. Glassow, editors, 1997, Perspectives in California Archaeology, vol. 4: Archaeology of the California coast during the middle Holocene: Los Angeles, California, Institute of Archaeology, University of California at Los Angeles, 187 p.

Grant, Campbell, 1974, Rock Art of Baja California, with notes on the pictographs of Baja·California by Léon Diguet (1895): Los Angeles, California, Dawson's Book Shop, 146 p., translated by Roxanne Lapidus.

Grant, Campbell, 1993 (reprint of 1965 edition), Rock paintings of the Chumash: A Study of a California Indian culture: Santa Barbara, California, Santa Barbara Museum of Natural History and EZ Nature Books, 163 p., 31 color plates and 120 b/w photos and illustrations.

Heizer, Robert F. and Adan E. Treganza, 1944, Mines and quarries of the Indians of California, Report XL of State Mineralogist, Chapter 3, p. 291–359.

Hudson, Travis, and Ernest Underhay, 1978: Crystals in the sky: an intellectual odyssey involving Chumash astronomy, cosmology and rock art: Santa Barbara, California, Santa Barbara Museum of Natural History Cooperative Publications, Ballena Press, 163 p.

Jaeger, Edmund C., 1957: The north American deserts: Stanford, California, Stanford University Press, 308 p.

Miller, Bruce W., 1988, Chumash: a picture of their world: Los Osos, California, Sand River Press, 140 p.

Moerman, Daniel E., 1998, Native American ethnobotany: Portland, Oregon: Timber Press, 927 p.

Moratto, Michael J., 1984, California archaeology: Orlando, Florida: Academic Press, Inc., Harcourt Brace Jovanovich, Publishers.

Ocean, Suellen, 1999, Acorns and eat 'em: A how-to vegetarian cookbook: Complete directions for harvesting, preparing, and cooking acorns: Potter Valley, California, Old Oak Printing, 86 p.

Patterson, Alex, 1992, A field guide to rock art symbols of the greater southwest: Boulder, Colorado, Johnson Books, 256 p.

Polk, Dora Beale, 1991, The island of California: a history of the myth: Lincoln, Nebraska, University of Nebraska Press, 397 p.

Pratt, Kevin, and Michael Jefferson-Brown, 1997, The Gardener's Guide to Growing Fritillaries: Portland, Oregon: Timber Press, Inc., 160 p.

Reid, J. Jefferson, and David E. Doyel, 1986, Emil W. Haury's Prehistory of the American southwest: Tucson, Arizona, The University of Arizona Press, 506 p.

Roberts, Norman C., 1989, Baja California plant field guide: La Jolla, California, Natural History Publishing Co., 308 p.

Schoenher, Allan A., C. Robert Feldmeth, and Michael J. Emerson, 1999, Natural history of the islands of California: Berkeley and Los Angeles, California, University of California Press, California Natural History Guides, no. 61, 491 p.

Strand, Carl Ludvig, 1980, Pre-1900 earthquakes of Baja California and San Diego County: San Diego, California, San Diego State University, Thesis in partial fulfillment for the degree Master of Science in Geology, Fall 1980, 320 p.

Wilson, Lynn, Jim Wilson, and Jeff Nicholas, 1987, Wildflower guide to Yosemite National Park: Yosemite, California, Sunrise Productions, 143 p.

PACIFIC NORTHWEST AND ALASKA

Allen, D., 1994 (4th edition), Totem poles of the northwest: Surrey, British Columbia, Canada, Hancock House Publishers, Ltd., 32 p.

Burley, David V., 1980, Marpole: Anthropological reconstructions of a prehistoric Northwest Coast culture type: Burnaby, British Columbia, Canada, Simon Fraser University Publication, 82 p.

Chaussonnet, Valérie, 1995, Crossroads Alaska: Native cultures of Alaska and Siberia: Washington, D. C., Smithsonian Institution, 112 p.

Croes, Dale R., 1995, The Hoko River archaeology site complex: Pullman, Washington, Washington State University Press, 248 p.

Crowell, Aron, and William W. Fitzhugh, editors, 1988, Crossroads of continents: Cultures of Siberia and Alaska: Washington D. C., Smithsonian Institution Press, 360 p.

Kari, Patricia Russell, 1995 (4th edition), Tanaina plantlore: Dena'ina K'et'una: Fairbanks, Alaska, Alaska Native Language Center, University of Alaska Fairbanks, 207 p.

Klein, Janet R., 1996, Archaeology of Katchemak Bay, Alaska: Homer, Alaska, Katchemak Country Publications, 94 p.

Langdon, Steve J., 1993 (3rd edition, revised), The native people of Alaska: Anchorage, Alaska, Greatland Graphics, 96 p.

Neel, David, 1995, The great canoes: Reviving a northwest coastal tradition: Seattle, Washington, University of Washington Press, 135 p.

Niehaus, Theodore F., 1976, A field guide to Pacific states wildflowers: Washington, Oregon, California and adjacent areas: Peterson Field Guide Series, Boston, Houghton Mifflin, 432p., illustrated by Charles L. Ripper.

Oman, Lela Kiana, 1995, The epic of Qayaq: The longest story ever told by my people: Seattle, University of Washington Press, 122 p.

Paul, Frances, 1944, Spruce root basketry of the Alaska Tlingt: Reprinted 1991, Sitka, Alaska, Sheldon Jackson Museum, 82 p. plus appendix (1981).

Pojar, Jim, and Andy MacKinnon, 1994, Plants of the Pacific Northwest Coast: Washington, Oregon, British Columbia and Alaska: Vancouver, British Columbia, Canada, Lone Pine Publishing, 529 p.

Ray, Dorothy Jean, 1975 (Reprinted with new preface, 1992), The Eskimos of Bering Strait, 1650–1898: Seattle, Washington, University of Washington Press, 305 p.

Viereck, Eleanor G., 1987, Alaska's wilderness medicines: Healthful plants of the far north: Anchorage, Alaska, Alaska Northwest Books, 107 p.

JAPAN AND CHINA

Anonymous, 1994, The ancient art in Xinjiang, China: Urumqi, Xinjiang, China, Xinjiang Fine Arts and Photo Publishing House, 251 p.

Barber, Elizabeth Wayland, 1999, The Mummies of Ürümchi: New York, W. W. Norton & Co., 240 p., with maps and 16 plates.

Bonavia, Judy, 1999, The Silk Road: From Xi'an to Kashgar: Kowloon, Hong Kong, Odyssey Publications Ltd., 336 p. (first published, 1988).

Dyer, Carolyn, 1986, Tracing the silk road: Vestiges of the caravans of ancient treasures from the East to western lands can still be seen today: Fiberarts, January/February, 1986, pp. 22-25.

Fairbank, John K., and Edwin O. Reischaur, 1989 (revised edition), China: Tradition and Transformation: Boston, Houghton Mifflin, 561 p.

Imamura, K., 1996, Prehistoric Japan: Honolulu, HI, University of Hawaii Press, 246 p.

Li Xueqin, 1995, Chinese bronzes: A general introduction: Beijing, China, Foreign Language Press, 171 p.

Mallory, J. P, and Victor H. Mair, 2000, The Tarim mummies: London and New York, Thames & Hudson, 352 p.

Peifen, Chen, 1995, Ancient Chinese bronzes in the Shanghai Museum: London, Scala Books, 95 p.

Ren Xizhong, Chen Zhongquiu, and Naymu Yasheng, editors, 1999 (third edition), Xinjiang tourism: Quarry Bay, Hong Kong, Hong Kong Tourism Press, 135 p.

University of Washington, press release from Sandra Hines, 2000, Intriguing archaeological sites, isolated lake targets of Kuril expedition: http://www.washington.edu/newsroom/news/2000archive/06-00archive/k063000.html [accessed 12/13/04]. Based on research of University of Washington Assistant Professor Benjamin Fitzhugh and others.

Xinjiang Bureau of Geology and Mineral Resources, compiler, 1990, Mineral resources in Xinjiang: Urumuqi, Xinjiang, China, Xinjiang People's Publishing House, 32 p. of text, in English and Chinese, plus photos and maps.

Xinjiang Museum staff, compilers, [no date], Xinjiang Museum: Urumuqi, The Xinjiang Art and Photography Publishing Press, 120 p., with introduction by Li Yuchun.

Zhong Shude and Liang Digang, editors in chief, 1997 (2nd edition, revised), Petroleum Geology of China: Tarim Basin: Wulumuqi, Xinjiang, China, Xinjiang Artistic Photography Publishing House, 160 p., edited by Xiniang Petroleum Administration, Tarim Petroleum Exploration Command, and Petroleum Geophysical Prospecting Bureau.

CENTRAL ASIA TO ANATOLIA AND PALESTINE

Aksu, Ali E., Richard N. Hiscott, and others, 2002, Persistent Holocene outflow from the Black Sea to the eastern Mediterranean contradicts Noah's flood hypothesis: GSA Today, Vol 12, No. 5, May, 2002, pp 4–10.

Brosnahan, Tom, and Pat Yale, 1999, Turkey: Oakland, California, Lonely Planet Publications, 816 p.

Macleod, Calum, and Bradley Mayhew, 1999, Uzbekistan: The golden road to Samarkand: Kowloon, Hong Kong, Odyssey Publications Ltd., 328 p. (first published, 1996).

Macqueen, J. G., 1986 (revised and enlarged edition), The Hittites and their contemporaries in Asia Minor: London, Thames and Hudson, 176 p. (first edition, 1975).

The Museum of Anatolian Civilizations, Members of the Museum staff, 1997, The Museum of Anatolian Civilizations: Ankara, Turkey, self published by the Museum of Anatolian Civilizations, D nmez Offset, 256 p.

Özgüç, Tashin, [no date], The Hittites: Ankara, Turkey, Dönmez Offset, 64 p.

Ryan, William B. F., and Walter C. Pitman, 1998: Noah's flood: The new scientific discoveries about the event that changed history: New York, Simon and Schuster.

Seeher, Jürgen, 1999: Hattusha Guide: a day in the Hittite Capital: Istanbul, Ege Yayinlari, 184 p.

Wood, Michael, 1988, In search of the Trojan war: Berkeley, California, University of California, Berkeley, 288 p., illustrated. Originally published: New York, Facts on File, 1985.

EGYPT

Avedian, D., R. Ben Ismaïl, and H. Mikaelian, coordinators, 1985, The great pharaoh Ramses II and his time: An exhibition of antiquities from the Egyptian Museum, Cairo, at the Great Hall of Ramses II, Expo 86, in Vancouver, British Columbia, Canada: Montreal, Quebec, Canada, Canada Exim Group, 67 p.

Baines, John, and Jaromir Malek, 1980, Cultural atlas of ancient Egypt: New York, Facts on File, Inc., 36 maps, 530 illustrations, 240 p. Revised Edition.

Gore, Rick, 2001, "Pharaohs of the sun:" National Geographic, April, 2001, p. 34–57.

Hutchinson, Warner, 1978: Ancient Egypt: Three thousand years of splendor: New York, Grosset and Dunlap, 116 p.

James, T.G.H., 2002, Ramesses II: New York, New York, Friedman/Fairfax, 319 p.

Kitchen, K.A., 1982, Pharaoh Triumphant: The Life and Times of Ramesses II: Cairo, Egypt, The American University of Cairo Press, 272 p.

Lubec, G., et al, 1993, "Use of Silk in Ancient Egypt," Nature, Vol. 362, #6415, 4 March 1993, p. 25. (Cited by Wolinski, 1995, p74.)

Manley, Bill, 1996, The Penguin historical atlas of ancient Egypt: London, Penguin Books Ltd., 144 p.

White, J. E. Manchip, 1970 (expanded edition), Ancient Egypt: Its culture and history: New York, Dover Publications, 217 p. (first edition, 1952).

Wolinski, Arelene E., 1995: Ancient Egypt: Personal perspectives: El Cajon, California, Interaction Publishers, 87 p.

SHIPS, SEAFARING, COMMERCE, AND TECHNOLOGY

Barber, Elizabeth Wayland, 1994, Women's Work: The first 20,000 years: Women, cloth, and society in early times: New York, W.W. Norton & Company, 334 p.

Casson, L., 1971 (updated 1995), Ships and seamanship in the ancient world: Baltimore and London, The Johns Hopkins University Press, 470 p.

Closs, Michael P., editor, 1986: Native American mathematics: Austin, Texas, University of Texas Press, 432 p.

Drews, Robert, 1993, The end of the Bronze Age: Changes in warfare and the catastrophe ca. 1200 B.C.: Princeton, New Jersey, Princeton University Press, 252 p.

Heiser, Charles B., Jr., 1990 (new edition), Seed to civilization: The story of food: Cambridge, Massachusetts, Harvard University Press, 228 p. (originally published, 1973).

Hodges, Henry, 1992 (reprinted), Technology in the ancient world: New York, Barnes and Noble Books, 297 p., with drawings by Judith Newcomer (originally published, 1970).

Hornell, James, 1946, Water transport: Origins and early evolution: Cambridge, England, Cambridge University Press, 304 p., plus 45 plates.

Kaplan, Robert, 1999, The nothing that is: a natural history of zero: New York: Oxford University Press, 225 p.

Jones, Dilwyn, 1995, Boats: London, British Museum Press, Egyptian Bookshelf, 96 p.

Wilford, John Noble, 1982, The mapmakers: New York, Random House, Vintage Books, 415 p.

POSTSCRIPT

Gastil, Raymond Duncan, 1993, Progress: Critical thinking about historical change: Westport, Connecticut, T. Praeger Publishers, 212 p.

ACKNOWLEDGMENTS

Over the last five years of travel, Janet and I have spoken with many people in many countries, too numerous to name individually here. I must, however, name a few. Arelene Wolinski (Egyptologist, and Professor of History, Mesa College) guided us through Egypt, sharing her extensive knowledge. Dale Croes (Department of Anthropology, South Puget Sound Community College) showed us archaeological sites on the Hoko River and provided valuable insight on the ancient people of northwest Washington. Several of my friends have read the manuscript and made suggestions or corrections, and my colleagues in the Department of Geological Sciences at San Diego State University have offered their thoughts on this manuscript. Special mention goes to all of the members of my extended family and many long-time friends, including John Holden (free lance writer and illustrator), Thomas Bowen (Professor emeritus of Anthropology, California State University, Fresno), and Fred Talbert (Professor emeritus of Astronomy, San Diego State University). Without the assistance of all these friends, family, and colleagues, this book would not have found itself in print and in your hands.

SUNBELT PUBLICATIONS
"Adventures in the Natural History and Cultural Heritage of the Californias"
Series Editor—Lowell Lindsay

Southern California Series:

Geology Terms in English and Spanish	Aurand
Geology and Enology of the Temecula Valley (SDAG)	Birnbaum, ed.
Water for Southern California (SDAG)	Cranham, ed.
Gateway to Alta California	Crosby
Portrait of Paloma: A Novel	Crosby
Mining History/Geology of Joshua Tree (SDAG)	Eggers, ed.
Fire, Chapparal, and Survival in Southern California	Halsey
California's El Camino Real and Its Historic Bells	Kurillo
Mission Memoirs: Reflections on California's Past	Ruscin
Warbird Watcher's Guide to the Southern California Skies	Smith
Campgrounds of Santa Barbara and Ventura Counties	Tyler
Campgrounds of Los Angeles and Orange Counties	Tyler
Jackpot Trail: Indian Gaming in Southern California	Valley
Will Thrall and the San Gabriels	Woolsey
The Sugar Bear Story: A Chumash Tale	Yee/DeSoto

California Desert Series:

Geology of the Elsinore Fault Zone (SDAG)	Hart/Murbach, eds.
Fossil Treasures of the Anza-Borrego Desert	Jefferson/Lindsay, eds.
Palm Springs Oasis: A Photographic Essay	Lawson
Anza-Borrego A To Z: People, Places, and Things	D. Lindsay
Marshal South and the Ghost Mountain Chronicles	D. Lindsay
The Anza-Borrego Desert Region (Wilderness Press)	L. and D. Lindsay
Geology of the Imperial/Mexicali Valleys (SDAG)	L. Lindsay, ed.
Palm Springs Legends: Creation of a Desert Oasis	Niemann
Desert Lore of Southern California	Pepper
Peaks, Palms, and Picnics: Journeys in Coachella Valley	Pyle
Geology of Anza-Borrego: Edge of Creation	Remeika, Lindsay
Paleontology of Anza-Borrego (SDAG)	Remeika, Sturz, eds.
California Desert Miracle: Parks and Wilderness	Wheat

Baja California/Mexico Series:

The Other Side: Journeys in Baja California	Botello
Cave Paintings of Baja California	Crosby
Backroad Baja: The Central Region	Higginbotham
The Kelemen Journals	Kelemen
Journey with a Baja Burro	Mackintosh
Abracadabra: Mexican Toys	Martinez, ed.

Houses of Los Cabos (Amaroma)	Martinez, ed.
Houses by the Sea (Amaroma)	Martinez, ed.
Mexicoland: Stories from Todos Santos (Barking Dog Books)	Mercer
Baja Legends: Historic Characters, Events, Locations	Niemann
Sea of Cortez Review	Redmond
Spanish Lingo for the Savvy Gringo	Reid
Tequila, Lemon, and Salt	Reveles
Mexican Slang Plus Graffitti	Robinson

San Diego Series:

Rise and Fall of San Diego: 150 Million Years	Abbott
Only in America	Alessio
More Adventures with Kids in San Diego	Botello, Paxton
Mission Trails Regional Park Trail Map	Cook
Cycling San Diego, 3rd Edition	Copp, Schad
San Diego: California's Cornerstone	Engstrand
Place Names of San Diego County A to Z	Fetzer
A Good Camp: Gold Mines of Julian and the Cuyamacas	Fetzer
San Diego Mountain Bike Guide	Greenstadt
Louis Rose: San Diego's First Jewish Settler	Harrison
The Play's The Thing: A Photographic Odyssey	Jacques
San Diego Specters: Ghosts, Poltergeists, Tales	Lamb
San Diego Padres, 1969-2001: A Complete History	Papucci
San Diego: An Introduction to the Region	Pryde
Pacific Peaks and Picnics: Day Journeys in San Diego	Pyle
Coastal Geology of San Diego (SDAG)	Stroh, ed.
Campgrounds of San Diego County	Tyler
Thirst for Independence: The San Diego Water Story	Walker

Incorporated in 1988, with roots in publishing since 1973, **Sunbelt Publications** produces and distributes natural science and outdoor guidebooks, regional histories, multi-language pictorials, and stories that celebrate the land and its people.

Sunbelt books help to discover and conserve the natural, historical, and cultural heritage of unique regions on the frontiers of adventure and learning. Our books guide readers into distinctive communities and special places, both natural and man-made.

We carry hundreds of books on southern California
and the southwest United States!
Visit us online at:
www.sunbeltbooks.com